ELI

HURLEY

UNDER FLINT
SKIES

MUDLARK'S PRESS

First published 2019 by Mudlark's Press

First paperback edition 2019

ISBN 978-0993218095 (paperback)

www.lizhurleywrites.com

'You either get Norfolk, with its wild roughness and uncultivated oddities, or you don't. It's not all soft and lovely. It doesn't ask to be loved.'

Stephen Fry

1

Ari watched in horror as the beaker of juice sailed towards her in a perfect arc. The poorly fitted lid came off and the purple liquid poured out in an elongated streak of colour. Everything seemed to be moving in slow motion, from the snarl on her husband's face to the trajectory of the cup, and then it all sped up. The cup smacked her on the temple, the rest of the drink splashing over her face and down her top. Too stunned to be angry yet, she stared at Greg who was already grabbing his coat from the chair.

"And you can clean that as well, you stupid bitch," he spat, the final word in an argument that had started as soon as he'd walked in the door, half an hour earlier…

Ari had jumped as her husband shouted at her, her hand clasped around a little package she had found in his jacket pocket. Greg had come into the kitchen from the front room. Whatever had been on TV no longer appealed and he now wanted his tea. She was surprised he hadn't simply shouted. God knows their little terrace house wasn't big; whichever room he was in, he simply shouted out his commands. Just her luck that she should be going through his pockets as he walked in.

"What the hell do you think you're doing?"

She shrugged. "The clicker for the cooker has stopped working again. I thought you might have some matches or a lighter."

"Yeah, well I don't." Greg snatched the jacket out of her hands and walked past her, flicking on the kettle. Ari stood by the lean-to kitchen table, looking at his back as he fumbled his way around the cupboards trying to find where the tea and sugar lived. Her hands clasped the back of the chair, knuckles tightening as she gripped the wood.

How had she failed so badly? Nothing she did was right. When the boys had first been born her body had resembled a battleground. Months later, instead of improving she felt worse. Twenty-two was too young to feel so old. When she lay down at night she sank down through the mattress. The sheets and blankets wrapping around her like a shroud, falling past the bed springs, down through the floorboards, buried in layers of the house. Every morning she fought to rise up through them, to simply drag her legs off the side of the bed. The frigid taunts slid off her like everything else.

Greg had walked out at eight months when she was still weaning the boys. She had been devastated and her younger sisters had been distraught. None of them knew how to fix this problem. When Greg's fling chucked him out, he returned, to Ari's deep relief. All she'd wanted was to succeed. To ensure she provided her sons with a loving father. When he returned after the second affair, she was saddened to discover how disappointed she was. That had been a year ago. Despite his assurances, another affair was overdue. And now, with her new discovery, the moment had arrived. Her pathetic attempt to play at happy families lay in shreds beneath her fingers.

"Who's Kylie?" she asked carefully.

Greg's outstretched arm paused, then he continued his hunt for sugar in the cupboard.

"Who?"

"Kylie. She's written you a note and put it in your pocket."

"Oh her. Just one of the girls at work. She writes down everything, we all get them." Still, with his back turned, Greg spooned some sugar into a cup and poured water over the teabag. "It's no big deal."

"Does she put little kisses on everyone's notes?"

Ari's dismay at finding the note was quickly being replaced but she wasn't sure yet if it was with anger or relief. She knew the marriage was over, had known it for over a year if she was honest. If she was *really* honest, she had known it was over from the moment she had said, 'I do'.

Greg turned to look at her, blowing on his tea and trying to sip it nonchalantly.

"Yeah, probably. She's friendly like that. You should try it sometime. See what happens when you go through people's pockets? You're making two plus two into a whole shitstorm. Something else to nag about."

"Sorry," said Ari, shrugging her shoulders. When he called her a nag, she bit her lip. When he jeered that she was stuck-up, she turned the other cheek. When he complained that she thought she was too good for him, she brushed it off. Each and every time she had borne the insults. She thought she had shown resilience and fortitude, now she realised all that he saw was a doormat. What a fool she had been, but no longer. This was it. This was the moment when she was finally going to call time on her useless, pathetic marriage. Hot prickles ran over her skin, every part of her panicky and shaking. She was about to ruin her sons' chance at a happy family with a loving mummy and daddy.

Ari took a deep breath. "The note says it's for the next time, and it's wrapped around a condom." She held out the small packet. That was when he'd lost it. His face flushed red, whether through embarrassment or anger Ari didn't know, but on reflection, she was bloody glad he had thrown Leo's beaker rather than the cup of tea.

She cowered as he stormed past her and out of the house. Ari winced, hoping that he hadn't woken the twins up, though they had become quite practised at sleeping through raised voices.

Now she looked about her and then methodically moved around her tiny kitchen wiping down the sticky mess wherever she could see a splash. She tried not to think about what this latest outrage indicated. Eventually, the room was clean but she was unable to erase the fear and anger that was still drumming through her body.

She wondered where he had gone. The gym seemed unlikely, the only exercise he did was raising a can to his face, a dart to the board, or his voice to the television. He was body-conscious but lazy about doing anything to stay fit. At five foot ten he'd pointed out that Ari would look silly wearing heels. So, to try and humour him she didn't. His thinning sandy hair was shaved short, like his idol *The Rock*. In a rare moment of levity, Ari joked that *The Rock* was totally bald, not thinning. Greg had found the comment less funny and sulked. Leaving the house, he had made his feelings clear with a slammed door.

The slammed door was a common punctuation in their house. He had never thrown anything at her before though and it was that, that had finally brought her to her senses. This wasn't going to get better; theirs was a marriage that should have never begun. Pregnancy was no longer the driver that it used to be. The fact that both parties secretly acknowledged that their relationship was on the rocks prior to the pee stick, was dismissed in the light of the momentous news. Ari had been tired and vulnerable, and Greg had felt a sense of duty. They should have never married. Even that was a hurried, sordid little excuse for a ceremony. Ari had stood supported by her four sisters who all stared in hostile suspicion at the loud family to which they had just become joined.

And now here they were, four years on, scrabbling to make ends meets, two open affairs already on Greg's side, no sex, and two wonderful little boys. She had stayed out of desperation and hope. She made constant excuses for Greg lately, though she had realised that he simply wasn't interested in the children, they were too loud or too messy and basically too much like little boys. Equally, they weren't much interested in him. He would shout at them all the time, never took them out, and didn't even tuck them in. Surely it wasn't too much to ask that he didn't swear at them? That he didn't smoke in the house? That he didn't come home drunk? Nag, snob, cow. Apparently it was.

The last eight years of Ari's life had been more or less horrible, the future looked no more promising. Tucking her hair behind her ear she winced as she realised the cup might have left a bruise on her temple and that her hair was sticky with juice. To hell with it, she picked up her book, turned off the oven and headed upstairs for a bath. If Greg was still hungry when he came home, he could do it himself, she was having a bath and turning in for the night. Thank God, Aster was away, Ari would sleep in her room and then in the morning she would start to put the wheels in motion for a divorce.

Standing up, she flinched as she heard the front door open again.

"Halloo! Good timing, I just saw Greg leaving. Important meeting at the pub?" Aster's voiced trailed off as she reached the kitchen. Until recently Aster had lived at home and still had a room. The minute she was able to go to university she had sprinted out the door. She might deeply love her sister and her nephews, but she loathed her brother-in-law. At eighteen she was generally self-absorbed, unaware, and apparently uninterested in anyone else's life. Until they were trying to hide something. And then she was like a heat-seeking missile. Aster took one look at Ari and stopped.

"Has he hit you? Ari what's happened?!"

Oh God, thought Ari, she just didn't have time for her sister's histrionics.

"No. He didn't hit me. How come you're home?"

"I left my laptop charger here."

"Why didn't you say? I'd have posted it."

Ari attempted to deflect Aster's attention. She didn't need the third degree right now. She was so incredibly tired, she just wanted to curl up in bed and sleep for a hundred years.

Aster walked over to the sink and filled the kettle. "And prove how irresponsible I am. Again? Not likely." Looking over her shoulder, she locked eyes with her big sister. "But I don't care about that. I care about this. Whatever this is."

Ari raised her hand to her temple again, wondering how bad it looked.

"Exactly," said Aster, "and you look dumbstruck. What's happened?"

Ari walked out of the kitchen towards the stairs. "Honestly, Az, leave it. I'm tired but I'm going to deal with it."

"Can you change the locks? I can sort that out if you want. There was a talk at college the other day about women needing to be more assertive. That's you, you need to stop letting Greg treat you like a doormat."

Christ, now she was being lectured by her baby sister about women's rights. University had turned a stroppy know-it-all teenager into a superior know-it-all monster. But seriously, did everyone see her as a doormat? Did that explain her sisters' puzzled expressions? Could no one see the intense sacrifice she had made in trying to hold her marriage together, the insults and ignominies that she had endured?

"I said leave it for fuck's sake. Stop going on. Take your charger. I'm having a bath and going to bed." Walking upstairs she went into the bathroom banging the door behind her.

Aster stood at the bottom of the staircase looking up at the closed door, stunned. She could count on one hand, the number of times she had heard her sister swear. Maybe she'd handled it badly? Greg was a bloody pig. She'd had to live with him for the past four years after he moved in and she'd pretty much hated him for every single day of those four years. Her only regret when she went to uni was leaving with the snake still in the nest. She climbed upstairs to her bedroom, retrieved her cable and stuck her head around the boys' door. Her two gorgeous nephews were fast asleep. As tempted as she was to go and give them a hug, she decided not to risk it. If they woke up, Ari might slaughter her, the mood she was in. She knocked on the bathroom door and called over the sound of running water.

"Do you want me to stay the night?"

The taps stopped, and Ari hissed at her not to wake the boys. "I'm fine, honestly. Anyway, I'm planning on sleeping in your bed tonight, okay? Call you tomorrow."

Well at least she was taking some sort of action thought Aster, but it was a long way short of what needed doing as far as she was concerned.

"Are you sure? I'm just worried. You know, soppy stuff. I love you."

"I love you too. I'll call you tomorrow."

And with that, the taps began to run again, and Aster quietly let herself out of the house, worried and angry.

2

Waking the following morning, Ari found that despite the early night, her sleep had been unsettled and she felt exhausted. Sounds from the children's room suggested that they were already up so she dragged herself out of bed to prepare for another dreary, weary, miserable day. The day that was going to mark the start of a particularly unpleasant stage in her life. As if she hadn't had enough already.

There were no sounds from Greg's room. She couldn't even think of it as their room, so she knocked on the door. She didn't want him late for work—she had a lot to do today, starting today with the trip to the solicitor. Maybe they could help her, once she found out what their letter to her was about. It was suitably vague, just a polite but insistent summons. There was no reply to her knock, so she opened the door and saw with resignation that he hadn't bothered coming home last night—again. Oh well, that was one less thing to deal with.

An hour later she was dropping the boys off with Mrs Singh next door and heading into the city. She was wearing her smartest clothes, her interview outfit, that she had worn for every family court hearing as well as for interviews at the local supermarket and pub. It was a plain navy skirt with a cream blouse tucked in, she wore a neat little blazer over the top, in an almost matching navy colour, and a pair of old but well-polished court shoes. They had a hole in their sole, but no one could see that, and she could never justify the expense of repairing a pair of shoes she rarely wore. Having got the part-time jobs stacking shelves and pulling pints, the interview outfit went back into the wardrobe, along with the smart shoes. For now, she had lined the insoles with cardboard, which, as an added bonus, kept her feet warm.

Sitting on the crowded bus, she pulled out the solicitor's letter from her handbag and wondered again what it was about. It had arrived three days ago but today was the first swap she could get from work; securing a babysitter was a minor issue on a street like hers. The paper the letter was written on was thick heavy stock and the envelope had been handwritten, an unusual touch. It gave a sense of the familiar, of privacy and inclusion, but inclusion was not something that meant anything to her. She read the contents again, requesting her presence at a fancy West End Solicitor to discuss an issue that had arisen in her favour. So here she was, sitting on a bus heading into town, dutifully jumping to attention. Well in fairness, whilst she was responding because she was a dutiful daughter, even if her mother had been dead seven years, she couldn't deny the fact that the phrase 'in her favour' was enticing.

However, she was also fully expecting it to be something unpleasant; that always came after hope she had noticed, but it didn't stop her. Eternal springs and so on, but there was only one thing that this could possibly be related to and that was the Family. The Other Family. The Not Us Family. Them. And nothing good had ever come of that. Her father's family were unknown, raised in Irish foster families; he would proclaim that his wife and daughters were the only family he would ever need. His dynasty started with him. When he made such declarations, the family would generally fall into fits of giggles imagining their dada as a fearsome patriarch, when in fact he was a soft-hearted pushover.

No, the family in question was her mother's. When Elizabeth de Foix fell in love with a parentless Irish student, her family had failed to see the attraction. As their love strengthened, so did her family's antipathy until she was made to choose between them, and she chose love. At that point, her family had thrown her out never to speak to her again. Ari looked at the envelope, what on earth could they possibly want now after all these years. She switched her thoughts to matters that she could deal with.

Thinking back to the previous night she wondered if this solicitor would be able to tell her about anything as grubby as divorce and her rights. She didn't think Greg would fight her for the children, hell some days he couldn't even get their names right. They weren't identical or anything, he couldn't get their names straight because, quite simply, he just didn't care. She was concerned though that he might fight her for the house and that was simply not up for discussion. This was the house that her mother and father had bought and started their married life in together. It was the home where she and her sisters were born and raised. When their parents died in a traffic accident, it was the home that she'd fought to keep her sisters in, when social services tried to take them all away. It was the home she had brought her sons up in. She was not selling it so that Greg could have some sort of proceeds from it, but she honestly had no idea what his rights were. If she went to the police and told them he had thrown something at her, would that make any subsequent case stronger in her favour? But what would the police do? It was only a cup; he hadn't actually touched her. Even if he had, so what? Ari knew of lots of women whose partners hit them, and the police did nothing. She had no intention of waiting until he did hit her, and as sure as night followed day, Ari knew that was the path that they were now both on; and maybe always had been.

She was jostled out of her musings by the person next to her trying to get off the bus and as she looked up, she realised everyone else was getting off as well. Yet again the bus had broken down. Damn, she just couldn't get a break. The cold March skies were tipping down, she had no brolly and her destination was another two stops away. Great, thought Ari, I'm going to turn up looking like a drowned rat.

And now she was late; the heavens had opened and she was running along the wet streets in an attempt at punctuality. She couldn't even phone ahead as she was out of credit and she had no money left to top it up. Being away from the children without any way to be contacted was just adding to her stress levels.

Running just doesn't work when you are in heels and a skirt nor does having a shoe with a hole in its sole when it's raining. Ari arrived late, out of breath and leaving a little, damp cardboard patch on the carpet as she entered the plush foyer of the solicitor's offices.

There were two ladies in the reception; a young, well made-up woman sat behind a desk and an older well-groomed lady stood by her side talking something through with her. Their voices were soft and muffled in the intimidating reception area. There were fresh flowers in vases, heavy curtains and deep-pile carpets, oil paintings hung on the walls and throughout the foyer was an overwhelming sense of prestige. The receptionist took one look at her, confirmed her name and then directed Ariana to one of the chairs. All were upholstered so she had no choice but to perch on the edge, not wishing to soak the material.

"Mrs Paxton?" The older lady interrupted Ari's churning thoughts, "Isn't this weather shocking?" She stuck her hand out, "Penelope Smith, I'm Mr Fanshawe's private secretary. I've let him know that you are here, but he apologises, could you give him five minutes, he's running late?" She paused to give Ari a few moments to gather her thoughts. "You have a couple of minutes; would you like to make use of the bathroom? You can borrow my brush and make-up bag if you would like?"

Ari knew she was being steamrollered but just like that, those kind words and kinder smile helped her calm down. Looking in the mirror in the loos she giggled at the utter mess she saw in front of her. Admittedly there was a slightly hysterical tinge to the laugh, but it was better than nothing. Her dark brown hair looked as though birds had tried to nest in it and as she removed a leaf, she thought they were halfway to being successful. Nothing in the make-up bag could

17

ELIZABETH HURLEY

deal with the dark shadows under her eyes, and the blusher was too dark for her pale skin, but Ari dabbed on a little of the lipstick which added some warmth to her face. Thank God for female solidarity. With that in mind, she pinched her cheeks, brushed her hair and as she looked in the mirror a fragment of Eliot sprang to mind. Here she was preparing her face to meet the faces that she would meet. Fortified by her favourite poet she returned to reception and was soon ushered along a corridor and into a large book-lined office. It was a room that either reassured or intimidated you, from the leather and oak, to the high ceilings and tasteful views beyond the windows, this was a room where tsunamis were turned into ripples.

Ariana sat down on the plump, high-backed chair in front of the solicitor's large desk, her hands clasped in her lap, desperately trying not to pull at a hangnail. Having ushered Ari into the room, Mrs Smith returned with a teapot and some cups for her employer and his client. Ari reached for a cup, anxious to have something to do with her hands, besides shredding her fingers and letting her nerves reveal themselves. However, when she placed her cup on the saucer, the cup rattled, and it was all she could do, to not simply sit on them. Having pattered through a few empty pleasantries, the solicitor then cleared his throat.

18

"It is my sad duty to inform you that your Uncle David has died." He paused to allow Ari the obligatory moment of insincere regret. Instead, she looked at him concerned.

"Wow, that's harsh," she said, "my poor grandparents, to live to see both children die."

Her grief was not personal, merely an observation that no parent should outlive their child. How could she have grief for people who had disowned her mother and not even attended the funeral? Ari could still remember the shock she'd felt when she read the brief note from her grandfather. He'd acknowledged her letter, informing him of her parents' death, but said that no one from the family would attend the funeral. And that had been that for the past seven years. There was no interest in the wellbeing of the five orphaned girls; why would there be? If they weren't even interested in the death of their daughter, concern for the welfare of their granddaughters was non-existent.

Mr Fanshawe looked at her in confusion. "I'm afraid your grandparents died some years ago. I take it you weren't aware of that fact?"

So that was the way of it then, was it? Uncle David, Mum's own brother, had decided to carry on the family feud and had continued the wall of silence.

Ariana was beyond disgusted. Her mother's family were revolting; she got up to leave. "Please pass on my condolences to Aunt Cecily and thank you for informing me of my uncle's death."

Mr Fanshawe stood, alarmed, and asked her to sit again. He appeared flustered and poured a second cup of tea, a strong one this time. Ariana, sat, trying to restrain her temper, something was out of kilter. This solicitor seemed anxious, which for a man surrounded by such obvious displays of confidence seemed odd, but right now Ari didn't care much. Her face was hot from the discovery that she and her sisters were still being actively ignored by their own family.

Fanshawe took a sip of his stronger drink, cleared his throat once more, and continued. "My apologies. It is now apparent to me, that your uncle continued your grandfather's refusal to acknowledge your mother and for that I am sorry. Families should pull together, especially in hard times. You may find the following uncomfortable to hear." He cleared his throat again and continued. "Your grandparents died six years ago, about a year after your mother. Your cousins, Julian and Jacinta, also died under tragic circumstances. An overdose and a suicide I regret to say, and their mother, your aunt by marriage, died of grief the following year. Your uncle, as I explained, died last month."

He paused, and Ariana stared at him. "What? Wait! They're all dead? All that death and no one once thought to call us up? Blimey, well we always felt like we were alone in the world but boy, I guess we really are now."

Fanshawe was surprised that the penny hadn't seemed to drop yet. Was it possible that this young lady didn't understand the implications of what he had told her? Was it possible that her mother may have chosen not to tell her daughters about the family that they belonged to?

"I'm afraid there's a bit more."

3

Ari looked up, was there anyone left to die? This was incredible, all her mother's family gone just like that. She had so many questions, but she had no idea how to ask them without sounding callous. The solicitor interrupted her thoughts.

"Were you aware of who your mother's family were?"

"Not really, they had a big house apparently, and some servants and my father wasn't good enough. That's pretty much it. Oh, the house! Good grief, is that why I'm here?"

Ari was anxious not to appear too delighted, but the idea that she might have actually inherited something was too good to be true. She bit down on that line of thought. Given the family's treatment of her, her uncle's final act had probably been to burn the damn thing to the ground!

"Well, yes, in a matter of speaking, the house is why you are here. You are the closest, oldest, surviving relative of the Earl of Wiverton, and as such, you are next in line to the title. In fact, he changed his will last year to specifically name you as his sole heir."

"The Earl of What? I'm sorry, who are we talking about?"

Ari was confused, one minute she was discussing the death of family members, the next this solicitor was rambling on about some complete stranger.

"Wiverton. Your Uncle David."

Fanshawe looked at Ari's puzzled expression and poured another strong tea, a large one. Clearing his throat again, he continued.

"Well, my dear, this is a rather difficult thing to hear all at once, but it is my pleasure to inform you that you are now the Right Honourable Lady de Foix, Countess of Wiverton. Your family is an old and distinguished one. Your estate covers several properties across the UK as well as a few properties abroad, you own various companies, although your uncle had begun to mothball some of them, but all in all your accounts are in good order. You don't have any voting rights in the House as your uncle relinquished them, but you still sit on a few boards." Pausing, he looked at her dumbstruck face, "Drink your tea."

Ari didn't believe in wasting anything, let alone words, but she was so tempted to ask if this was a joke. She sipped her tea in silence. Eventually, she

23

became aware of the clock ticking, and she steadied herself to look up at the solicitor again.

"So, is that why my grandfather wrote Wiverton at the bottom of his letter telling us he wouldn't be attending his daughter's funeral? Instead of his actual surname?" asked Ari. Everything she had just been told was so overwhelming that she was trying to focus on a small detail. At the time she had assumed her grandfather might have had dementia.

"Ah, no," said Fanshawe, "I'm afraid at that point your grandfather was already dead so his son David, your uncle, became the Earl of Wiverton. And in turn, because Wiverton is a female title you are now Wiverton in your own right. You are the Countess of Wiverton. In addition, you have several other titles, some of which can be held by your children in their own right."

"And my sisters? I'm sorry, this is ridiculous." Ari could barely take it in and she was still waiting for the solicitor to confess to pulling her leg.

"Well again, that is down to you to decide. There are several titles they can use as favours, and the estate is considerable, so there will be plenty of property for them to live in if you wish. In their own rights, they have now moved from 'the Honourable' to 'Lady'. The form of address remains Lady, but you are 'The Right Honourable Lady Wiverton' rather than 'the Lady Wiverton'. 'The' with a capital T. You have all been Honourables from the day you were born. Your grandfather may have shunned your mother, but he didn't write her out of the family line, and neither did your uncle."

Ari stared at him in silence. What on earth was he talking about?

"I'm a lady?" Ari was completely non-plussed.

"No, you are a countess. Your sisters are ladies."

Ari sniggered, "I'm sorry. That sounds ridiculous. Is this a joke? Are you sure about this?" She had grown up in a terrace house in the East End of London, where she shared a bedroom with her sister. They walked to their local comprehensive. They were on free school meals and hand-me-downs were just the normal way of acquiring clothes. Their phones were state of the ark, they didn't have pudding or treats, and they never went on foreign holidays. Ari shuffled about in the chair, her bare legs rubbing against the velvet padding, her feet cold from the hole in her shoe. The Countess of Wet Cardboard. And yet the solicitor seemed incredibly earnest. If this was a joke, then probably the best thing to do was to play along until someone laughed at her. The alternative, that he was actually telling the truth, seemed too implausible.

"Go on then. What next?"

Fanshawe admired her poise. If this was anything to go by, the estate was going to be fine. He had run a quick background check on her and her sisters, and they appeared to have done admirably, given their abandonment by the rest of the family. Admittedly, she had got pregnant and married quite early on, but then young love will sweep even the most level-headed off their feet. Pulling some files towards him, he explained everything to be dealt with; bank cards and chequebooks were in the process of being drawn up in her name, that he would get the keys to her presently, and she now needed to sort out a will, if she didn't already have one in place. He assumed from the suppressed snort that no will was in place.

"Might I suggest that we meet again next week when I have everything ready for you? I'm sure that you would like to share the good news with your husband and sisters? No doubt by then things will have begun to sink in, and you will have a lot more questions. Although I am, of course, at your disposal, day or night, should you need to phone me with a question." Mr Fanshawe now leant back in his chair. A difficult conversation had become trickier than he expected but all seemed to now be back on course. He was relaxing into the knowledge that he liked his new client. "In fact, I encourage you to do just that. My firm has worked for your family for over a hundred years; we can probably handle anything that you need. Now, in the meantime, whilst we wait for the bank accounts to transfer into your name, may I wire some money to your current account?"

Quite a lot of his words had just become buzzing, but an offer of money was never to be ignored. Ari paused, she didn't want to seem greedy and she was reluctant for the joke to be finally sprung but she may as well ask.

"Would fifty pounds be possible?"

If this was real, that would give her a nice cushion for the electricity bill. The constant rain recently had meant drying the children's clothes and bedding indoors, and she was ploughing her way through the coin meter.

"Oh, I think we can do a bit better than that," smiled Fanshawe. "Shall we say a thousand, but let me know if that's..."

His voice trailed off as Ari burst into tears. Finally embraced into the arms of the family, to find there was no family left but an apparent fortune instead.

27

After a lot of toing and froing, Ari recovered her decorum and was soon sitting in the back of a taxi. She had tried to point out that she had a return bus ticket but Mr Fanshawe, and more importantly, Mrs Smith, wouldn't hear of it. She had had a massive shock and shouldn't be standing around, squeezed in on public transport. Ari wanted to point out that a taxi was also public transport, but she wasn't up to making jokes at the moment, her head was reeling. She was rich. She had a title. The whole family was rich, she would be able to take care of everyone properly. Which led her back to Greg. How was she going to keep this a secret from Greg? Could she keep it secret? She should have asked Mr Fanshawe for advice, but it seemed a little bit sordid and an awful lot greedy. Hopefully, she could just buy him off.

The taxi pulled up two streets away by the bus stop. She wasn't sure how to proceed. For now, she wanted to keep things to herself whilst she got on top of the situation. Turning up outside her front door in a taxi would be akin to throwing kerosene on a barbeque; curtains would twitch, tongues would wag, and scenarios would be speculated upon.

She loved her street; it was a proper community made up of families from all over the globe. Their only common strand being a desire to do well, living in the poorest area of London. Growing up, the five sisters had ended up with mamas from Africa, aunties from India and a whole extended family consisting of most of the street. Everyone knew everyone's business, and all had an opinion on it.

No, she would walk the last section. As she turned into her terraced street, she saw a police car outside her home. Despite living in London, theirs was a safe neighbourhood and they rarely saw police cars parked outside. Her first thoughts were that something was wrong with the children but then she realised she was being ridiculous. If something was wrong with the children, an ambulance would have come instead. She needed to calm down. The twelve hours since her fight with Greg had been so momentous that she was jumping at shadows. In fact, not so much jumping as pole vaulting. As she got closer, she could see that the two police officers were talking to Mrs Monjareet, next door. She made a note to pop over later and see if she could help in any way, Mrs M's English wasn't perfect, but her pride was. Ari would offer some assistance in a discreet manner later and leave her neighbour to the police. If she needed her now, Ari knew she would call out. Indeed, as she approached, all three turned towards her but the look on their faces brought her to a standstill. A feeling of utter dread rooted her to the spot, this was what always happened to good news. It was destroyed.

"Is it the boys? Mrs M, is it the boys?"

Ari realised she was shouting. She couldn't take another step, utterly immobilised by fear. She didn't want to get any closer to them, as if by getting closer, it would make it more real. The female police officer walked towards her.

"Is it the boys?" Screaming now.

"No, Mrs Paxton, it's not your children. Where are they and I can get them on the phone to you? Mrs Paxton. It's not your boys."

Slowly and calmly, the policewoman reached her hand out towards her. She was aware that the officer was trying to say something to her, but she just couldn't take it in. Ari tried to recover herself.

"I'm so sorry, I don't know what's come over me. It's been a long day. How silly of me, do please excuse me." She realised she was gabbling but the shock had been so great that she had been briefly undone. "If you'll excuse me, I need to get my children."

My God, how embarrassing, creating a scene in public. Wait until she told the girls how their calm and collected big sister stood in front of Mama Vy's house screaming at the police. She knew she would laugh later but for now, she just wanted to grab the boys and hug them until her heart calmed down.

"Mrs Paxton. Did you hear me? We need to speak to you about your husband." The police and Mrs M continued to look at Ari in concern and Ari realised that she still hadn't moved and now she looked at the officer with familiar resignation.

"Greg? Is this about him?"

Ari watched as the officers exchanged glances. The male officer just shrugged his shoulders, whilst Mrs M continued to stare at Ari in pity.

"Please, Mrs Paxton, can we go indoors?" The officer was quiet but insistent. Ari looked back at her but just couldn't get a handle on the situation. The boys were okay, so why was everyone treating her like spun glass. God knows she was used to Greg doing something stupid.

"No, I don't think so. Just let me know why you're here and I'll deal with it. I want to go and get my children. Now!" She wondered dully if he had been in another fight, or maybe there'd been a misunderstanding about whose wallet he had picked up. Again. Whatever, she was sick of it and sick of the association and now, following her inheritance, she finally had a means of escape.

The policewoman looked uncomfortable and looked back to her colleague for support. However, he just grimaced and made no effort to join her. She took a deep breath.

"Mrs Paxton. I'm afraid to tell you that there was an accident last night. Please, can we go inside?"

Hell, thought Ari, had he hurt someone? "Was it a fight, or was he driving drunk again? Is anyone hurt?"

Again, the PC tried to persuade Ari into her house, but she wasn't moving, she was fed up of police officers in her house telling her how her husband had been involved in this or that misunderstanding.

"Mrs Paxton, I'm sorry to have to inform you but your husband is dead."

She stared at the officer. Incomprehension slowly giving way to realisation.

"Dead?"

And for the first time in weeks, Ariana laughed her head off.

4

The boys fidgeted on either side of Ari, uncomfortable in their formal clothes. They were flanked by their aunts as the small family sat in one pew at the front of the chapel of rest. Behind them sat various friends and neighbours of the family. Today, the whole community was out to support Ari. Given where Ari had grown up, her neighbourhood was a natural melting pot of nationalities. One thing all cultures understood was the need for rituals, regardless of the faith or the culture, and a funeral was one of the greatest rituals there was. Today they were out in force. Solemn and respectful. Across the aisle, Greg's friends and family cast hostile glances.

Funerals could only be endured thought Ari, but this was nearly over. Greg's coffin had slid behind the curtains to an Elvis Presley track selected by his mother. The entire event had been handled by her and Ari was grateful to let her do it, not that Annette had given her any choice. Since his death, Annette had assumed the role of principal mourner giving Ari no say in the matter. God knows, she wasn't grieving for him and she had her hands full with her unexpected inheritance.

33

Telling her sisters had been a nightmare. In fairness, trying to tell them that Greg was dead and that they were rich, in the same call, was a difficult task. Clem was Ari's second sister, two years younger than her, and her saviour. Through every setback, Clem had been supporting Ari and fighting all the battles she could, desperate to take some of the strain off her older sister's shoulders. When she heard about Greg she went for honesty and said how delighted she was. She also liked the idea of being a Lady, which made Ari laugh. Clem was more of a Rottweiler than a poodle, but each were pedigrees in their own right. Paddy cried and tried to reminisce with Ari about the good times with Greg, but she stuttered to a halt. Her sobs starting again when she asked how the boys were managing. She had only been fourteen when their parents had died and had suffered greatly at the time. But that was Paddy all over, caring and emotional, she was easily swamped by the distress of others. The death of her own parents had possibly affected her the worst of all the girls. Certainly the most obviously. When Ari told her about recent events, she hadn't even asked a single question regarding the inheritance. Unlike her twin, Nick, who had failed to comment on Greg at all, but went straight to the nitty-gritty of liabilities. Really thought Ari, Nick was well suited to her job in the stock market. She didn't waste any time on false sentiment and cut straight to the heart of the matter. It was funny, thought Ari, how chalk and cheese the twins were, yet challenge either of them and the other sprang to her sister's side. When she had told Aster, she could almost hear the shrug over the phone, followed by a query asking if she was expected to attend the funeral. Ari snapped that it wasn't an invitation it was an instruction.

And during all this, the bits of paperwork flew back and forth to the solicitor, various documents were signed. Bank accounts were being set up but other than that the sisters had kept the matter entirely between themselves. Ari hadn't even told the boys. It seemed wrong to be excited and optimistic when Greg wasn't even in the ground. The sisters were desperate to celebrate but they understood Ari's position and that of the boys. They had readily agreed to let it simmer in the background until the funeral had passed. Ari was relieved that it was almost over. As the music died down, Annette stood up and turned to face the congregation.

"Thank you all for coming today. This has been the worst time of our lives and Nigel and I are grateful to you for all your support." She sniffed and dabbed at her eyes avoiding making any eye contact with Ari or anyone on that side of the chapel. "As you know, Greg was never one to let an occasion pass without the odd drink." There was polite laughter from the chapel, which astounded Ari, after all, they were here because he had fallen in the canal and drowned because he, as usual, was drunk. "And so, I'd like to invite you all back to our house to raise a final glass to Greg and send him on his way." Annette paused, and finally looked at Ari. "Everyone that is except for his wife and her two bastard children."

There was an audible gasp amongst the mourners and for a second Ari could not believe that Annette had just said that out loud. Turning to Aster and Paddy, she told them to take the boys outside immediately. Quickly their aunts grabbed the little boys' hands and smartly pulled them out of the chapel. As soon as Ari saw the children had left the building she stood up, reminding herself furiously that Annette was grieving.

"Thank you, Annette, for hosting Greg's wake." Her hands were to her side and she could feel Clem and Nick on either side of her giving them a little squeeze. "As you wish, we shall not attend. This is a sad and painful day for you, we don't want to add to it." She paused, she knew she was sounding formal and stuffy, but she had to speak. "But, for the record, my sons are your grandsons."

"My sons are your grandsons," mimicked Annette in a nasty little sing-song voice. "No, they're bloody not. Greg always suspected you were sleeping around and lied to him to get a ring on your finger."

Ariana recoiled; this was appalling. She knew Annette had never liked her much, but she hadn't appreciated the depth of her venom. And to say such wicked things in front of all these people.

"They are your grandchildren," Ari repeated in a shaky voice.

Nigel was now standing by Annette. "Leave it alone, Ari, can't you see how much you are upsetting Annette. God, if Greg could see what you are doing, he'd be ashamed of you."

Ari cleared her throat aware of a small movement to her left, praying that Clem kept her mouth shut. She spoke to Nigel instead. "I'm sorry, Nigel, obviously I don't mean to upset either you or Annette, but the boys are Greg's sons."

"Oh, right love, and do you reckon that we are going to support them now he's dead. Is that your angle?"

Shocked that Nigel also clearly held her in the same opinion as his wife, Ari didn't know how to continue.

"I don't want any money from you. But they are your grandchildren!"

37

The rest of the congregation were now sat in a stupefied thrall. Whether gleeful or horrified, no one could move as this abysmal scene unfolded in front of them.

"You're a bloody liar who always thought she was too good for my son and tricked him into marrying her," spat Annette. "Well, you won't get a penny out of us. Not for you or for your bastard brats, and that's our final say on the matter."

Glaring at her, the couple seemed almost pleased and puffed up, having made this pronouncement. Regardless of the fact that the corpse of their son lay not ten metres away. Losing her temper or bursting into tears was not going to help in any way despite Ari's great desire to do both. She breathed in deeply, "If that's how you feel about it, I would be grateful if you could put it in writing. But I hope you don't. I hope tomorrow we can put this behind us."

Not waiting for a reply, she turned to her side of the congregation.

"We're leaving now. Thank you for coming here today but the boys and my sisters are now going to spend some time together. As requested, we won't be at the wake."

Mama Vy, the matriarch of the street, stood up, "You do what you need to do, dearie. But we won't be attending the wake either." She paused and looked around the pews, eyeballing everyone to make sure that they knew that this applied to them as well. "If you are not welcome then neither are we."

"Good," crowed Annette from the front stage. "I don't want your sort in my house anyway. I never knew how Greg could bear to live among you lot."

There was some unpleasant sniggering from Greg's family and friends. Mutters about smells and thieves could be heard and Ari flushed to hear such openly racist slurs against her friends. In a clear show of disapproval, her entire side of the chapel stood up. There was some quiet rustling as bags were picked up and coats put on but other than that not a word was spoken. As they filed out, each made a point of thanking the presiding official. His mortification was bitten down as he received the thanks and compliments for a lovely service from a group of individuals that held themselves with dignity and pride. In the background further jeering and laughing could be heard.

The first to thank him had been Nick, pulling at Ari and Clem. Both girls looked ready to start a fight on behalf of their neighbours. Nick wasn't sure what Ari was capable of at that moment but knew that

Clem could kick off in a paper cup without any provocation whatsoever. Just now they had witnessed more provocation than you could shake a pointy stick at.

Once out in the fresh air, Ariana stepped to one side and threw up. She was surprised to notice how many cigarette butts there were in the gutter that were self-rolled. What a silly thing to notice she thought, and then burst into tears. Nick hissed that the others were now coming out, so she quickly wiped her mouth on her sleeve. Pulling herself together, the three of them joined Paddy, Aster, and the boys by one of the funeral cars.

As they all piled in the car, Aster took one look at her sisters' expressions and brightly declared to everyone that she fancied pizza. The boys cheered and soon their funeral car was pulling up outside a nearby Pizza Hut. As the car pulled to a stop, five elegant young women stepped out. All dressed head to toe in black, they were accompanied by two smartly dressed little boys and as they swept into the restaurant, the waiting staff quickly re-arranged some tables for them. God knows they'd seen all sorts, from stag dos to bar mitzvahs but this was the first time that anyone remembered hosting a wake.

Looking at her sisters, Ari felt exhausted but also so grateful for their presence. The future was bewildering but she knew that with the four of them by her side she could do it. She stood and raised a glass of water, ignoring the curious glances of nearby diners

"May I, Countess Wiverton, offer my thanks to the Honourable Lady Clementine, the Honourable Ladies Nicoletta and Patricia, the Honourable Lady Aster, and to the Honourable Viscounts William and Leo."

She had meant it to sound funny, but the sisters looked at her in silence as they finally came to terms with their new lives. Pushing her chair back, Nick raised her glass.

"To us."

The other three girls stood, the boys looking on. Clem cleared her throat, her eyes bright.

"Here's to Mummy and Da." And finally, the tears that no one was prepared to shed for Greg ran down the girls' faces.

ELIZABETH HURLEY

5

For the next few weeks, there was little to laugh about. The children had started to wet their beds again. They didn't seem to be sad about their father not being around but every visitor to the house kept telling them how awful and tragic it was, and they were miserably confused.

The funeral had been horrific and through everything, she and her sisters had to sit down and come to terms with how the paths of their lives had suddenly altered. Like Ari, they at first thought the news was one giant practical joke, but as they received new bank accounts in their new names with fat bank balances, the reality sank in.

And now, she was finally on the road. After the first half hour of driving the van, Ari relaxed. A little. At least her knuckles were no longer a vivid white. Both boys were strapped in the cab beside her, and they were enjoying the views and looking down on the other cars. So far boredom hadn't set in. The huge roads leading out of London had been terrifying, and whilst she knew she was bigger than a car and with better visibility, she kept checking in the non-existent rear-view mirror and spooking herself. Despite being perched up higher than most drivers, it oddly made her feel more exposed and vulnerable. At every opportunity, she hugged the inside lane, driving like a little old lady. The van wasn't particularly large, nor was there much in it, but Ari was convinced that despite all the straps, the load was going to swing and tip the van over. It also had the manoeuvrability of a wardrobe; she felt that it was wallowing along the lanes of traffic, pitching and swaying like the Mary Rose before she succumbed to the waves. If she didn't get a grip soon, she would be a nervous wreck before she arrived—more of a nervous wreck. Just at the point when Ari felt she was going to have to pull over and calm down, the roads became easier. The M11, despite being a motorway, was pretty empty which helped dispel the feeling of everyone hemming her in and glaring at her as they overtook.

That was less a feeling and more of a reality. One man had drawn level whilst overtaking and was clearly gearing up for some Anglo-Saxon gestures, when he looked across and saw a young woman sat bolt upright, her neck tense and a death grip on the wheel. Beside her sat two cherubs waving planes around in the air. He quickly tried to change his hand signals to a salute and drove on. What sort of husband left the driving to his wife when she was so clearly out of her depth?

Once in the countryside, Ari relaxed but now there were fewer things to occupy the boys' attention and soon the aeroplanes began to accidentally hit each other. To accidentally bump into each other whilst both children were strapped in their car seats showed an impressive effort, but Ari had never underestimated the boys' ability to start a fight when bored. She pulled into the next services for a break in the play area and ordered herself a very large coffee.

As she sat at the table, she wondered how many other parents had sat shivering on these damp wooden benches, their legs tucked uncomfortably between the fixed seat and top, hands wrapped around a cooling cup, waiting for their children to wear themselves out. Ari thought she could probably fall asleep right now if someone put a pillow in front of her. But that wasn't going to get the job done and reminded her that she wanted to arrive in the daylight. It shouldn't be an issue but driving a wardrobe in unfamiliar dark country lanes was not on her list of firsts for today. Will had stopped to look at a crisp packet, but Leo was still going strong on the climbing frame. Only chocolate bribery was going to work, but thankfully such a rare treat did the trick, and soon both boys were once more encased in their little shells of styrofoam, fabric, buckles and belts. After a short while both boys' heads were lolling, little chocolate drools smeared across their chins. The Suffolk countryside gave way to Norfolk countryside, and soon the ground fell away from the horizon, leaving

45

the sky in all its glory dominating the view in every direction. For a girl that had grown up in the shadows of tower blocks, this vastness was something amazing to witness. She remembered feeling the same when her mother took her into St Paul's Cathedral for the first time, and she and her sisters had stood silently in awe of the space above them. She smiled at that memory suddenly surfacing and couldn't wait to take the boys. It would be a few years yet, though she imagined the first thing they would do on seeing all that space would be to try and fill it. As loudly as their lungs could bellow, they would play with the space and try to cram themselves into every last gap of air that they could occupy. They would have great fun, but Ari felt certain that they would be in the minority enjoying their noise. Maybe churches should have a bellowing session where people could just come in and shout, yawp against the day, fill the echoes with their cries. It had a whispering gallery, why not a shouting dome?

The satnav was beginning to make frequent adjustments now, and Ari realised she was within a few miles of the postcode and her new life. The land around here was a bit hillier than before, and there were also some woods about. Every so often she spotted patches of yellow flowers in the underbrush and at the sandy verges. As she got closer to the postcode, she spotted lots of fence posts and doors painted in the same colour. Russet was a popular choice and blended in nicely with the redbrick and flint walls she saw from time to time. Largely though, this area was countryside and apart from the odd driveway or cottage, she saw little evidence of houses or people.

Then to her right, she saw a massive gateway with a cottage built alongside one of the giant pillars. A stag stood high up on the top of one pillar, a lion on the other.

"You have reached your destination," chirped the satnav with unnecessary drama.

Ari pulled off the road, past the gate posts and parked the van. She leant over to wake the boys; good or bad, whatever lay ahead was theirs too, and she wanted them to remember this moment.

"Darlings. We're here. Are we ready to go exploring?"

The children looked around, curious but not seeing anything special. Then Leo spotted the house by the gate.

"Look our house has a big horse on the top!"

"No silly, Mummy said it was a big house. Didn't you, Mummy?"

"That's a pretty big horse!"

Leaving the boys to bicker about the size of houses and horses and reminding herself to tell them about stags, Ari jumped out of the van and knocked on the cottage door. She had been told that the whole estate was vacant but quite frankly she felt rude not checking and she simply couldn't rid herself of the feeling of trespassing. However, there was no reply and as she looked through the window, the place whilst furnished, looked unloved and unlived in.

Hopping back into the van she could hear the children still rumbling on and now asking if they could also get out.

"Just a bit longer. This isn't us; I think ours is a bit bigger, but we're almost there and then you can run around. Okay?"

"Is it as big as Vihaan's?"

Vihaan lived with his parents and grandparents. They had bought three terrace houses and had made a clever knock through. From the outside, everything appeared normal, but behind the front doors, there were little passageways running back and forth. They had even converted the three attics into a long den for the children. It was an ingenious solution to rising house prices and a family that wanted to live near each other, but not necessarily in each other's pockets.

48

"I think it might be even bigger than that but be warned it might be ever so messy and run-down looking. But we can fix that can't we?"

"Yes, we can!" cried out Bob the Builder One and Two. And with the children prepared for the worst, Ari drove down the drive.

"Are we there yet?"

Leo had a point; this was a very long drive with lovely green pastures on either side. The wide green parkland was dotted with the odd large tree and the tarmac drive cut through the green swathe but still there was no sign of a house. Just as she was convinced she had taken a wrong turning, the van crested a small hill and before her, standing behind a second set of smaller gates, was the prettiest house that Ari had ever seen. She stopped the van in wonder.

"Wow."

The overwhelming impression was of a jumble. Roughly it seemed to be three storeys high or maybe four, and at least twelve windows wide along the front of the house. There appeared to be one initial large building with others built on to the side and then a wing at a right angle on the other side. A large bay window fronted one section of the house and just continued up past the roofline to become a tower. It sat along the skyline with an array of chimneys bristling against the sky, each set of chimneys built in ornate red brick patterns. At the other end of the house at the edge of a wing was another tower, round this time with arrow slits in it. Sections of the building had tall panels of narrow elegant windows, other areas had lower rectangular windows with lead lines crisscrossing over them like a black and white harlequin. Throughout this mishmash of features ran red bricks and capped and cobbled flint stones lending the entire structure an exquisite harmony. The evening sun made the red brick walls glow and the many panes of glass twinkled back a warm light.

She looked at the boys, her eyes as wide as plates. "That's it then. At least it's got a roof on!" And then she burst into laughter, with possibly a slightly manic edge. She'd been convinced, despite Mr Fanshawes's reassurances, that the estate was in rack and ruin and that she had actually inherited a great big pile of dung.

The boys weren't sure what the joke was, but a joke's a joke and their mother was laughing, so it was clearly a good one.

"And it's got windows!" piped up Leo. Not wanting to be left out, William joined in, "And a door."

"At least it's got walls!" Laughing, they drove forward whilst the joke was being played out to a rattling death, "At least it's got its garden on!" Everyone was happy.

"Which bit is ours, Mummy?" asked Leo.

"Um, all of it."

"We don't have to share it with anyone?"

"I'm not sure. There may be some other people living here." Although again, Mr Fanshawe had told her that Uncle David had dismissed all his live-in staff after his wife died.

"We'll have to find out."

"I bet ghosts live here," said Leo. Great, thought Ari, he never misses a moment to alarm his brother.

"That would be brilliant! Wouldn't it, William? I bet the ghosts here are the friendliest happiest ghosts in the whole wide world. What do you think, Leo?"

Leo, catching his mother's scowl quickly agreed that they had the best ghosts, if there were any ghosts, and that they would all make friends. Will seemed a little concerned, so Ari pulled out another chocolate bar. Honestly, she could crown Leo.

Parking on the gravel in front of the house, Ariana rummaged in the vast box of keys that Mr

Fanshawe had given to her until she found the one with the label Front Door. Unbuckling the boys, she heaved them out of the cab. The March wind bit into them and she was surprised by how cold it was—noticeably chillier than at home—and they hurried toward the huge front door. She had been told that no one would be there, but it seemed strange that such a large place would be so still and silent. Slotting the key into the lock, Ari wondered at the size of the doorway, you could probably ride a horse in through it and she wondered if anyone had in the past. She could imagine the screeches of protest from whoever had to clean it and decided not to say anything to the boys, just in case it gave them ideas. Shaking her head, Ari and the boys all turned the large key together, pushing the door inwards.

As they walked in, they were greeted by a tall wide room. Large dark floorboards spanned the room and were covered by a huge rug. To one side was an enormous hearth and to the other, a wide shallow staircase climbed up to a large open gallery. Both the gallery and the staircase were also carved out of dark oak, and the walls were lined in oak panels. The newel post at the bottom of the stairs had a carved bird of prey proudly holding a family shield. Along the balcony were several more animals bearing crests looking down on the newcomers staring up at them. The hearth was empty and as the boys stood in it, they shouted that they could see the sky at the top. Two large doors stood to the left and right and a corridor snaked off in the corner of the hall towards the back of the house. The edges of the room were home to various side tables with vases on them and there was a pleasant inviting feel to the room despite its size. Something about the proportions and offset doors and architecture seemed to show a house that had grown and adapted over the centuries for the families that had lived within.

As the family explored, they found doors leading to cellars and doors leading up into towers, they found loads of bedrooms, but only two upstairs bathrooms. There were more staircases than she could keep track of, the narrowest and steepest leading down from the attic floor to an enormous kitchen. They found an outdoors loo and a downstairs bathroom that seemed to have been installed in the 1930s and then abandoned. There was a library or study, something with lots of books and a big desk. Leading off the library was a smaller room, full of display cases of every sort of oddity. There were pretty china plates, standing up on show like in a museum. Next to them was a small stuffed armadillo, and then on to a carriage clock and a collection of rocks. Shrugging their shoulders at each other, they retreated and continued to explore. There seemed to be a few rooms with sofas in them and a formal dining room with a large polished table sitting in the middle of it, the walls covered with gloomy paintings of fields and hedges.

Her favourite room so far though, was the kitchen. At one end, was a big heavy table with two long benches running down either side. Looking around, Ari thought she could probably drag one of the many sofas she had come across into this room as well. She would work out how to live in the other rooms as time progressed, but for now, she knew where she was in a kitchen, and this was where the new family would grow out from.

Finding a grand bedroom with a bathroom attached to it she suggested the boys slept in there for the night and she would join them as well when she came up. Within seconds they were fast asleep, overwhelmed by their new home.

Although she was tempted to join them, she still had a lot of work to do. With great reluctance, she began unloading the van, swearing about the awkwardness of it all, and missing the help she had had from her neighbours as they had loaded it up for her. There had been so much laughter and noise, and some of the aunties had made her trays of food, to tide her and the boys over for the next few days. However, in their enthusiasm, Ari was convinced that she now had enough meals to take her through the next ice age.

At least there was no furniture. She had left it all in the house until she and her sisters decided what they were going to do with it. Paddy had suggested giving it to a homeless family. The sisters loved the generosity of the gesture and had agreed to look into it in more detail, as they settled into the idea of their newfound wealth.

Gradually, she had emptied out the black bin bags of stuff belonging to her and the boys. She had called Greg's parents and asked if they would like to come and collect his stuff. It had been an ugly scene as they had first refused, insisting that Ari come out to them. When she pointed out that they had a car and she'd have to do the journey, laden down with bags, two small boys and three bus changes they didn't care. She was again reminded of their hostility at the funeral. Ari hadn't told them about her change in fortunes, and they simply assumed that she was just getting rid of his stuff, rather than moving house. Reaching an impasse, Ari asked what charity they would like the items donated to; amongst a backdrop of name calling, they relented and arrived the next day.

They had stalked around the house looking for things that belonged to their son. Each time they claimed an item Ari had to point out that it had belonged to her parents. Maybe they would like to see the photo albums with the object in the background? Finally, they stuffed the bags in the back of the car and were preparing to leave when Ari pointed out that they hadn't even seen the boys. The children had been out on a playdate when Annette and Nigel had arrived earlier than expected. Ari had got on the phone and asked her friends if they could bring the boys back as soon as they could. She knew she was asking a lot, but she didn't want the boys to miss out on seeing their grandparents. And as much as she didn't like them, she felt that they deserved to see their son's sons.

Annette glared at her. "Are you taking the piss? Didn't we make ourselves clear at the funeral?" She flung a letter at Ari, no doubt confirming their disavowal in writing. With that, they both got into the car, slammed their doors and screeched up the road, narrowly missing Julie who had driven back as quickly as she could, through rush hour traffic. On discovering that they had been taken away from their playdate for no good reason and that they had missed their grandparents, both boys had started to cry and fight, throwing a massive tantrum on the pavement. Ari and Julie had had to pick them up and bring them into the house—Ari's neighbours knew all her dirty laundry but there was no need to air it so frequently.

An owl hooted, startling Ari. She had been so busy thinking back to those last painful days in

London that evening had gently fallen around her. Now she was going to have to try and find the fuse box in the disappearing light. She didn't mind going to bed in the dark but if she didn't get the fridge on, all that good food was going to go to waste. Grumbling, she went off exploring, her phone lighting the way. Finally, she found a small cupboard near the back of the house and flipping a big switch was relieved to hear a quiet whirr, rather than a massive bang. As the evening progressed, she unpacked the food and brought all the other bags and boxes into the hallway. Tomorrow they could return the van to the local depot, grab a taxi home and start to live their new lives. For now, shattered, she climbed the stairs patting each wooden animal on its head and clambered in with the boys. The sheets felt slightly damp and had a musty smell but within seconds the two little bodies warmed her up and she fell into a deep and exhausted sleep, unsure of what her tomorrows looked like.

6

Wendy was in the community centre pouring out cups of tea and coffee for the mothers and toddlers' group. It was her turn on the rota to run today's session and she had been looking forward to it all week. Since being laid off, time had hung heavy on her hands. Happiest when she was working, losing her job had left her reeling. Over the months she had picked up odd jobs and voluntary work, but it was still a source of concern. The drop in household income hadn't helped either but her husband had picked up a second shift whilst she applied for jobs on a daily basis. She was wondering about her current batch of applications when the hall doors opened, and a young woman, about her own age, walked in with two small boys. The woman was tall and thin and dressed in a neat pair of jeans and flat pumps with her hair tied up in a ponytail. Her navy jumper had a fashionable slashed boatneck and three-quarter length sleeves. All in all, it was a nice outfit and Wendy was convinced that the woman in question was unaware of the smear of strawberry jam across the side of the jumper. She also thought that she spotted some peanut butter in the ponytail, but she'd have to get closer to be sure. Certainly, she'd seen worse. The two little boys gripped onto their mother's hands and stood as close to her legs as they could without actually hiding behind them. Both were dressed in little, tailored shorts and shirts and looked adorable. Wendy missed seeing small children in formal wear, in fairness they usually destroyed their outfits in about five minutes. But for those five minutes, you could kid yourself that they were little angels. With those blond curls, it was easy to imagine they were perfect, but Wendy had seen enough small children to know that few were, and those that looked it the most, were often furthest from the pearly gates.

As she went to greet the newcomers, she saw that Ellie had got there first and was already crouched down inviting the boys to come and play with the others. Wendy sighed, Ellie was a good person, but she was quite clueless at times; those children would not be leaving their mother's side any time soon. Clearly, Ellie finally realised this and encouraged Mum and the boys to sit at a table near the other toddlers and brought them a box of cars to play with. As she watched, Mum immediately sat on the floor and tipped the whole box out and gradually the family began to play alongside the others. After a while, she sat back up on the chair and observed the boys whilst a few other children inched closer to play nearby. Before long there appeared to be traffic jams involving Barbies, Noddy, Thomas the Tank Engine, some cars and an elephant. A little girl appeared to be trying to straighten out the confusion, but the elephant was oblivious to the mayhem he was causing.

Wendy tapped the new woman on the shoulder and invited her to join the other mums for a cup of coffee. The boys seemed remarkably calm about their mother's departure to the next table and continued to add a giraffe and dog to the traffic jam. The little girl was unimpressed.

"Thanks for that," she said. "People are always in such a rush to separate us, but all they need is a few minutes to find their bearings before they settle down."

Whilst the new mum didn't exactly look or sound like she belonged, she was friendly and down to earth and gave a horrified groan when Debbie pointed out the jam, which was quickly followed by a shriek, when Debbie also pointed out the peanut butter, with possibly a bit too much glee. Still, that was Debbie for you, always happy to pull someone down if she could manage it.

The new mum walked over to the boys and waved her ponytail at them laughing, then headed off to the loos. A few minutes later she returned with wet hair and a damp jumper and a more relaxed air.

"Sorry about that, what a mess. I swear half the time you can see what we've been eating all week."

"Baked beans in our house," piped up Tracey.

"Oh, me too! Or for a treat, tomato soup!" laughed the new mum who introduced herself as Ari.

"Yeah, why is everything red? Jordan just has to look at spaghetti hoops, and he's covered, I'm covered, the cats are covered, the whole fucking house is covered."

Wendy coughed.

"Whoops, my bad. Sorry, all. Hi, I'm Daisy Foul Mouth."

Ari smiled, "No worries, I'm Ari Peanut Ponytail."

It was a lame joke but everyone smiled and started to swap their worst public embarrassments, and it was widely agreed that no one would ever top Monica's poo tipped ponytail, which had then smeared the back of her top and dripped down the back of her legs.

The new girl relaxed into the laughter and agreed that peanut butter might look bad, but it was far from the worst that could happen. Soon the focus swung back to Ari, and Tracey asked if she had just moved to the area.

"Yes, I've moved in near one of the villages, and I saw this sign up in the town library. So, I thought I'd come along and see what the coffee was like." Given how awful the coffee was, everyone grinned. Wendy may be a demon at cooking and organising things and had the kindest heart when it came to children, but she made an appalling cup of coffee, and her tea was even worse. Wendy was proud of her ability to make a teabag stretch to four cups. Wendy was the only one that was proud of this fact.

"So, what does your partner do?" chipped in Debbie; typical thought Wendy, always ready for the kill.

Ari paused, "He's not around anymore."

It was clear to the other women that this was a recent issue and one that was still raw. "Neither's mine pet, and good riddance."

"Nor mine."

"Never had one."

"Never kept one, more like!"

"Cheeky cow."

"Single mum, scourge of society."

Ari grinned, "Blimey, are we all single mums?" Everyone laughed, and those with partners volunteered their names and their opinions of them. Janice's Dan was hard working, Julie's Simon, wasn't. Wendy's husband was apparently a paragon of virtue, even making tea and buying her birthday presents, but Debbie's husband who was apparently perfect in Debbie's eyes, seemed to cause mirth amongst some of the others.

"Part-time brickie, part-time husband!" laughed Kylie.

Wendy coughed again.

"What?" demanded Kylie, "It's okay for her to slag me off but not the other way around?"

The two women glared at each other. Clearly a long-running feud.

In an attempt to change the subject, Wendy reminded everyone of the bring and buy stall for the town market. "It's to raise funds for this group," said Wendy, "so if you have anything in the house you don't need, just bring it along."

Ari spluttered and Wendy quickly changed tack, "Don't worry love, lots of us don't have anything to spare, but if you wanted to volunteer to man the stall for a few hours you'd be most welcome." Wendy was instantly drowned out by the others deploring her for trying to co-opt a new volunteer before they'd even had their second cup of coffee.

Ari looked at her watch and realised that she was going to have to go if she was going to get all the other chores done before the boys needed their afternoon nap. Agreeing to volunteer if she was free, Ari took Wendy's number and waved goodbye to the rest of the group, pleased for once that she could just leave a pile of toys on the floor for someone else to clear away.

"What do you reckon?"

"No ring on her finger."

"She was quite twitchy, and she didn't say where she lived."

"Maybe he used to hit her?"

"Maybe she's never had a bloke."

"Don't be daft, look at her, posh girl like that, she'd have them lining up."

"Well, maybe she's one of those 'don't need a man' types."

"Depends what sort of man. There's many I could do without."

"Are you starting again?!"

"Keep your knickers on. Just saying she might be one of them Women's Libbers."

"Lesbian?"

"No, wally, women's lib."

"Well, she seemed nice enough. Mind you, did you see her phone? That belonged in a museum."

"Poor love, I thought she was going to choke when you asked her for donations."

"Don't! I feel awful. It's just her clothes were nice, and she spoke so proper that I figured she might have a nice house too."

"Didn't the boys look adorable. Right little princes."

"It's the curls, my Jordan looks like Prince George."

"Do you reckon Prince George bites?"

"Oi!"

Ari walked down the high street and wondered how long she'd be discussed before the conversation moved on. They seemed like a fun bunch, but she wasn't sure if she fitted in; they all seemed younger than her, except for Wendy, who seemed a little older. However, they were welcoming, well, most of them were, but she wondered if that friendliness would change when they discovered where she lived. At some point, she wouldn't be able to hide it, but for now, she enjoyed the anonymity. She wasn't a fool, she knew that plenty in this town were probably

ELIZABETH HURLEY

connected in some way to the big house but until she
knew more about those ties, she didn't want anyone to
know who she was.

Daydreaming, she and the boys spent the next
few hours trudging in and out of shops, grabbing
essentials, signing up for the library and doctors.
Exhausted they headed off to the bus stop only to
discover that the next one wasn't for another hour. Life
in the countryside was going to take some adjusting
to. Instead, she could catch the next bus which went
roughly in the right direction and walk the last two
miles. She considered a taxi, but she still wasn't used
to having that sort of money. As she got on the bus,
she explained to the driver that she would need him to
shout when she was closest to home, and she would
jump out. Bribing the children with a packet of
sweeties they stepped off the bus and headed down the
lanes, following the driver's instructions.

Looking up at the sky Ari was beginning to
regret her decision to not take a taxi. She had
anticipated walking home with the boys across the
fields following the new path she had found.
However, that cloud looked like it had other ideas. In
a quick recalculation, she decided the quickest route
was straight across the fields; it was shorter but more
exposed. If they were lucky, they could beat the rain.
She was unsure who the fields belonged to, but she

66

had a sneaky feeling that they were probably hers anyway.

As the wind picked up, a few faint spots caught their faces. All three sets of legs sped up, but soon there was no escaping the fact that they were quick marching through the grass in the pouring rain, telling each other what they were going to put in their hot chocolates. Just as Will had mentioned his tenth layer of marshmallows, there was a huge crash of thunder, and the sky flickered into X-ray images as the heavens lit up with a huge flash of light. All three shouted in alarm and exhilaration and then they legged it as fast as they could, as huge pails of rain began sheeting out of the sky. Ahead of them, Ari noticed that someone was standing in the front door of a cottage and shouting at them to come in. In a quick change of direction, all three headed towards the little house on the other side of a country lane and in an explosion of water and laughter piled into a small front living room.

"Oh my God. This rain! Look at you!" A young woman started handing out towels, flicked the kettle on, pulled out a bucket of Lego from behind a sofa, and gave the boys a biscuit. Ari stood drying out her hair, impressed with her saviour's ability to take control.

"Hello again," said Ari, recognising her from the playgroup that morning, "Wendy?"

"Yes, Wendy and you were Harry? Did I hear that correctly? Do you fancy a coffee while you wait for the rain to pass?"

Ari followed Wendy into the kitchen. It was a welcoming, if overcrowded room, the fridge was covered in notes and drawings as well as bills and postcards; comedy magnets holding them in place. On the windowsill was a collection of thriving and dying plants, some jam jars with yellowing water in them, some with twigs in them, others with paintbrushes. The table was again covered in stuff which was promptly re-arranged into stacks to make way for the two cups of coffee. As Wendy pulled out some chairs to sit on, she had to move a pile of ironing off one and tip a cat off the other. She grinned and apologised for the mess, "Mind you, even if I did know you were coming it would probably still look like this!" Ari looked about her with a smile. It reminded her of home when her folks were still alive, and all seven of them were living there.

"How many children have you got?" Ari asked, and was embarrassed when Wendy said none.

"Oh, don't apologise. This house is full of kids, neighbours and nieces and nephews. We can't have children, so this is a nice solution. Plus, I lost my job recently, so I get to help out more."

Ari knew better than to commiserate but it was a hard thing for a woman who so clearly enjoyed the company of children to be without her own. However, she wasn't sure what to say about the recent redundancy either, so with no clear conversational opening, she resorted to small talk.

"I bet you're really popular, my boys love Lego." Taking a sip of her coffee and wishing she'd asked for a glass of water instead she moved the conversation away from any further uncomfortable topics. "So, does it always rain like this in Norfolk? That was a bit intense!"

"Ah, don't let it spoil your first impressions," said Wendy, offering her another biscuit. Checking with Ari that it was okay to offer another to the boys as well, she went into the front room. Ari could hear excited, "Yes pleases," and visibly relaxed, glad that the little monsters had remembered their manners and hadn't simply grabbed the entire packet. As Wendy came back through Ari commented that Wendy had now made two best friends for life. "Lego and homemade biscuits, you have all the best things!"

"Life is so simple at that age isn't it?" she said ruefully. She seemed about to say something else but paused, and instead in a brighter tone, asked Ari how well she knew the area.

"Not at all. I've always lived in London and I'm still trying to get a grip on everything."

Wendy whistled, "Ah, that explains it, I didn't think you sounded local. Well, you sure aren't in Kansas anymore Dorothy!"

Ari laughed, "I know! I mean it's not that far away and all that, but everything here is so different. The buses, for instance, only a handful a day, how do you cope? And the supermarket, where the hell is the spices section? And what's with everyone smiling at each other and saying hello?!"

Both women laughed and Wendy pointed out that hourly buses were a summer highlight. In winter they had to manage with just two or three a day, or none at all, depending on where you lived.

Ari had to check if Wendy was joking and was alarmed to discover she wasn't.

"But how do you cope?"

"You learn to drive."

"But what if you can't afford a car?"

"Well, then you struggle."

God, thought Ari, there was so much to living in the countryside that she had absolutely no idea about. She thought back to the various cars in Uncle David's garage and realised once again that she had stepped from one side to the other of the Them and Us divide.

Wendy noticed the concern on Ari's face. "Where have you moved to? I can look it up and see what their bus network is like if it helps. And don't worry, everyone's ever so friendly here. Just ask for help and someone will pitch in. Even for outsiders," she said with a wink.

Ari pondered if she was indeed an outsider, even if she felt like one. "My mother grew up here and her family have always lived here so I suppose I'm sort of coming home? A half and half outsider?" Ari wasn't sure about being part of her family, but the idea of belonging was a beguiling one.

"Where does your mother live now then?" asked Wendy.

"Nowhere. I mean to say, she's dead. So's Da." Seeing Wendy's distress she was quick to reassure her. "It's okay, it was eight years ago." She rushed on, "then the other day I got a letter from a solicitor saying her brother had died and I needed to get up to Norfolk. So here we are. Fresh start and everything."

"God, I'm so sorry. I didn't mean to put my foot in it. Is your uncle's place nearby? I could give you a lift home if you like?"

Ari paused and then thought to hell with it, at some point she was going to have to come out of hiding, "He lived at Wiverton Manor."

Wendy looked unsure, "Really? No one lives there, only Lord Wiverton himself, and he, thankfully, has just popped his clogs. Miserable old bastard. Oh, hang on!" said Wendy in dawning horror, "Please don't say. Oh, God. Please don't tell me you're Lord Wiverton's niece?"

Ari cringed, "Who? Uncle David, the miserable old bastard?"

Wendy looked at Ari and groaned and then swore and then groaned again and started to try and apologise.

"Please," begged Ari, "I never met him and for the record, I suspect your description of him is one hundred per cent accurate."

"So, are you the heir?" asked Wendy, and looked thoughtful when Ari confirmed that apparently, she was. "Well there have been de Foix at Wiverton for the past five hundred years, so I think that settles the issue of whether you are a local or not. Wow! Another coffee, your ladyship?"

"Don't!" exclaimed Ari in a horrified laugh. "In all honesty this is all totally new to me, we grew up not knowing anything about our mother's family. When I said *Fresh start and everything*, the *Everything* bit is still a bit unbelievable. Just call me Ari, no H, it's what everyone else does. It's short for Ariana but that was always a bit of a mickey take in school, so it soon got snipped down."

The two were soon chatting about life when the phone rang, Wendy ignored it, but the answerphone kicked in, and the voice on the other end sounded full of distress.

"Wendy, love, are you there? The bastards are evicting Jim; they're at his flat now!"

Wendy lunged for the phone, "I'm here! Hang on, I'll be there right away."

Wendy turned to Ari. "I know this is a long shot, but this is sort of your problem. Want to fix it?"

ELIZABETH HURLEY

7

Ari looked concerned; how could anything possibly be her fault? She had been here less than a week. However, one thing she was good at, was solving problems.

"Okay. Explain in the car. Come on boys."

Thankfully the twins sensed that this was not an occasion for delaying tactics and obediently left their Lego and were happily bundled into the back of Wendy's car.

As they drove along Wendy explained. "Jim was one of your staff. Lord Wiverton stopped paying him, and others I might add, a few months ago. Lots of us have been dipping into savings and making do with our partner's wages if they didn't also work for the estate, but Jim has no one and no savings. So, he's been running behind on his rent, and now it looks like it's come to a head, and the bastards are kicking him out."

Ari's stomach churned, she had never met Jim, but she knew exactly how he was feeling. That awful hand to mouth existence, underlined by the constant fear of having everything taken from you. The sheer bloody powerlessness of it all. Wendy's car sped along country lanes and gradually headed in towards the outskirts of town, and rows of terrace houses. It was clear that neighbours had rallied the troops, as a small group of people stood in front of a door, blocking the way of two large aggressive looking men, one of whom was on his phone. Ari told the boys to stay in the car and then strode towards him.

"Are you speaking to your boss? May I?"

The bailiff looked at Ari's outstretched hand with wary surprise. Her voice was the sort that was used to being obeyed immediately, she was calm and quietly spoken, but nothing about her stance seemed soft.

"Hang on, guv, someone wants a word."

Passing the phone over to Ari, he and the small crowd listened in silence to the one-sided conversation.

"Good afternoon. This is Lady Wiverton. To whom am I speaking?"

The crowd now muttered and nudged each other, so this was the new owner.

"I understand your men are here to settle an outstanding balance. What is the amount please?"

The crowd winced in sympathy with Ari's grimace.

"And what exactly does that cover? Right. What form of payment will you take right now so that your staff can leave my employee in peace?"

Tucking the phone under her chin, Ari opened her bag and pulled out her wallet. Soon she was reading out a string of numbers and then passed the phone back to the bailiff.

"Your boss would like a word."

Ari and the crowd watched as the man nodded on the phone. Then the two of them climbed back into their van and drove away, each with a matching bemused look.

A huge cheer erupted from the crowd, and everyone started talking at once. Wendy knocked on the door, "Jim, love. You can unlock the door, they've gone. For good, I reckon."

There was some noise of furniture being pulled about, and then the front door slowly opened. An old man peered out from around the door, hesitant to open it too wide in case this was some unpleasant ruse.

As the door opened the crowd calmed down, they smiled and nodded at Jim, and then began to disperse; a proud and quiet man, they left him with his privacy until just Ari and Wendy were left on the pavement with the boys peering out of the car window.

"Mr? Um, Jim. Hello, I'm Ari, I owe you an apology. I am extremely sorry for the position that my family put you in. May I call on you when I don't have my sons with me? I'd like to understand what went wrong and what I can do to help you?"

The old man looked at Ari with suspicion but was reassured by Wendy's encouragement. A date was agreed once Wendy had made sure that he was alright and needed nothing else right now.

Back in the car, Wendy offered to drive the family home. Ari sat in silence as Wendy chattered on in excitement. "Did you see their faces, and Jim's. Oh my God, you have made his year, you were like a whirlwind! You don't come across like one of them, but then wow, on it flicks!"

Ari's misery deepened as Wendy burbled on. How many more people had her uncle let down? She doubted that Jim was an isolated case, but it looked like she had bigger problems on her hands than blocked gutters and no staff.

"Wendy, I need help. I have no staff, I don't know who they are, or who they were, or even what they did. I don't know where they have all gone, or what happened to everyone. I've been in the house for days now, and I haven't seen a soul. Now I'm worried that others may be in a similar position to Jim, and I don't have a clue."

"What about Dickie?"

"Dickie?"

"Your housekeeper. Runs the place with an iron fist? Terrifying woman, puts Vlad the Impaler to shame."

Ari smiled weakly, "I suspect I'd have spotted her if she had been around."

"Blimey. Did he fire her too? Right, let me ask around."

By now, Wendy's car was heading up the driveway to the front of the house.

"You know, this morning when I asked you for donations, I didn't mean anything fancy. I didn't realise."

"Please, it doesn't matter." Ari thanked her for the lift and with her help lifted the boys out of the car and in through the front door. "I'd love to help out, it's just, at the moment, none of it feels like mine to give away. If that even makes sense? Not much makes sense right now."

The women each carried a boy into a large room off the hallway and lowered them still sleeping, onto a pair of sofas and then Ari walked Wendy back to the front door.

"If you find Dickie, please ask her if she would be happy for me to get in touch."

Once Wendy had left, Ari headed into the kitchen. She looked at the laptop and the paperwork laid out across the large refectory table. No wonder the accounts had looked so good this morning, they weren't paying anyone for anything. Were there also debts that hadn't yet been revealed? What a bloody mess. She wasn't sure what to do, but the first plan of action was to call Mr Fanshawe. He might be able to shed some light on what had just happened. Moving into one of the rooms with a collection of comfortable sofas, she put the call through.

"Lady Wiverton, how are you settling in? How may I help you?"

She smiled, picturing him in his office, waiting for Mrs Smith to bring him his cup of tea and a rich tea biscuit, a chocolate hobnob if she felt he deserved it. Mrs Smith was concerned for his health and was only distributing hobnobs if he walked into work.

Ari explained the afternoon's events and the fact that she hadn't seen a soul anywhere around the grounds or estate buildings.

"Well, I did wonder, but I understand from the accountants that over the past two years your uncle had started to pull in the drawstrings across the whole estate. He was even beginning to discuss selling off parcels of the estate. These are all matters that you and I do need to discuss, but I was hoping that you could have at least a few days to settle into your new home."

Ari looked around this ridiculously large room; nothing felt like home yet. Dear God, she had rooms that she didn't even know what their function was. She had a sneaky feeling that this room was a second or third living room because obviously, one wasn't enough. At the moment her home felt like a large, cold box, full of beautiful things she didn't dare touch.

Mr Fanshawe carried on and explained to her that there was a sale of land that was in limbo following her uncle's death. The parcel of land was essential for the plans of a property developer and they had been badgering him to process the sale. Mr Fanshawe assured her that he would do no such thing until the two of them had discussed the matter and the wider ramifications.

"The fact of the matter, Lady Wiverton, is that this is not a thing to be rushed. They are offering a substantial amount of money for the land, but I need to talk with you about it. They are having a launch presentation in a fortnight, here in town. I have your invitation and would suggest that you and I meet the day before to talk things through? No matter what they say or suggest, this will proceed at your pace. Not theirs."

Thanking Fanshawe, she then spoke to the accountant. After a long and wearying phone call, she realised that the figures were, of course, too good to be true. She didn't understand the extent of an estate's needs but knew it needed constant upkeep, and that meant staff and stuff. And that meant money. The accountant felt that run at the levels it had been two years ago they wouldn't be in the red, but they wouldn't be much in the black either. The estate had to grow. It was time to call the girls as well. Ari knew when she was out of her depth.

Reaching for her phone she made a group call to her sisters and explained the eviction scene earlier as well as some of the other problems she was uncovering.

Nick was quick as ever to sort out a plan. Everyone would come to Wiverton, then the following day Ari could go down to London and stay in the London flat. She could visit the solicitor and the following day, after the developer's meeting, she would return to Wiverton and then the five sisters could work out what to do next.

Ari was unsure about leaving the boys, but her sisters pleaded that they were missing them. As the conversation moved on Ari could hear in the things that her sisters did and didn't say how much they were all struggling with their new lives. A few days in the company of family sounded like the tonic that they all needed.

She was also desperate for some adult conversation that had nothing to do with children. She missed her sisters so much, especially Aster with whom she would have long chats about her homework and various ideas and topics. Now that she was in Cambridge, Ari was enjoying living vicariously through her, but Aster was incredibly busy with her studies and Ari was incredibly busy with the boys and nowadays long chats arguing and putting the world to right were gone. Da had used to make them play a debating game where he would put forward a discussion point and two of the sisters would have to take opposing sides. At a random moment, he would shout switch and they then had to instantly start arguing the opposing point of view. Ari had loved this game, she loved having to think fast on her feet, Clemmie hated it, she just couldn't see the other side in any argument. Paddy would end up crying because she'd got so passionately involved and Nick would laugh that everyone should just get along, but Aster, even at ten, Aster was the best at the game. No matter what she argued, she was a demon at getting everyone to agree with her and then seconds later when she had to change position, she would destroy her previous argument and get everyone cheering for the new point of view. Mummy and Da at that point would throw their eyes to heaven and make her promise never to go into politics or start a coup.

Eventually, Ari hung up, reinvigorated simply by chatting to them. Well, it looked like it was going to be another night of jacket potatoes and baked beans then. She laughed, here she sat in a house with so many bedrooms that she had lost count and yet still seemed to be as poor as before. But single, she whispered to herself, happy to finally be shot of Greg.

8

The following morning Ari and the boys were setting out a wooden train track in the hallway and a marble tower running down the staircase. The rain had settled in, and the children were getting restless, Ari didn't want them exploring on their own, and lots of the rooms were still ghost rooms, strange shapes hidden under white sheets. Yesterday they had found a room on the top floor full of children's toys, a whole room just full of toys. The boys were desperate to explore but Ari was unhappy leaving them up there on their own whilst she went through the paperwork downstairs. As a compromise, they'd piled all the Brio train track pieces into a large tub and dragged it along the wooden floorboards and down the various staircases to the large open hallway. Now the train track was running under a sideboard and had several junctions leading off in all directions. Despite the junctions, the boys seemed to be able to make the trains smash into each other with alarming regularity.

Happy that they would entertain themselves for a while she got up to get on with the paperwork when the doorbell rang. Given that they were practically under the bell they all jumped; she didn't realise a bell could be quite so loud but, in a house this large, she supposed it made sense. Wondering if a bell was also ringing elsewhere in the house, like in the movies, she went to open the door to her first visitor. A short older woman was standing on the doorstep; her coat was buttoned up, and out in the driveway sat a little shiny Corsa. Ariana was instantly put in mind of the Women's Institute and if this woman was a member she was almost certainly in charge. In fact, the way she was looking at Ari was disconcerting. It's quite a thing to open your own front door and be met with a look of disapproval. Maybe it was the pyjamas?

"Good morning," the woman began but then faltered, looking Ari up and down. "Please, could you tell your mistress that she has a visitor?"

"Okay. Duly informed," smiled Ari, "How can I help?"

"Are you Lady Wiverton?"

"Yes."

"But you opened the door?"

"Well, how else was it going to open? I don't have a magic wand!"

The woman looked confused and then seemed to gather herself.

"Maybe I should call at a more convenient time; I just wished to thank you on behalf of Jim. I was worried how he was going to cope after the late Lord Wiverton let him go."

Ari was finding the conversation perplexing. She had clearly fallen short of some standard in this stranger's eyes. However, she also wanted to hear how her old tenant was doing.

"Look I'm afraid you have the advantage over me. Would you like to come in? I should like to hear how Jim is doing and maybe you could tell me who you are?"

The stern little lady stepped in through the doorway, and her face broke into a huge smile as she saw the boys laying on their tummies pushing the trains around. One boy had one sock on, the other was barefoot, little toes waving in the air.

"Oh, I remember Master Julian doing just that! Although not in the hallway. That would have been up in the nursery."

Ari rolled her eyes, "We found that yesterday, but it's too far away for me to watch over them. Wait, Master Julian? Does that mean you used to work here?"

And that's how Ariana met Dickie. It turned out that Wendy had got straight on the phone to Mrs Dickens when she had got home and told her to get up to the big house. The new owner was in, and it looked like she might not be cut from the same cloth as the rest of the family. Plus, she was desperate for help.

Having introduced herself as Dickie, just Dickie, she headed towards the kitchens leaving Ari to follow along behind in a faintly amused manner. Ari watched as the woman moved around the kitchen gathering everything together for a pot of tea. Her protestations were swept away as she was told to sit down and relax. This was clearly a room that Mrs Dickens knew her way around.

"I'm afraid we only have teabags," said Ari, as she saw a teapot being pulled out. Mrs Dickens frowned briefly and walked off into the pantry, returning with a tea caddy. "There's always tea somewhere in this house. Lady Wiverton would never run out. My apologies, the previous Lady Wiverton."

A thousand questions skated through her mind, but as she watched Mrs Dickens work, she realised that the housekeeper was also trying to ask a thousand questions and with surprise, Ari realised that she was the one who was actually in charge, not this older efficient lady. This was going to be delicate.

"When you stopped working here, was it voluntarily, Mrs Dickens?" Mrs Dickens was still, her back to Ari, as she placed cups and saucers on a tray.

Taking a breath, she turned and walked to the table with the tea set.

"It's Dickie, and not exactly, no. I'm sure your uncle had his reasons, and I'll not speak ill of the dead, but when he told me to go, I was shocked. I had thought I would be here for life. Then a month or two after that, I got a letter saying that as I was no longer an employee of the estate, my preferential rent would return to market values. I was welcome to stay on in my home but only at the new rent. As I said, I won't speak ill of the dead, but that caused me some sleepless nights."

Ari sipped her tea and listened as Dickie explained how over the past few years Uncle David had gradually dismissed the workforce, cancelled staff picnics, withdrew permission from various bodies to use the grounds for events and slowly, but surely, like the receding tide, he pulled away from any and all commitments.

"I don't doubt that losing Jacinta and Julian broke his heart, we were all devastated, but it also brought out the worst in him. Then Lady Wiverton died last year, and that seemed to be the straw that broke the camel's back. We thought your mother might turn up for the funerals, but they came and went, and we never saw a glimpse of her."

Ari bristled at the implied censure.

"My mother and father died when I was eighteen, no one came to their funeral, and no one told me or my sisters about the death of our cousins or our aunt." She pushed her chair back and walked toward the kitchen door. "Thank you for calling, Mrs Dickens, I shall start to try to fix some of my uncle's mistakes, but now I do have rather a lot to be getting on with."

Dickie remained seated, but as she looked up at Ari, she had tears in her eyes, "Lily's dead?"

It was the first time Ariana had ever seen anyone care about her mother, beyond her father and sisters, and it utterly disarmed her. She stood in the kitchen doorway not knowing what to do. She didn't want to talk about her mother, especially when she was feeling so raw, but this woman seemed genuinely upset by the news that Ari had just dumped into her lap. Doing the only thing that she could think of, she returned to the teapot and poured herself a fresh cup.

"Look, do you mind if we don't talk about it right now? I'm sorry if I was a bit defensive just then."

"Oh, my dear, I'm so sorry, of course not, but did you say, sisters? I bet she was a wonderful mother?"

"There are five of us. But can we talk about something else? I'm exhausted, and quite frankly, I'm in over my head."

"Right," said Dickie, "this is going to be a two-pot problem then is it?"

Hearing 'two pot' problem, Ari was snapped back to her old family kitchen, with her mother, making a cup of tea, whilst Ari poured her heart out over a boy who didn't know she existed. Clearly, a 'two pot' problem. And now here was the source of her mother's favourite saying for when the chips were down. Ari was flooded with memories of the warmth of that small room and the love in her mother's face. Tears welled up in her eyes, and a sob broke free, a dam that had been held tight for months cracked and Ari, overwhelmed, found herself crying, a howling mess of tears. In alarm, William came running in from the hallway, quickly followed by Leo and both glared at the strange woman whilst hugging their mother.

Dickie was horrified that she had triggered such distress and quickly tried to remedy the situation.

"Come on, boys, Mummy's tired and needs a biscuit. Where are the biscuits?" And giving Ari time to compose herself, Dickie and the boys proceeded to make a noisy examination of the cupboards with bangs and laughs as Dickie tried to eat the teabags and

Leo tried to eat a plate. Eventually, Will found a packet by the coffee and having been reassured by Ari that she was now fine, they returned to the train track with a biscuit in each hand.

She was just about to apologise when Dickie dismissed her and went to a drawer and pulled out a block of paper and a pen. She pushed it towards Ari and said they needed a plan of attack. Ari would tell Dickie what she needed, and Dickie would tell her how to go about it. Two pots turned to three and some soup for lunch. By the end of the day, an action plan had been launched.

ELIZABETH HURLEY

9

Over the next fortnight, Ari got to work getting the house back in order. Mrs Dickens was re-employed, and Ari got into the habit of just calling her Dickie; gradually various staff were offered their old jobs back. She was particularly pleased to discover that Wendy, her saviour from the rainstorm, used to run the kitchens and was eager to come back to work. Tenants were sorted out; rents were adjusted and the word went out that Wiverton had an open policy once more. The boys were due to start school part-time in September but right now she didn't even know what schools were around. It could either be a disaster or just what the boys needed to settle down. She knew they were also missing their London life; as William said, everyone in the country looked the same and it was hard to remember who they all were. She couldn't wait to tell Mama Vy that, God she would laugh. Like Ariana and her sisters, her sons had grown up in a multicultural landscape. Faces, dress, customs, languages, music, food, there were so many varieties and all jostling alongside each other. It was a happy mix in which they had thrived. Now everything seemed one note.

Ari's thoughts of London life were interrupted by a text alert on her phone. It was from Wendy. Ari thought she was a nice person with a kind heart, but she was prone to interfere. It was clear to Ari that Wendy pitied her. Ari would sometimes catch Wendy turning down the radio when she came into the kitchen, presumably there was something Wendy deemed sensitive on it. Ari thought she was just overcompensating for having called Lord Wiverton an old bastard and learning that her husband was dead. Clearly, in Wendy's eyes nothing was worse than not having a partner, and to be a widow? So tragic. When she walked into rooms, conversations about husbands and families would suddenly dry up. Ari didn't want anyone to think she was a pitiful or tragic figure but equally, she didn't want to tell anyone that the boys' father was a douche and that she blessed the day he died.

Ari looked at Wendy's text. A fancy dress party? No doubt Wendy was hoping that Ari might meet someone. Ari snorted to herself. That wasn't going to happen in a million years. Once bitten. But a party sounded exactly like what she needed. She couldn't think when she last went to one and the more she thought about it the more she realized that she had never been to one, at least not an adult one, one with actual alcohol and stuff. She texted back saying sure and then realised she didn't have a clue what to wear. In a flurry of texts, Ari discovered that the theme was

'Eurovision' and that Wendy had a costume she could borrow, a Dutch flower girl.

Once Wendy had agreed to keep Ari's identity private, she decided to go. She fancied a night away from being Lady Wiverton. Not too many people recognised her yet, so she still had a level of anonymity to let her hair down. Maybe she could incorporate a mask into her costume?

When the weekend arrived, she arranged for Dickie to stay the night. Ari then booked a cab and headed over to Wendy's. She wasn't sure how good an idea this was, but she had already looked at all the escape routes. If she wanted to leave the party early, she didn't want to spoil Wendy's evening. Since she had arrived in Norfolk, she had gone out for walks every day with the boys. They were beginning to build up an idea of the landscape and villages around them. She particularly liked a boardwalk that led from the village pub through a wetland area and then out on a lane near the estate. It cut through a wide, open reed bed, and wherever she looked, all she could see was sky above and occasional pools of water amongst the reeds. If she couldn't get a taxi, she'd walk that way home.

Despite their mother's concerns, her father had taught all the girls how to fight dirty and how to stay safe. Her mother thought they simply shouldn't be out at night; their father knew there wasn't a hope in hell of enforcing that. Instead, he had protected his girls as best he could, by showing them how to defend themselves, when they were on their own. Considering her mother's privileged and sheltered upbringing and her father's itinerant traipse through Irish foster homes, she knew which of them had a better take on personal safety. Walking through the countryside offered Ariana no concerns—she acknowledged that this was probably ignorance and that there were dangers here too, but they were negligible compared to London's crime rates.

Ari knocked on Wendy's front door and was greeted with a glass of something pink and fizzy, and a bag with her costume in it. Sitting down in the front room Wendy tipped out the bag and Ari looked at the small pile of clothes in front of her.

"Is that it? Where's the rest of it?" She flourished something white and frilly at Wendy, "What the hell is this?"

"Your knickers," laughed Wendy

"Knickers! With frills? Who the hell puts frills on their knickers? They'll be so uncomfortable to sit in."

"I don't think they are designed for comfort," said Wendy, "consider it an artistic flourish."

96

Ari spat her drink out.

"What are you on?! Who's going to see them under my skirt?" Looking around she asked where her skirt was anyway. A wisp of blue and red silky fabric and ribbons sailed over as Wendy threw her the rest of her outfit.

"Are you kidding?! I thought that was a hanky. Oh my God, this is a slutty Dutch costume, isn't it?"

Ari groaned in horror. Holland was the home of Lutheran doctrines; she didn't think this is what they had in mind when they introduced their puritan black and white dress codes.

"Let's see the top then." Another suggestion of broderie anglaise and wishful thinking sailed over, along with a bodice top with straps and laces that completed the ensemble.

Despite serious misgivings, Ari decided to just go with the flow. Wendy promised her no one would recognise her once she had her face painted up. Knocking back her fizz, she and Wendy began to get their outfits together. The doorbell rang again and a few more of Wendy's friends joined them. Ari recognised some of them from the playgroup. Daisy was dressed as a Russian Cossack dancer, who appeared to be wearing high heels and shorts, and a girl called Julie was dressed as a nun, with sequins!

Again, Ari felt the veracity of their outfits was lacking a certain something. And she was certain that that something was decency. Thank heavens for her clogs. At least she was holding out a bit. She shuffled on her fluffy bottom as Daisy made up her face. Gradually, she disappeared behind layers of foundation and a doll-like character emerged. Daisy was a whizz with the make-up and was painting a fabulous character on Ari's face, there was no need for a mask, soon she was indeed, unrecognisable.

Her phone rang, and she saw it was Nick. Rather than replying she sent a selfie and was immediately rewarded with a screaming gif. Her phone rang again.

"Is that you?!!!" Nick screeched down the phone.

"Hang on, let me show you the whole outfit." Ari was enjoying her new phone and held it out now, so that her sister could see the entire look.

"Ari, you look amazing. God, I wish I was there! Have a bloody blast. I want all the details. Now, go and get hammered and let your hair down."

Hanging up, Ari grinned to herself and went to study her reflection in the mirror. Putting her yellow wig on, she adjusted the upturned plaits and Daisy added some freckles to each cheek. Laughing and dancing to the music, the girls finished their drinks and when the taxi tooted outside, they all piled out into the street. Climbing into the back of the car with the other girls, Ari thought how much she'd needed this. She couldn't remember the last time she had acted like an idiot, had behaved irresponsibly or simply didn't give a damn. It was so much fun.

By the time they got to the pub, the party was in full flow, dodgy Europop was blaring out of the speakers and Ari was relieved to realise that she and her group were not the most outrageously dressed people there. One set of boys had come as the Village People, there were lots of Vikings, as well as Starship Troopers and a pantomime dame. When Ari asked what the dame had to do with Eurovision, Wendy rolled her eyes.

"That's Harry Fields, one of the local policemen, he plays the Panto Dame each year. He's brilliant at it but quite frankly I reckon he volunteers each year because he likes the dress. Come on, let's get a drink!"

Dubious cocktails were being offered for the price of a raffle ticket and a donation. Ari hoped that they were going to raise a lot of money tonight for the local community centre. She planned to match-fund the amount, anonymously, but tonight it was all about letting her hair down. As the pub filled up, groups piled out into the street and the garden. However, the temperature wasn't kind on some of the outfits so, shivering, Ari danced back to the bar, whooping to the strains of ABBA and having a bloody good time.

#

After a long and frustrating week in the City, Sir Sebastian Flint-Hyssop was looking forward to a quick drink in The Bull in the little village of Wiverton. He didn't know how his brother could love London so much; Geoffrey thrived there; London, New York, Tokyo, wherever there was money moving around, he was there behind the scenes pushing the pounds in the right direction. Despite being pretty woeful with human beings, Geoffrey was a world-class businessman, he was able to track a column of figures to their last variable and figure out which way they were going to jump. He could do this before the rest of the market even woke up to the fact that something was in the wind. It was Sebastian, the younger of the two brothers, that was considered to be the more persuasive of the two; his open and engaging manner invited confidences and he was generally able to sway any matter to a path of his choosing. But not this week, and his failure meant that people were going to lose their homes.

He needed to gather his thoughts before going home to discuss the issue with his father. He couldn't see a solution, but failure wasn't an option either. Some quiet reflection was needed. For the whole journey, ideas had been tumbling through his head, each as hopeless as the last, as the car tore through the long dark miles. At six foot three most of Seb's height was in his legs so he appreciated that his low-slung Daimler allowed him to properly stretch out in comfort as he drove. Tonight though, his shoulders ached, and he realised that he must be even more wound up than he had realised. He would go for a swim tomorrow; some bracing North Sea action would soon thrash out any knots and aches in his torso. For tonight however, he decided to settle on a nightcap in The Bull. It was a nice quiet pub and not too close to home. He should be able to have a drink without bumping into anyone he knew.

As his car turned the corner, he swerved to miss a couple standing in the street. Swearing at them, he parked the car, ignoring their shouts about speed and headed towards the pub. To his dismay, he realised an event was taking place. Dammit, this was all he needed, what on earth were they thinking, the place was chaos. Maybe the snug would be empty but heading towards the bar he saw that the snug appeared to be full of Vikings and gondoliers as well as what could only be described as a sexy bullfighter and a rather rough looking older pirate.

"John, is that you?" asked Seb incredulously. "Whatever is going on?"

The pirate looked startled and then a bit sheepish as he looked up at his landlord. In embarrassment at being caught out in fancy dress, he mumbled, "Fancy dress, sir. Eurovision."

"But you're dressed as a pirate!"

"Yes, sir, bloody thieving Euro bureaucrats and their subsidies."

Realising that John hadn't quite understood the party theme and was warming up for another one of his blinkered rants, Seb wished him an enjoyable evening and headed towards the bar, to the relief of both men. Two girls stood beside him, clearly drunk and shouting over the sounds of, dear God, was that Falco? He couldn't help but be party to their conversation. Both appeared to have children, the taller of the two was boasting that her children were fast asleep and that apparently, she could just go home whenever it suited. There was no ring on her finger so clearly, these little ones had been left home alone whilst their teenage mother went out boozing it up. He assumed she was a teenager given her behaviour, although it was hard to tell under that ridiculous doll-like make-up and upturned yellow plaits. Her friend looked older but that was likely down to the overflowing cleavage that seemed an integral part of her Cossack outfit.

"Did you just tut at me?"

Snapped out of his musings, Seb realised that he had not been as subtle in his observations as he could have been.

"Hello? I asked you if you just tutted at me?"

Sebastian was startled by the girl's accent, if he was honest, he hadn't expected her to talk like that. She also appeared to be slurring less than he'd anticipated. The girl next to her joined in.

"What the fuck are you looking at?"

Oh great, just what he needed at the end of the day. A bar brawl, with a couple of trollops.

"Can I suggest you sober up and go home to your children? What sort of example do you think you are setting?" He paused and looked them up and down, "leaving them home alone, dressing like tarts and getting wasted."

Aware that any hope of a quiet drink was going to be futile, he decided to drive on home. He was angry and tired, and he didn't want to go to his own local as too many people knew him in there.

Especially people that were counting on him to save their homes. Turning away from the girls, he headed back outside. Out in the fresh air, he realised that the two harpies had followed him. The taller one looked like she was going to be sick, the shorter one he realised, was still shouting and swearing at him.

"For God's sake, go home, you're drunk!" he snapped at them.

At this moment the fresh air seemed to hit the taller girl and as she leaned over, he thought she was going to vomit. Seb got a distinctly odd view of stockings, thighs and white frilly knickers.

As she straightened up, having picked up her phone, she turned to look at him and realised that he had been looking at her exposed behind. He flushed, but before he could explain that he wasn't staring, she had drawn herself up and let rip. He only caught one word in four but given that the ones that he had heard were: stuck up, arrogant, stupid, ugly, and the rest were a vivid explosion of Anglo Saxon, he didn't need to hear any more. And in such clipped tones, it sounded like he was being told off by his mother. If his mother ever got drunk and swallowed a swear book. He smiled at the image, but this was like lighting a fire under the girl, she now stepped towards him, jabbing her finger at him and screaming that he had spoilt her night, that she had been looking forward to this forever, and that basically, he was the worst person in the whole universe. Her friend tugged at her arm, appearing startled at the fury pouring out of her mate. He also had a feeling that she might have just recognised who he was.

It was no good, this gorgeous girl was on a roll. He was surprised that he viewed her as gorgeous, he couldn't even tell what she looked like, but she was magnificent in her fury, it was elemental. Her vocabulary was glorious, he wasn't sure if he had ever been called a piece of corpusculent, ragged filth before, he wasn't even sure if it was a real word, but it was astounding. Realising that he wanted to fight back he was aware that the only thing he could think to do would be to kiss her and stop the tirade. She was so close to him and her slender figure looked like it would easily wrap against his taller frame if he pulled her towards him. She was older than he had first guessed, possibly in her mid-twenties looking at her frame, but the way she handled herself, she appeared many decades older. Her silly painted face and fake blonde plaits were tilted up towards him, the snarl on her face at total odds with the rosy cheeks, freckled nose and yellow bobbing plaits.

He shook his head, this was ridiculous, clearly, he was more tired than he realised and not thinking straight. There was no way he was going to dignify the situation with a response and he walked towards his car. As he got in, there was an almighty bang on the metal work. He shot out of the car to see a wooden clog lying beside the hub cap, the light from the local pub suggesting a dent in the bodywork. In horror he and the Dutch doll stared at each other and then grabbing her other clog, she flung it at him and legged it towards the dark expanse of Withy Mere. Seb chased after her, but despite the booze, she was fast and was sprinting off along the causeway, her path illuminated by moonlight. Seb stopped and wondered what the hell he was doing, chasing some drunk girl across the mere. What the hell did he intend to do if he caught her? Drag her back? And how well would that go down? Local peer of the realm assaulting a young mother at a charity do? Coming to his senses he stopped and watched her back receding until all he could see was her white frilly knickers disappearing off into the dark.

Bemused, he wondered where she was heading and if it was worth visiting her in the morning. He was certain that the damage to the car was going to be expensive and the quiet relaxing drink had totally failed to materialise. When he returned to the Daimler, he noticed that the other girl had also legged it. He picked up the clogs and wondered if he could return them to their owner with a bill for the damages. Getting back into his car he noticed some of his despondency seemed to have lifted. Despite an abysmal end to an awful day he inexplicably found himself smiling every time he thought of that little white tail bouncing along the causeway off into the darkness.

10

"Honestly, Father, it's no good, I tried everything, I even spoke to the Minister. Shining Horizons are promising the moon and the stars, and that's all anyone is paying attention to. With their promise of a fully funded hospital, we are looking at the very real likelihood of a compulsory purchase of Lower Lane, Withies Common and Labourers Row. Hell, at this rate, they may even go after the whole damn estate!"

"Sebastian, mind your language," Lady Flint-Hyssop chided. Mary looked at her youngest son in concern; she didn't doubt that he had done everything that was possible. He had arrived home an hour earlier full of bad tidings. After a quick shower, he was now sitting with his parents in front of the drawing room fire, explaining just how bleak the situation was. She remembered how he'd loved to play down in those fields with the local children when his older siblings were away at school. The fact that a solution wasn't yet obvious was irrelevant. Between him and her husband a way would be found, she was certain of it. They were from a long line of fighters after all, but right now the struggle did seem overwhelming. It wasn't helped by how ridiculous the whole situation was in the first place, subsequent generations weren't made aware that the land no longer belonged to the Flint-Hyssop estate and by the time they did it had been sold, pending planning approval, to a property developer.

"I don't understand why the Minister won't see reason, Seb," said Lord Flint-Hyssop, "Surely the Whitehall mandarins can see this is all smoke and mirrors. Who do we know in the department?"

"Makes no difference, Pa. The big problem, that I only discovered yesterday, is the Wiverton estate. It turns out that David agreed to sell the lower carriage drive to the developer."

"But that would provide a near as dammit, direct route from the new development to the A14!"

"I don't believe you. David would never do that," exclaimed Mary.

Seb's parents were thunderstruck. No wonder the government was acting like this was a done deal. If the developer could provide easy road access to their development, half their battle was not so much won, as the foundations for the second homes already built.

"But the Burbidges have lived on that land all their life! And what about the bitterns, and the dormice? Oh, dear God, this is a disaster. Tony, what can we do?" The situation was indeed dire. Whilst no one would become homeless—the estate would rehome them in an instant—it would be the first time in over two hundred years that any land would be lost.

"Oh why didn't your grandfather buy back Hyssop Lakes when he had the chance?"

It was a fair question, and the simple answer was complacency. The lakes were completely surrounded by Flint-Hyssop land but lost in a card game centuries before. Over the years, a sort of gentlemen's agreement had stood, and each successive owner of the lakes and surrounding land, let the family estate take care of them. Ten years ago though, someone with an eye for location had noticed the rather glorious setting and that it was near to a local town whilst sufficiently distant enough to remain exclusive. Even better was the private sandy beach that was flanked by dunes and then lakes. Now the plan was to build an eco-village, with certain facilities on the tick list of the urban planners' wish lists. A hospital being the jewel in the crown.

Anyone with half an eye into Shining Horizon's portfolio would see that they were in the habit of building gated communities with luxury facilities. Promises of playgrounds and village stores, time and again mysteriously vanished as the go-ahead to build was given the green light. Hedgerows were torn down, gates and fences put up instead. Seb had visited one of their developments out on the Broads. It certainly looked beautiful, but clever loopholes meant that even the affordable housing that they had built was beyond the reach of the locals. The same people who had been duped into signing petitions endorsing the need for the development, based on the promise of cheap housing for locals. There was a lot of bad blood in the area, and Seb could see exactly the same thing happening again at Hyssop Lakes.

"Well, we have to stop the road then."

"Do you intend to lie in the road in front of the diggers?" Tony smiled at Mary; he could see his wife doing just that. As a young girl, she had always seemed so prim and then she would sweep the legs out from underneath him. He remembered that time he thought she had gone on a shopping spree to London with the girls, and it turned out she'd been camping out at Greenham Common with the 'wimmin' instead. Maybe he should have sent her, instead of Seb, to fight their corner. She might wave a Hermes scarf rather than her bra at the ministers, but by God, she'd still make them quiver.

"If I must, but shall we first let's establish if that land has actually been sold?"

"How do you mean?"

"The developer may be playing fast and loose. Given David's unexpected death, the transaction may not have been finalised. It may be a proposal in principle only. We need to talk to the new Lord Wiverton, whenever he deigns to turn up."

Seb looked at his whisky and realised that his mother was right. He had been so horrified by this sleight of hand that he hadn't paused to consider that it might not actually be in place yet. A solution may yet exist.

"I did hear the other day that the issue of inheritance had been resolved and that the new heir had been informed. They may even be in place. Do you think it's Lily?"

"Unlikely, she'd have already been in touch I would have thought. Surely?"

"I thought she was written out of the estate altogether."

"No idea actually, you know what they were like. Woe betide anyone that brought up her name in conversation."

"Well if not Lily, then who? Mary, you're a dab at old family lines. Who gets the estate next?"

"Do you think I haven't already looked? That family line was dying out, withering on the vine so to speak. I fear the next in line is either Canadian or German."

Tony shuddered. He had nothing against the Germans or Canadians, and of course, it could be worse, it could be French or Americans. The problem was that if they weren't British, would they want to take on the estate? It was vast, with responsibilities everywhere across the country. Would the duty of their blood sing louder than the ring of the cash register?

"Let's ask Jenny in the morning."

"Maybe I should go over there instead?" suggested Seb.

"And say what?" queried his mother. "How do you do and by the way let me tell you how to run your affairs? No, Seb, I think this is going to require a little bit of covert operations."

"Let your mother do her thing and let's take it from there. In the meantime, I'll ask the firm if they can investigate the Land Registry and see if anything is on the move in terms of deeds."

A plan of attack decided, the three of them sat in silence, returning to their thoughts. Mary was writing a piece on the breeding habits of bitterns, but her heart was no longer in it; little avenues of investigation were coming to her as she considered the day ahead. Tony watched the flames in the fire and stroked Ralf's head as he considered what losing the lakes would mean to the people who worked on the estate. Seb breathed in the fumes of his whisky. The fragrance conjured up the fresh air and large open skies of the Scottish moorland. In his mind, he could see the heather and peat bogs where this whisky came from. Disturbingly though, his moorland seemed overrun with rabbits, their white tails bobbing off into the shadows.

#

Lady Flint-Hyssop moved slowly towards the breakfast table. She hadn't slept well; the nights were still chilly, and she had a lot on her mind. She was delighted, however, to see a small plate of fresh strawberries on the table. Old Diggory had been saying all winter that he thought he and the other gardeners might be able to have an early batch of strawberries in the hothouse this year, and he'd been as good as his word.

"First strawberries of the season," smiled Jenny. "His Lordship is already out with Bill making a tour of the building."

Every Saturday, Tony and their estate manager would take a quick turn around the immediate estate. Discussing what had happened that week and what plans were in place for the following one. As

114

important as that was though, neither of them would be able to help Mary with her plan of attack. Jenny was just the person Mary had been hoping to see. Certainly, she wasn't a local, nor had she been with them as long as other staff but if there was a story about, Jenny would know all the ins and outs. Mary was convinced Jenny would earn a lot more as a Fleet Street runner or a blackmailer but for now, she seemed happy enough living at the hall and making sure that the place ran like clockwork. Mary and Cathcart, her housekeeper, both hoped Jenny might be the next housekeeper, and all three ladies were working towards that goal.

"Now, Jenny," Mary began, her first sip of coffee warming her bones, and the heat of the porcelain unbending her stiff fingers, "I heard from Seb last night, that there may be a new heir in place over at Wiverton. Have you heard anything?"

Jenny looked conflicted, "I have, ma'am, but Mrs Cathcart said I shouldn't bring it up. That it would upset you."

That was curious so she asked her to fetch Cathcart. As she left the room, Tony swept in bringing all the chill and excitement of this morning's fresh air with him, as well as a tribe of dogs all full of nervous energy.

"Really, Tony! In this state? They'll destroy the place."

"I know, but it's so pretty out there that I thought we could take a stroll around the grounds together. The sun is warming up nicely. What do you say?"

"That sounds lovely but not before I've finished my coffee and not before I speak to Cathcart. It turns out the new heir is in place at Wiverton Manor, and the news may upset me?"

"Dammit, they're American after all!"

"I think that would be more a body blow to you, not me, darling. Now tell me how's the old girl doing, anything new flaked off?"

They chatted for a few moments about the never-ending list of repairs that a house of this age required, before Jenny reappeared with Cathcart. Before Mary had even begun to open her mouth, her housekeeper rushed ahead, desperate to confess.

"Lady Flint-Hyssop, please accept my apologies for not informing you sooner about Wiverton Manor. I made a judgement call, wrongly, and then the days went past and here we are."

Cathcart looked more upset than Mary and Tony had seen in many years, and they were alarmed that they had distressed her in some way.

"Come on now, Bridie, it's not as bad as all that, surely?" said Tony, although Mary thought that calling Cathcart by her first name, suggested that it might, indeed, be as bad as all that.

"Sorry, sir, it's just that when I heard about the new resident, I knew that you would be upset."

"Do they have an accent?"

"An accent, sir?"

"Yes, is it possible that he's, a Yank?"

"Oh no, it's a woman, your Lordship, and British. You see that's why I thought you would be upset, ma'am. Whoever she is, she's not Lady Elizabeth; she's too young. And I thought given what we found in the family trees and that there was no other British family member's that she had to be a daughter of Lady Elizabeth's. And that means that something had happened to her. Otherwise, why isn't she here?"

Cathcart would never have referred to Lady Elizabeth as Lily, given that that was a family nickname. However, that didn't stop her from knowing all the local family trees. It was the sort of information that any good housekeeper could summon up at a moment's notice. Such knowledge was invaluable for invitations, seating arrangements and basic diplomatic issues. Not a loquacious woman, she seemed nervous and anxious. That was quite a speech for Cathcart and yet having delivered it, she seemed as distressed as before. Jenny stood behind her, her face also suggesting that there was more to come.

"Well, come now, that's surely not the only explanation, this girl could be an estate manager or someone from the solicitor, she could even be the English wife of the new Earl."

A small groan from Tony.

"Oh, she's definitely the Countess, whether she's married or not I don't know but that's how she described herself to the bailiffs," explained Cathcart.

"Good God! Surely David didn't let the estate fall apart? Maybe that's why he's selling the land?"

"Sorry, sir, these bailiffs were trying to evict one of the estates ex-labourers, and she swoops in, pays the rent, and sends them off with a flea in their ear. It caused quite a scene, and that's how I got to hear of it."

"Oh, how exciting, I do love a good mystery, I wonder who she is?" said Mary. "I must invite her over; won't do for her to think I'm rude. When did you say this happened?"

"A fortnight ago," mumbled Cathcart.

Mary looked aghast. "A fortnight?" The penny dropped.

"Oh well, no harm done. I shall drop her a little note today. Maybe we could get Bill to pop it into her? Thank you, ladies, I think Tony and the dogs are champing at the bit for a walk, so I shan't hold you up anymore."

They left the room downcast, and Mary looked at Tony, "Well that explains a lot, poor Cathcart."

"Does it? I'm afraid I don't follow you, why was Cathcart looking like she was about to get whipped?"

"Because she forgot, dear. Jenny must have come to her with the news, she told Jenny not to say anything whilst she either thought about it or investigated more, and then promptly forgot. Which she is beginning to do more frequently."

"Oh, it never rains, but it pours. Well, I'll leave that in your hands, indoor stuff and all that, but what shall we do about our neighbour? They'll think we're ignoring them. Shall we drive past later and pop in?"

119

"Pop in? Heavens, they might think that we are rude now but let's not confirm it by calling in unannounced. No, I'll have Bill drop a little invitation in to call on us at their leisure and to welcome them to the neighbourhood. Whoever they are, they are unlikely to know much, if anything, about the house and the area. I imagine they are still finding their feet."

"Right. And then will you ask them about this preposterous plan to sell the lower carriageway?"

"Yes, Tony. Should I ask them about their preposterous plans before or after they've removed their coats?"

With a harrumph, Tony stood and offered his wife his hand.

"Come on, old girl, I know you'll take care of it, let's take a stretch down to the greenhouses and congratulate everyone on the strawberries."

Mary squeezed his hand, acknowledging the concern in his voice. They headed out into the cold fresh air, a pack of hounds bouncing around them, steam gently rising from the vegetable gardens ahead.

#

Seb parked his car and walked across the gravel. His mother's investigations had paid off and it appeared that the new heir was, in fact, Lady Elizabeth de Foix's daughter. This had given his father great satisfaction, but his mother had been unable to find out what had happened to Elizabeth herself. She had sent an invitation, but as yet, the new heir hadn't replied, and time was running out. The developer's presentation was in two days' time and Sebastian still hadn't been able to arrange a meeting. Lady Wiverton's solicitor was apologetic but firm, he would do nothing to influence his client, nor was he prepared to give him a telephone number. He had dropped a few notes in to Wiverton Manor, but the housekeeper had politely taken them in and then told him that the Lady of the House wasn't available. It was terribly awkward, and he knew he was behaving like a bore. The problem was he was running out of time.

The front door was open and despite his knocking and calling out no one answered. There were clearly voices within, but no one came to the door and so he wandered in, calling out as he went. The last thing he wanted to do was start by appearing as a burglar or have the housekeeper run him out. A radio was playing off to the left, and he followed the sound into a study. A girl was sitting at a large desk, scribbling on a pad whilst tapping away on a calculator, looking to and from between, as far as he could see, a laptop, a pc, a tablet, another pc and possibly a phone. If this was The Countess Wiverton, she was clearly deep in thought, and he was uncertain how to announce himself without disturbing her.

"Give me a minute," she muttered and continued scribbling and tapping until she sighed and turned to meet him.

"Hello? Can I help?"

"Yes, hello," said Sebastian, clearing his throat, "I'm looking for the daughter of Elizabeth and Michael Byrne?"

"Well, at last, something that I can help with. How do you do."

"Ah, wonderful. I wanted to pop over and introduce myself, I'm Sebastian Flint-Hyssop, one of your neighbours. I was hoping to introduce myself and given tomorrow's meeting I wondered if we could go over a few things?"

Another girl wandered into the room and eyed Sebastian up and down.

"Hello, I'm Paddy, who are you?" There was no denying these two were sisters and they looked so alike that Seb couldn't tell who might be the eldest. His money was on twins. The one sat at the desk had her hair scraped back in a low ponytail, whereas the other girl had her hair loose, her dark hair fell in curls beyond her shoulders, and she had sparkling blue eyes. If her twin was all restraint, this one was unbridled.

"Hello, I'm Seb, your neighbour. Do I have the pleasure of addressing Lady Wiverton?"

"Typical," exclaimed the first sister, "turns out I couldn't get that right either."

"Oh, I do apologise, are you the eldest?" said Seb turning away from the slightly hungry gaze of the second sister.

"Of course not, Paddy's the eldest." Confused, Seb turned back to Paddy who was smiling at him wolfishly.

Just as he was about to try and sort it out another girl walked into the room. Nodding a smile Seb's way she spoke to the girl at the table, "Nick, Clem wants to know if you are winning with the figures."

"Nowhere near, but I think I'm beginning to get a clearer look at things. Aster, may I introduce our neighbour, St John Fitz, Something."

"Sebastian Flint-Hyssop, pleased to meet you. I gather you are another sister?" This one seemed somehow less than her sisters, she was shorter than them, her hair was short and strawberry blonde and whilst she also had blue eyes, he knew that if he were asked to describe her tomorrow, he would be hard pressed to. Trying to gather his wits and work out who was who he tried again. "And you are all the daughters of Elizabeth and Michael Byrne?" Maybe he had got the details of Elizabeth de Foix's marriage incorrect. No one seemed to know what he was talking about. "I was just trying to work out which of you is Lady Ariana, Countess Wiverton?"

"God, that sounds so weird. Countess Wiverton. Anyway, it's not me; I'm the youngest, Aster. Hi."

Seb shook her small hand just as a fourth girl strode into the room. This one looked a little older than the others but was also the shortest of the lot. She was curvier than her sisters and had an enormous mane of red hair. She also looked completely fed up.

"Where the hell did you all disappear to? I swear we could lose the Tabernacle Choir in this place. Oh, hello," she said, looking Seb up and down, "Now I see what caused the distraction. Can we help? We are rather busy at the moment."

A chorus of protests came from the other girls. "Clem, don't be so rude. This is our neighbour, and he's come over to say hello. Now he's going to think this is a house of termagants."

"What's a termagant?" queried Paddy.

Aster laughed and pointed at her big sister, "Harridan, shrew, bully. Clementine, basically!"

"Not fair!" protested Clem. "Look I'm sorry, St John is it? But we have a lot on right now, so maybe you could pop back at another time?"

"Clem! Seriously, you are so rude."

"For fuck's sake, Paddy, we are drowning in paperwork, and you are flashing your eyes at the first thing with a pulse."

Aware that a full-on sibling feud was about to explode, Sebastian cleared his throat, "Are you the Countess Wiverton?"

"Christ no, do I look like Ari? She isn't here; she's out with the boys. Why don't you phone to make an appointment? She should be back in an hour or two."

And with that, she gestured towards the study door and saw him out to the front steps. Walking towards the car, he heard the door bang closed behind him; bemused he got into his car and tried to gather his thoughts as he drove home.

He felt that he had been outflanked. Perhaps not deliberately, but whether by design or accident, that first meeting had not gone according to plan and he hadn't even met the one person he had meant to.

God, how many girls were there? His best guess was that there must be five; two of them were twins, and there were no brothers. Otherwise, he would have inherited, knowing David. In fact, there could be two sets of twins. Ariana could be a twin with the short, rude one. Seb groaned, the idea of having to deal with, what was it the youngest one called her, 'a termagant', made his heart sink. The other sisters seemed more approachable although he felt he might need a chaperone if he was going to be left alone with the one with all the hair. He decided he was just going to have to go to the meeting without having put his case forward to Lady Wiverton. It was clear from their conversation that the sisters were currently going through the estate finances and didn't seem overly thrilled with what they had found. Selling the land might be just the godsend they were looking for. And his downfall.

11

The following day and miles away, Ariana stepped out of the cab and stood in front of her solicitor's building. It was hard to imagine how much things had changed in just under two months. Now she was a widow, a peer of the realm and the owner of a vast estate. Two months ago, she was wet and had cardboard in her shoes. Admittedly she was still in second-hand clothes, but she was grateful that her aunt and cousin were a close match for her, even if she did have to work with belts and hemlines. Soon she would go shopping properly, but she just didn't have the time and she wanted to go with Clem, who had a much better eye for outfits than Ari.

Ari climbed the steps and waited to be buzzed in. Mrs Smith smiled at her with a polite enquiring smile, but then her face changed to a genuine one as she recognised Ariana.
"Lady Wiverton! How lovely to see you again," and then remembering Ari's recent bereavement, she offered her condolences. Ari always found this situation awkward; it was impossible to say how delighted she was, so she would simply nod her head in acknowledgement. Accept the condolences and change the subject. However, she was aware that this gave the entirely incorrect impression of a grieving

widow, nobly struggling on, not someone having the time of her life. For all that she had loathed Greg, he had once been a decent human being, if not to her, and he didn't deserve his final epitaph to be written by a girl who was full of bile and hatred towards him. And he was the boys' father, and for that fact alone, she would remain eternally grateful for him.

Ari presented Mrs Smith with a pot of honey and a box of lavender chocolates. "A little gift from Norfolk to say thank you for last time. You have no idea how much those small gestures helped me."

"Really, I was just doing my job."

"Nonsense, you were a lifesaver."

Penelope smiled and took the gifts; lavender chocolate was vile, but the thought was well meant, but she did love honey, so she would pass the chocolates on to the school raffle and enjoy the honey on her toast tomorrow morning. She walked with Ari to Mr Fanshawe's office and returned to reception. Ari had told Mrs Smith she had no idea how nervous she had been. That was true then, but after their first meeting Mrs Smith had pulled up Google maps and had a look at the area where Ariana was living and had grown up. The screen showed street after street of houses whose doors opened directly onto the pavements, tower blocks looming over waste ground that only seemed to grow burnt out cars and shopping trolleys. It was hard to imagine the heir to the Wiverton Estate growing up here, and she thought that Ariana's mother must have loved her husband very much indeed, to give everything up to live in such circumstances. Mrs Smith didn't know the de Foix twins, but she had often seen them in the society pages and had had to regularly post out cheques to cover up indiscretions and breakages, as they tore their way through wherever they were. She tried to imagine how those two would have turned out if it had been David banished and living in one of London's most deprived boroughs. She was pretty certain that would have turned out the same, death by drugs and fast cars. Only the labels on their clothes would be different, the drugs in their veins enhanced by something fizzy in a can rather than something fizzy from a magnum.

Mr Fanshawe shook Ari's hand and returned to his desk. She made herself comfortable, asking for a coffee when it was established that this would be quite a long meeting. The first hour passed in a tedium of signatures. Stretching for a second coffee break, Ari phoned to check on the boys and then returned to the table. The second hour was spent discussing her responsibilities and staffing issues across the whole estate. As they headed towards lunch, Mr Fanshawe could see that Ari was tiring and was beginning to glaze over every now and then.

"Shall we have lunch? My club is nearby, and the food is excellent. I don't know about you but I'm flagging a bit, and we still have a few important matters to discuss and one that's rather pressing."

Ari smiled. "I don't believe for a second that you are flagging. You are completely in your element, but yes, I could definitely do with a break."

Heading towards the club it was indeed just a few streets away. Ari appreciated the chance to stretch her legs, though much farther and her calves would begin to protest in her high heels. Arriving at the club she saw that it was much like the other properties on the street. A large Regency building, overlooking a green square, set back from a wide pavement. It was a quiet area of London, no takeaways or tourists, just a mix of hotels, offices, and apartments converted from large residential townhouses. Most had steps leading up to front doors with brass plaques beside them. As she entered the hallway, she appreciated the choice of paintings and furnishings; nothing was intended to provoke opinion or alarm. This was a place to rest and relax, free from conflict or desires beyond a good lunch and the opportunity to grab an uninterrupted forty winks. In a room to her right newspapers were rustled from behind deep leather armchairs but no other sound disturbed the oak panels and soft carpet. Ari wondered whether Mr Fanshawe had chosen this club after he settled on his offices or the other way around.

"Penny for your thoughts, Lady Wiverton?"

"I was just wondering which came first for you, the club or your offices?"

"Oh, most definitely the club," he laughed. "A colleague brought me here once, and when I was setting up my own business, I made sure to find somewhere close by. Come on, let's eat and you can see why."

Leading her along the corridor, he was pleased by her insight; an intelligent client was always more rewarding to work with. They certainly weren't as easy to manoeuvre, but he had enough of those. It was never in his best interests when his clients made disastrous decisions, and he did the best he could to help them avoid those missteps. Intelligent clients rarely made those sorts of mistakes though they tended to have ideas, and whilst ideas were undoubtedly noble things to have, they always led to more work. However, risks brought rewards and he felt that this partnership with the new heir was going to be an enjoyable venture for himself. He knew that his assistant, Penelope, approved of their new client and she had never yet got the wrong take on one. Certainly, she would still work to the best of her ability, she was far too professional for anything else, but for the clients she liked and/or respected she went that extra mile. It had not passed his notice that the first time he met Ariana she was wearing Penelope's lipstick.

Ari was pleased to note that when Mr Fanshawe had used her title, none of the staff had reacted. She was taking time getting used to it, and it helped when it was treated as a normal thing rather than something to twitch eyebrows.

They headed towards a lovely table set with linen, silver and crystal, and bathed in spring sunlight. Sitting down she saw that the window overlooked a garden laid out with box hedges and early blooms; first roses, resting in the shelter of the walled garden, their faces turned up to the early May sunshine.

Ari looked at the short but sumptuous menu and groaned when her tummy rumbled loud enough for Mr Fanshawe to hear. With a grin, he invited her to help herself to the bread before recommending the soup followed by the fish.

"I think in my current state I shall disgrace myself and drip soup all down my top. Would you recommend the terrine? That's like pâté isn't it?"

Mr Fanshawe found Ari utterly enchanting. He didn't know many young women, but those that he did seemed terribly concerned by what others thought of them. Indeed, Lady Ariana seemed a bit nervous, but she was not easily embarrassed by things she couldn't help and was determined to learn, rather than feign ignorance.

"Now there is only one rule at lunch," he said, "and that is 'no business', so I propose that you tell me all about your delightful children, and then you shall indulge me, by listening to the proud boasting of a grandfather. We shall both nod appreciatively and agree that the other has a delightful family."

"I accept your proposal," smiled Ari, "but only on the condition that you stop me going on beyond a polite period of gushing."

"Accepted."

The following hour was spent in enjoyable conversation, and as the food came and went, Ari felt herself fully relaxing. She was glad she had declined the wine though; she suspected that if she had had so much as a sip, she would join the gentlemen in the lounge, pretending to read behind the newspapers.

In fairness, there wasn't much to say about Mr Fanshawe's granddaughter given that she had only been making her mark for the past ten months.

133

"She's just at the stage when she is pulling herself up onto the furniture; she'll be walking any day."

"Oh Lor' It's all go from here on in! God, I remember when William started to walk, everything was something new that had to be explored by teeth and drool. All my books had to go up a level, but then they were in the way, so they were thrown out."

She paused and then frowned, she hadn't meant to reveal so much, but she had got caught up in the moment. There was no way that Mr Fanshawe would have failed to notice how upset the disposal of her books had made her and all that could be inferred from that. Too polite, professional, or kind to comment on her hesitation, he stepped in and rescued her from a clearly painful memory.

"So, was William walking first? What did Leo make of that?"

"Not much! He watched his brother for a bit then promptly tried the same thing. I can't decide if it's competition or companionship. Whatever one is doing the other has to join in. I came into the kitchen once, and both of them were sitting in front of the cupboard door, rubbing flour into each other's hair and pickle over their faces. God, I laughed, and then they did my face and hair as well. After that, I put child locks on all the doors."

Walking back to the offices Ari was pleased with how lunch had gone. Mr Fanshawe appeared to be an intelligent and kind man, shrewd as well. These were good traits to have, in her mind, and he was right, his club provided an excellent lunch, she would have to try an ensure that future meetings were scheduled near lunchtime.

"Tell me," she asked, "Is there a similar sort of club that I could belong to? I loved the peace and privacy you seemed to enjoy there."

"I'm not sure about the Ladies Clubs, let me enquire for you, or would you like to be terribly modern and have a mixed club instead? I hear they are all the rage."

Ari smiled inwardly. Mr Fanshawe seemed to consider the modern world as something of a whim. "I don't think I care? Maybe send me a list of places, and I'll see if any of them suit me?"

"Your grandfather and uncle were both members of Whites, but that is strictly Men Only. In fact, I shall need to get in touch with them as they no doubt have expectations of the next heir of Wiverton joining them."

"I think you may safely assume that anything that suited my grandfather and uncle will not suit me," remarked Ari as they arrived back at the offices.

"Which rather neatly brings us round to the final topic of our meeting. Let's get Mrs Smith to bring in some coffee and we'll have a look at it."

Exercised and fed, Ari joined Mr Fanshawe for what she suspected was going to be her first proper decision about the estate.

An hour later Ariana left the solicitor with her mind reeling. In what world could they turn down ten million pounds?

12

Leaving the house early the following day, Ariana decided that if they did sell the London townhouse, they would replace it with a flat in the same area. This was incredibly convenient, and the boys would enjoy visiting the park opposite. She'd talk it through with Nick. What suited her and the boys may not suit her sister.

She arrived nice and early at the venue that Shining Horizons had hired for the presentation. The room was already set up, and as she walked in, she was greeted by a friendly host who presented her with a professional set of brochures outlining a bright new tomorrow. She was embarrassed to realise that she didn't know the landscape well enough to see if this was an accurate description of the countryside that was going to be affected. On giving her name to the host, an assistant peeled away and shortly Ariana was being welcomed personally by the head of Shining Horizons. Standing in a pinstripe suit and exuding old school affability he introduced himself as Peter Ghrab and welcomed Ariana, offering her a glass of something fizzy to celebrate.

"Celebrate? What are we celebrating?" Ari was confused, she had been up all night going through consultation meeting minutes, proposals, architects' plans, treatments and outlines but nowhere had she noticed any final decision, even in principle.

"Well, our wonderful new partnership. With your lower carriageway confirmed for the project, this is going to be a marvellous venture, and we will all make lots of money. Which is the main thing, what?!"

Another man joined him. "Lady Wiverton, may I introduce my partner Gavin Bogett. He's our details man; I do the vision stuff, he does the nuts and bolts. Isn't that so, Gavin?"

Gavin looked as sharply dressed as Peter, but a receding hairline and encroaching waistband lent a sense of seediness to his appearance.

"Couldn't have put it better myself. How do you do? Can I just say how excited we are to be working with you." He held out his hand, and it was all Ari could do to not flinch under the warm sweaty paw. "Pleased to meet you Mr Bogett. Mr Ghrab mentioned that my carriageway was confirmed?"

Gavin Bogett stalled, "Please, there's no need for formality between partners, you must call me Gavin. And, of course, Peter. And we shall call you...?"

Ari paused, she didn't want to sound rude or stuffy, but she also didn't want to be overly pally.

Something about these men gave her the creeps. She decided on semi-formality.

"Please call me Ariana. Now, what's this about me selling the lower carriageway?"

"Well yes, your uncle did agree."

"But I am not my uncle, and nothing has been signed?"

The smiles on the developers' faces became a little more static, "Well no, of course, dear lady, nothing has been signed, I merely assumed that you too, would be eager to honour your uncle's wishes. A man of great insight, putting the needs of his estate before his own pecuniary interests," said Peter.

"Oh, was he giving it to you for nothing then?"

"Ha ha, very droll. I can see we will have to mind our P's and Q's here, Gavin!" chuckled Peter in an extremely patronising manner. All laughed politely, although by now Ari was feeling remarkably cross as well as somewhat grubby.

"Gentlemen." Ari smiled politely, "Would you excuse me, please? I need to freshen up before the meeting." Anything to escape this uncomfortable conversation. Ari wanted to meet some of the other people in the room and chat with them about their feelings before the presentation started. She headed into the bathroom, unaware that a young woman had followed her.

"You lot are all the same, aren't you?"

Ari looked around in alarm at the accusatory voice. A young woman was glaring at her, her clothes were a bit tight and she was wearing more make-up than she seemed comfortable with. She looked like someone that had dressed for an occasion where she was completely out of her depth and aggressively uncomfortable.

"Sorry?"

The woman put on a silly voice, "I'm so posh, it's all so funny, ha ha ha, tread on the poor, make more money, rah rah rah! Well, what about me and my kids? If we get evicted where are we going to live? You don't have a bloody clue, do you? It's all just one big joke to you. Stupid bitch." And just like that, she stormed back out of the loos leaving Ari feeling bewildered. Who the hell was that? Before she could gather her thoughts, another woman came in and cleared her throat.

"Hello, I saw you chatting to Peter and Gavin just now. I can't wait to be working with you; it will be so nice to have another girl around to help keep those boys in line. I'm DeeDee."

Apparently, DeeDee didn't have a surname or a job title, so Ari wasn't sure what to do next without sounding rude.

"Hello, DeeDee, I'm Ariana. So, how are you involved in all this?"

"Oh me? Barely involved in anything," simpered DeeDee, " I'm head of Urban-Rural Synthesis." She rolled her eyes, "I know, what a mouthful, but actually it's an essential position. Basically, it's my job to make it all look pretty."

"Oh right. How interesting." Ariana paused, "Make what look pretty?"

"The countryside."

"Make the countryside look pretty?"

"Yes, you know, I mean no one wants to come home, actually covered in mud, do they?"

"I see your point," said Ari, completely not understanding the point, and attempted to change the subject.

"A minute ago, there was a young woman in here shouting at me about being evicted. Would you have any idea who she was?"

"But that's dreadful!" exclaimed DeeDee

"I know."

"Let me call security. If a Countess can't use the facilities without being pestered by protestors, I don't know what the world is coming to. I do apologise."

"No," said Ari, "I meant it was dreadful that she is being evicted. Is this really the case?"

"Of course not! What a thought. At Shining Horizons, we are all about the synergy of man and landscape, creating an oasis to retire to after a long day at work, this is where you come home to unwind in carefully curated, natural wellness."

"So why does she say she's being evicted? Who is she?"

"She's not being evicted; she and her family are being offered a state-of-the-art apartment at no cost. Close to Saxburgh, so she's close to all the shops, landscaped gardens for the residents, a shared leisure facility area. It will be wonderful. A huge improvement from the little hovel she's in now, let me tell you."

Ari wondered if the young woman's hovel had a garden and hens. A sunrise and a sunset. Did its garden back on to fields?

"Well, quite," murmured Ari, "lovely to meet you but I had better get a coffee before we begin." Ari edged out of the loo wondering if she was going to be pestered for the entire length of the presentation.

Sebastian was looking around the room trying to see if he could work out who Lady Wiverton was. He didn't want to ask and reveal his ignorance, but it was vital that he at least introduced himself before the meeting began. Chairs were beginning to fill up; from the look of the crowd there were a lot of potential investors and buyers in the room, but he could also spot quite a few familiar faces. In fact, his eyes caught on Janet Burbidge, one of the tenants that was facing eviction. Her face was flushed and angry and as she saw him, she made a beeline for him, her husband, Paul, catching up with her.

"Morning, Mr Seb. I see the place is filling up with people ready to throw us out on our ear."

Sebastian smiled; Janet had always called him Mr Seb. She had said when she first met him that Sir Sebastian made her lisp, and despite his request to just call him Seb, she said she was more comfortable with Mr Seb. As she put it, she was always putting her foot in it. If she called him just Seb, she might forget that she was speaking to her landlord and boss when she was ranting on. "That don't mean you're better than me," she'd said, "but you pays the wages and it don't hurt for me to remember that." Seb never felt entirely comfortable with this summation but if it worked for Janet then he would happily be Mr Seb.

"There's one of them stuck up developers now, over by the ladies. I gave her a right piece of my mind."

Paul looked alarmed, "Which one, Janet?"

Seb was now looking at the two ladies that Janet had pointed at. One was DeeDee Withers, Head of PR for Shining Horizons. The other was familiar but for the life of him, he couldn't place her. She was quite tall and slim with dark hair and pale skin. She looked to be in her mid-twenties and in Seb's eyes, was extremely good looking. Given the way she was catching the attention of others in the room, he wasn't alone in thinking her one of the prettiest women present. It might be that she was benefitting from the comparison of standing next to DeeDee who, as ever, was draped in gold chains, lots of make-up and some terribly expensive designer top. In contrast, the other girl was in a pale pink blouse and a pair of old-fashioned high waisted trousers. He was put in mind of Katherine Hepburn. For the life of him, he couldn't place her; it wasn't her face so much as the way she stood, the angle of her shoulders and head as she spoke to the other woman. Janet interrupted his thoughts.

"The tall one in the trousers. Why?"

"Oh God, Janet," groaned Paul, "tell me you were friendly."

Silence. Her husband groaned again.

"Christ, at least tell me you were polite?"

More silence.

"Oh, sweet Jesus, Janet, she's not a sodding developer, that's Lady Wiverton! Are you bloody stupid? Seb here, is trying to get her on our side, and you go in there and start giving her a hard time?"

Janet was bereft. "I didn't know it was her," she muttered sullenly. All she could think of was losing their house, the one her children had been born in, losing the fields she had grown up in. She couldn't help herself, foot in mouth Janet strikes again. But this time she may have actually contributed to the loss of her family's home.

"Right," said Seb in a calm voice, "don't panic, I'll go over, introduce myself and see if we can't fix any damage caused." As Janet made to come with him, he stopped her. "No, Janet. Let me, please?"

Leaving Paul and Janet behind, he went to join the two women. Lady Wiverton had been fidgeting and casting her eye around the room giving Seb the impression that she might enjoy the interruption, but as she caught his eye, he could see a wave of total alarm cross her features before being quickly suppressed. Surprised, he wondered what had caused that reaction, maybe she had seen him with Janet and thought he was coming over to shout at her as well. God, he could murder Janet at times. Her heart was in the right place, but her foot seldom was, and she spent most of her life extracting it from her mouth.

Unable to shake DeeDee, Ari re-entered the conference room to see many more people had now arrived. How could she politely ditch her minder and go and mingle? Having this society harpy on her shoulder would lead everyone to assume she was in the developer's pocket already. In fact, Ari thought, that was exactly the impression DeeDee was trying to impart.

She looked around the room to see if there was any obvious diversion when she caught sight of a tall man looking at her. Her skin went prickly, and she felt sick, memories of schnapps and clogs came flooding back. Dear God, what was he doing here? And he was looking straight at her. He was going to spoil everything. Who was he? This was a disaster. Oh God, he was walking straight towards her. People nodded at him as he easily cut through the crowd and Ari realised that this time, she had no means of escape.

13

The gorgeous, terrifying man approached DeeDee with a familiar air. "DeeDee, what a delight."

Clearly, his advances were appreciated as DeeDee simpered and gave him a loud air kiss. As much for her benefit as for anyone that was in the vicinity.

"Sir Sebastian, I'm so glad you could make it. I do hope you find this educational."

"Educational? Yes, I suppose we could say that. Are you going to introduce me?"

He turned smiling warmly at Ari.

"Oh, I do beg your pardon, I thought you knew each other? Not very neighbourly, are you?" She took the opportunity to lightly touch him on the arm in reproach. "Poor Lady Wiverton, fancy your neighbours not even coming to offer you a bowl of sugar! The very idea! Lady Wiverton, may I present, Sir Sebastian of the Hyssop Estate. Your neighbour."

Seb tried not to scowl at DeeDee; it was hardly her fault that he had given her an open goal. "Lady Wiverton. My sincere apologies for not catching up sooner."

Ari was so relieved that he hadn't recognised her that she almost gushed in response. "Nonsense, I was chatting to your folks just the other day. Your mother has been most charming and welcoming. And of course, the girls have all met you and think you are super. I think we're practically old friends by now." She smiled at DeeDee. "Do you think you could give us a moment? I think Mr Ghrab is looking for you."

"But of course, Lady Wiverton, shall I come back for you when we kick off?"

"Why?"

"Well, we should love you to join us at the front. It would be our honour."

Ari paused. "Gosh, how generous, but I'm a terrible chatterbox. It's probably best if I sit in the cheap seats."

"Oh, you are funny, but I insist."

"Likewise."

There was a pause and DeeDee realised that the other woman wasn't going to budge.

"Ah, well I shall let Peter and Gavin know, they will be terribly disappointed, but hopefully you will be able to join us for lunch afterwards? I'm sure there will be some fine-tuning to be discussed." She walked away, greeting and kissing people as she made her way back to the main platform.

Relieved and amused that DeeDee had been dismissed so smartly, Sebastian turned to Ariana, "Have you met my mother?"

"No, not a peep but I didn't want that woman to think she had scored a point. Although, I have been receiving lots of invitations, so maybe one was from her? Really though, I don't know why people don't just come and knock on the door."

Seb smiled. He didn't know how the wind blew with this self-possessed girl, but he liked the fact that she wasn't a pushover. Something about her seemed familiar, but he couldn't place it, no doubt it was to do with meeting all her sisters the day before.

Now that the frightful woman had gone, Ari was left standing next to this tall, beautiful man and waited for him to start shouting at her about clogs and cars. She decided the best thing was to remain calm and silent, see what he did next. Surely, he wouldn't shout at her, not here in public. She realised that she was beginning to panic, memories of Greg shouting at her for the state of the house, for the clothes she wore, for the way she spoke, for the time of day, for the bad weather. All of it came back in a rush, combining with the memory of her loss of control the other night, getting drunk and getting into a fight. She felt ill and looked around for a free chair.

"Are you okay?"

Her small face looked up at him in alarm, her expression panicky. Seb wasn't sure what was wrong, but the girl clearly looked like she was about to either burst into tears or faint. "Here, sit down and let me get you a glass of water."

Ari inhaled deeply, her hands gripping the side of her chair. She looked around, but no one seemed to be paying her any attention. Seb had chosen a chair in a discreet corner. Ari wondered if that was on purpose. Before she had time to ponder his actions, he was sat beside her with a glass of water, blocking her from the view of others.

"Would you like to step outside for a moment? It's rather stuffy in here."

Either this man was remarkably kind and forgiving or else he hadn't realised who she was. And why would he? Her face had been painted out, it was dark, and she was hardly wearing the same clothes. Right, that was a problem to consider at a later date. For now, Ari needed to buckle down and focus solely on this meeting.

"No, I'm fine, thank you, I'm feeling a lot better now. Please, I just don't know enough about the issues of this development. I've read all the developer's stuff, and it would seem they plan to build paradise. How are you involved? And is that woman over by the food something to do with you?"

Looking over, Sebastian could see that Janet was picking up the canapes, staring at them suspiciously, then pulling faces after she bit into them.

"Ah, Janet, yes she is indeed something to do with me. She and her husband and their four children live in Downside Cottage, one of my properties that is targeted for compulsory purchase."

"Compulsory purchase? I don't follow?"

"If a development is deemed to be essential, the government can step in and force you to sell your land. It's often used in the cases of airports and railway lines."

"But that's outrageous. Are they planning on building something like that here?"

"No, not a bit of it, but the developers have promised the government a hospital, and that was almost enough to convince them to give the project the green light."

"Almost?"

"Yes. They still had the issue of access, the lanes around the area were not considered suitable for the amount of traffic that the development would produce. However, a newly built, direct-access road ticks all the boxes and makes the project a viable reality."

"Ah. Right, and that's where I come in. Although, just so you know, the road, or carriageway, whatever it's called, hasn't been sold yet." Ari noticed his face sag in relief as he reacted to that piece of news. "I understand your objections to having your land grabbed away from you, but how do you balance that against the hospital and the new community services that they plan to bring to the area?"

Seb's initial delight dwindled as he listened to her dismiss his concerns as a land grab. What did he expect? She hadn't grown up at Wiverton; it might be in her blood, but it wasn't in her bones. Instead, he decided to explain about the so-called hospital. The hospital that was most likely a massive smoke screen. These things cost billions and never made any money for anyone other than the financiers. The developers just wanted the land to make millions selling the exclusive gated community. They would build a small housing development on the edge of town, some maisonettes over a row of shops, maybe a doctor's surgery, maybe a branch library, a small park, and that would be their community commitment taken care of.

And then a few years later, oh dear no hospital, for whatever reason they could think of.

Ariana listened to him in silence, as he explained his worries. His passion was clear, but she was uncertain how much came from simply not wanting his land taken off him. Which was a reasonable concern, but she needed to balance that against the community needs, shops, doctors' surgeries, libraries these were all good things, and a hospital was an enormous incentive, despite his scepticism. There was also the case that the sale of the land would bring a massive cash injection into her estate.

Seb interrupted her thoughts. "Look they are about to start. Would you excuse me whilst I rejoin Paul and Janet? Maybe we could meet up afterwards?" Seb was reluctant to leave her side, she was clearly open-minded, and he was delighted to discover that the road sale wasn't the done deal that the developers assumed it was. However, it would be wrong to try and bully her into the right decision, and so he left her, although before making himself comfortable, he returned with another glass of water and some food from the table. She still looked a little too pale and despite having only just met her, he felt oddly protective of her.

Deep in thought and scribbling away in her notebook, Ari was startled by an oily voice.

"Oh dear. Have you been abandoned? Please join me; I have a chair for you on the dais." Ari looked up; did Mr Ghrab have to loom over her so closely? It was intimidating, well that was probably the point, but his aftershave was also rather overwhelming and was making her feel ill all over again.

"That's a terribly kind offer, but I think it might give off the wrong signal. I'm quite happy here."

"Very wise, I'm sure. Always good to look impartial." He winked at her. "Now look, we should be able to wrap this presentation up after an hour or two, and I've booked a table at Claridge's for us. I can introduce you to some of the other partners and you can pry all the details out of us over lobster. Doesn't that sound lovely?"

That sounds like you are a patronising arse thought Ari. "How kind, but I'm afraid I already have plans for lunch. Oh, look, I think they are about to start!"

"Not without me, they're not," he laughed. "Well, what a pity but it can't be helped. Didn't you receive your invitation? No? Well, I do apologise. Maybe we can fix another date, yes?"

Ari was aware that the room had now settled, waiting for the meeting to begin and many were becoming aware that the chairman was deep in conversation with her. She admired his tactics but not the fact that she was being used to manipulate the crowd. Quickly she agreed, to get rid of him, and the meeting began.

Seb watched. As that creep loomed over Lady Wiverton, he was tempted to go and rejoin her, though he suspected that it might only make things worse, but it was ridiculous, look at the poor thing having to crick her neck up; where were Ghrab's manners? More alarmingly, what were they talking about? She wasn't smiling or laughing, but she did seem to be nodding her head a lot. Oh God, what if he offered her a chair on the dais, that would be the smart thing to do and how would she resist? He'd heard Peter turn on the charm before, place of honour, valued partner et cetera, but as he returned to the stage without Ari, Seb felt he should recalibrate his opinions of Peter. He had clearly given him too much credit. The smart thing would have been to get the Countess up on the platform by his side.

The meeting began with a welcome and then, in Peter's first misstep, he introduced the panel and the project. There was a small cough from the

audience as someone cleared their throat and then
Ariana spoke from her chair at the back of the room.

"Just a little clarification. I think when you
said that bit about the access across the Wiverton
Estate, it may have been interpreted by some here in
the room, as a fact. Just for the record, the Wiverton
Estate has not, as yet, entered into any deal to sell the
lower carriageway. It has been proposed, and we are
currently looking at it. I do apologise for interrupting,
just trying to help."

Peter looked startled at having been interrupted
and then his mouth twitched in annoyance as he found
himself being publicly corrected.

"Quite so, quite so, and I apologise if anyone
misunderstood my meaning. It is essential that we
have full trust and disclosure here. I am indebted to
you, Lady Wiverton."

Seb looked over at Lady Wiverton, sipping on
her water, and realised that he might not have
overestimated Peter after all, but he might have wildly
underestimated the Countess.

The meeting plodded on, and then the room
opened up for questions.

Lots of people living in Saxburgh, the nearby
town, seemed delighted by the prospect of a new

hospital, but Seb queried the need for a doctor's surgery if a hospital was just down the road.

"Oh dear, Sir Sebastian," said Gavin, "I'm afraid hospitals aren't built in a day. We can't just tell our labourers to get on with it; it's not the eighteenth century anymore." Gavin was gratified by some sprinkled laughter, although he had hoped for greater support.

Ariana read the room and decided that she needed to be careful, she didn't know what Seb's reputation was like in the area, although Gavin had got fewer laughs for that jibe than he might have expected, so maybe Seb was popular with the audience? Ariana, however, was pretty certain that the reputation of her estate was in the mud after her uncle's recent behaviour. If she joined in now, Gavin would be able to play the 'them and us' card with ease. Ari knew how easy it was to blame others; she had no intention of offering herself up as bait. She had to be smarter than that. She raised her hand.

"I think a hospital is wonderful, but of course you are so right. It certainly can't be built in a day. With that in mind can you let us know what the legal commitments in the development plans are for the doctor's surgery. That's also greatly needed and can be built much quicker. I think everyone would be thrilled to discover a cast-iron commitment to that, regardless of any hospital development."

"Of course, they're not going to build a hospital," someone shouted out. "They just want to build a load of fancy homes and make shed loads."

Peter was quick to jump in and pacify the crowd, grateful for the chance to dodge Ariana's question, "I understand your concerns, but this isn't simply a housing development. This is the creation of a new community, one that will embrace and support the current one..."

Damn, thought Seb, as Peter rattled on with his spiel, that protester had given him an opportunity to ignore Ariana's question.

"Rubbish," cried out the same protester.

"Oh, pipe down, Jim," a woman with a broad accent called out, "you're always arguing against anything. What do I care about some bloody crested newt when there's nowhere for my kids to play and no decent shops? I'm all for this development, you've seen the pictures, it's going to look well nice."

Ariana groaned, what did she mean, nowhere to play? In all her life Ariana had never seen so many green spaces. And now the momentum had moved away from securing the doctor's surgery.

"Why don't you answer the lady's question?" This was addressed to the panel.

"Absolutely. We will be building a state-of-the-art playground with all the latest safety equipment as well as a separate area for skateboards and scooters. In addition, we are also considering a combined-use court for netball and basketball."

"Thank you," said the man again, "but I meant the other lady's question. Will you give us a cast-iron guarantee about the doctor's surgery? Even if you don't get permission for the road and hospital?"

"Yes of course," smiled Gavin smoothly, "and I think our commitment to that point has already been made clear. As I said earlier, this isn't the Victorian era, we can't just make the labourers do what we want because we have a title."

The response was less favourable this time, and Gavin realised that he might have lost the crowd. Time to wrap things up smartish before it turned ugly. These things often flipped on a single sentence. Luckily, he had avoided that.

Bloody fool thought Peter, always going one step too far, and now he'd flipped the mood of the crowd. Time to call it a day. Standing up he thanked the audience over the growing hubbub and called the meeting to a close. He invited them all to look through the proposal and to make an appointment to discuss any investments in person. He also reminded the room that a prestigious development like this came along rarely and that people should secure their interests early. Ari got up and made her way quickly over to Seb.

"Lunch, now, quickly before I get nabbed again." Surprised but pleased, Seb steered Ari out through the crowd before Peter and Gavin noticed who she had left with. With a quick flick of his wrist he hailed a cab, "Borough Market, please."

That made Ari smile, she loved the market, but she didn't think she could be more overdressed if she tried.

"I know we're a little overdressed," said Seb, "but I love Borough Market. Do you know it? It's a lovely spot, and we can chat without fear of being interrupted or overheard." The taxi pulled away just as DeeDee dashed out onto the pavement looking about to see if she could spot Ariana.

14

Borough Market was a fabulous hotchpotch of large areas sheltering under the iron girders of a large open-air Victorian structure. People had been buying and selling food on this spot for over a thousand years and whilst the Victorians had brought a sense of scale and organisation to the market, it remained wonderfully chaotic and eclectic under the heavy ironwork. Despite the heaviness and darkness of the market, Ari always felt that the energy of the place was vibrant and exciting. Conversely, despite the shade, it always felt light and airy. Whilst she waited for Seb to return with some coffees, Ari glanced around and decided that she would do a bit of shopping when they were done. Norfolk was lovely but the only cheese the local shop had was cheddar and when she'd asked for the spice section the nice chap behind the till told her that they had salt, pepper and mustard, in a tone that suggested nothing else was required.

"Hello, daydreamer?" Ari was startled. God, she had been lost in thoughts of spiced puddings and what she was going to cook tonight.

"Sorry, boring stuff," she said, reaching for her coffee, "I was thinking of doing a spot of shopping here when we finish. I was trying to make some gulab

162

jamun the other day for the boys and the only 'spice' the local shops seem to stock is mustard!"

Seb grinned, "Well you'll have to forgive Norfolk the mustard bias, Colman's Mustard originated in Norwich. It was a huge industry, there's even a museum about it."

Ari laughed, "Yes, of course there is, is that next to the Marmalade Museum"

Now it was Seb's turn to laugh. "No, I'm serious, in Norwich, there is an actual Mustard Museum, let me take you and then you can apologise for laughing at our noble Norfolk ways. But seriously, there isn't much in the way of 'foreign stuff' in the local shops, try Burnham Market, it's a village along the coast from us. It has lots of little independents."

Ari spluttered, "Let me stop you right there. I've been to Burnham Market, it's so pretty but the prices are outrageous. Do you know they are selling fancy pots of turmeric for the same price that I can buy a whole sack of it from my old corner shop? And I know here isn't as cheap as them, but it's a damn sight cheaper than some incredibly pretty little village in North Norfolk. And another thing; why is bread displayed in a fancy wicker basket suddenly twice the price? What gives? Sorry," she paused for breath and grinned, "I'm ranting. Culture shock, I guess. But yes, an invitation to a Mustard Factory sounds delightful."

Seb loved the sound of her voice and the more she spoke the more convinced he was, that he now knew where he had met her. Especially as she built up a head of steam.

"I can't tell from your sceptical tone if you are serious or not, but I shall, of course, be happy to give you a guided tour of Norwich, and I can also introduce you to the delights of throwing pennies down a well, playing with Snap the Dragon and finishing off with the best chips in the world from the market."

"It's a date then," said Ari, "and sounds like more fun than the past few hours. I still have a headache from that ghastly man's aftershave, talk about malodorous!"

Seb choked on his coffee and roared with laughter. "J'accuse! Malodorous! I thought it was you! What did you call me? 'A malodorous piece of jumped up excrement'."

Ari looked at him in horror. He remembered their first encounter outside the pub.

"Oh my God. I'm sooooooo sorry. I know I should have confessed the minute I saw you walking towards me, but you didn't recognise me, and it didn't seem like the best time to bring it up."

Still laughing, Seb agreed that that wouldn't have been a good time to mention damaging his car and swearing at him, but then he couldn't think when a good time would be.

"I really am so, so sorry. How much do I owe you for the car, did I do a lot of damage? Have I mentioned how sorry I am? It was my first time out in years without the children and I just meant to let my hair down a little bit, but I got carried away."

"You didn't let your hair down, it was stuck up in those bright yellow upturned plaits. What were you supposed to be by the way? All I saw was a lot of ribbons, and scraps of shiny fabric. Oh and of course lots of flesh."

Ari was mortified. She had never behaved so outrageously in her life, and here was the recipient of her appalling behaviour apparently laughing at her. God, could this be any more embarrassing. "I was a Dutch flower girl."

"Ah, yes that explains the white frilly knickers, the Lutherans were famous for their black and white dress code."

"I know! That's what I said!" Both Seb and Ari were now laughing loudly enough to catch the attention of neighbouring tables and passing shoppers.

"Look seriously. I do need to apologise, I was incredibly rude and I damaged your car, there's no excuse for it so please let me make amends."

Wiping tears from his eyes, Seb dismissed her apology. "Honestly, that laugh was payment enough. I was a bloody bore that evening. I was downright rude to you and your friend when I walked into the pub and I don't even have the excuse of being drunk. I deserved all the vitriol I got, so please let's call it quits. But I have kept the clogs as a reminder not to be a stuck-up bad-tempered bigot. Unless Cinderella would like her footwear back?"

"Cinderella, I like it! No, I've already replaced them for my friend. Although I haven't seen her since. I think she recognised who you were and doesn't want to be associated with, as she put it, 'a nut job'. Boy did I mess up that night! At least I can go and tell her that I have now set things right by her and that it's all resolved."

Realising that the coffee was now finished, Ari was disappointed to discover how much time had flown, she needed to get on with the shopping before she returned to Wiverton Manor. She couldn't remember the last time she had fallen into such an easy conversation with someone and she would have loved to spend the rest of the day with him.

"Didn't you say you needed to do some shopping? How about I come with you and carry the bags? Then you can tell me what goes into gulab jamun. It sounds intriguing."

"Oh, I'd love that. Better yet, why not come for tea this evening and share some with us? Although you might have to fight the boys for them?" God thought Ari, what was she thinking, she'd only met him this morning and now she was inviting him to dinner. But of course, he was her neighbour, she was just being neighbourly, and they still had a lot to talk about. Yes, that was it. Which didn't explain how disappointed she was when he explained he already had a prior engagement that he couldn't break.

They spent the next hour weaving in and out of the crowds. Ari would say where she wanted to go next and Seb would then make a path through the throng of people. Gradually, she loaded Seb up with bag after bag. She bought lots of store cupboard essentials and bags of treats that she knew the boys would love, then she added some cheeses and dried meats. As they shopped, Ari chatted about the boys. Seb was impressed that they had such an educated palate to be eating the things that she was buying. She scoffed at him, it wasn't exotic, it was what everyone on the street ate. When you played at your friend's house you ate what was put in front of you. Ari

167

explained that she and her sisters had grown up exactly the same way. You ate what was put on the plate. It had been the same for Seb, at boarding school it was pretty much whatever slops were given or starve. Ari laughed, she wouldn't have called what her folks cooked, slops, but the consequences were the same. You'd eat it and say thank you or go to bed hungry.

As Seb groaned under the weight of the bags he pointed out that she still had to get them all home. He had a point, where was her shopper when she needed it? Ari smiled at the idea of her pulling her shopping trolley along the gravel drive at Wiverton Manor, back from a day at the market. Happily, however, she only had to get a taxi to the train station and then her car was parked at the other end. God, having money was lovely. Realising that the day was drawing to an end, she asked Seb to look after the bags whilst she popped off to powder her nose.

On the way back, she could see that he had his back to her and was on the phone. As she got closer, she caught a brief snatch of his conversation.

"She's docile and easily led." He paused, listening to the other side of the conversation, "I wish." Another nod, then, "No I think it's going to be plain sailing. Just keep her in the dark for a bit longer and then we should be home free."

Horrified, Ari stepped back and approached Seb from another angle so that he could see her approach. As she did, he smiled at her and quickly ended his phone call. Ari left the market feeling hurt and stupid. She had thought Greg was a temporary lapse in judgement. Now here she was again, overwhelmed by the task ahead of her and trying to lean on the first charming man she met. A charming man who was apparently playing her. It was clear from his phone call that his behaviour was all an act, he was just trying to manipulate her into not selling the land. Ari was desperate not to believe it. She had had a lovely time with him, and he hadn't brought up the meeting or the issue of the land once. Could she have misread him?

Noticing a change in her mood, Seb suggested that they should arrange a date to have a site visit to discuss the actual planning in question. In all the fun of coffee and shopping, they had forgotten what they were about. Politely Ai agreed then clambered into the back of a waiting cab, leaving Seb a little puzzled at her cold demeanour. He had thought things were going well. Frustrated, he sent her a quick text, having got her number over coffee and suggested a meeting in three days' time.

As Ari sat dejected in the back of the car, she saw that Seb was wasting no time in getting on with his real agenda. Fine, she thought, getting on the phone to Shining Horizons, two could play at that game.

#

Clemmie took one look at Ari's face as she walked in the house and flicked on the kettle.

"Was it awful?"

"Oh, you know, sycophants and bullies. But at least this time round, I have power. Trouble is I just don't know how to use it yet."

She paused and called out for the boys who soon came shouting towards her running and waving wooden swords at her. Just as they got to her, they threw them to one side and leapt on her, all of them collapsing onto the sofa, giggling.

"Did you bring us presents?"

And then there were more shouts of excitement as their mother opened her suitcase and pulled out packets of sweeties and cakes. They weren't the sort of presents that she would normally encourage but the boys enjoyed them all the more because of it.

"So, what have you been up to?"

The boys ran off and came back carrying loads of pictures that they had been drawing over the past few days. They had also named all the carved figurines around the house, made fudge, and started a small vegetable patch in the kitchen gardens.

"My word, you've been busy. Will you show me everything you've done after I've had a cup of tea?"

The boys promised they would and picking up their swords again they went off to play hide and seek with Wendy. The five sisters now gathered around the dining room table and closed the door. Ari pulled out various portfolios and forecasts and passed one to each sister. She told them everything Mr Fanshawe had told her and then explained the scheme being put forward by Shining Horizons.

"Gut feeling, Ari, should we sell the land to the developers?" asked Aster.

"God, I wish it were that easy. Gut feeling is an easy no. They are slimy, greasy, patronising bastards, but that's not the point is it? There are other issues at play. Will this be of a genuine positive benefit to the community and how badly do we need the money?"

"Okay, that one I can help you with," said Nick, and she went on to outline how her day had been. Mothballing the estate had caused it some damage, but nothing appeared to be too critical financially. Looking at it, Nick figured it would take a year or two to get back on the same footing that the estate had been at about five years ago. But it would be hard work and relied on the general economy staying stable. She also wanted to explore avenues that the estate had never entered into before. Ari breathed a sigh of relief, but Nick wasn't finished.

"The problem is the soft stuff, Ari. The people, the staff. Uncle David treated them with ruthless disregard. I've checked how it was all done, and every dismissal was above board, no one is going to come after the estate for wrongful dismissal but, Ari, there are so many, and their letters of appeal are heartbreaking. Some of these people have been linked to the family for generations. You should read them."

The sisters looked at Ari with concern. Nick felt guilty for telling Ari this because she knew how her sister would respond and it seemed to her that she had always been fighting for the underdog. She deserved a break herself, to just spend time playing with her children and helping them to cope with the loss of their father. She needed time to grieve, not play lady of the manor.

Trying to change the tone, Paddy asked Ari if she had finally met up with her neighbour?

Apparently, she had missed him when he had called around, and according to the housekeeper and solicitor, had been trying to see her for the past two weeks. The sisters were clearly impressed with him and wanted to know what she had made of him. Ari scowled. Sebastian Flint-Hyssop was not an issue she wanted to discuss. Getting up from the table without answering their questions, she asked her sisters to think about what she had discovered and suggested that they all sleep on it. As she left, her sisters gave each other some quizzical looks. Something was afoot.

Following a hearty breakfast, the boys were settled with some paper and colouring pencils and the sisters sat around the large refectory table. The low morning sun made the oak planks shine with a warm, comforting solidity. Generations had sat here, planning, celebrating, gossiping, doing homework, eating dinner. It had been the heart of many a conversation and would be at the heart of many more for centuries to come. Its simple strength reassured Ari, and as she looked at the others, she felt that it was going to be okay, no matter how tough things may become. God knows they had been through worse. This problem might be vast, but it wasn't deep, and this time she had her sisters to help in a way that they couldn't when she was fighting for their custody.

"Right. This is the way I see it."

Over the next hour, the sisters discussed the family's plans. Clemmie was up in Scotland trying to sort things out up there. Nick was trying to get to grips with the Wiverton enterprises, Paddy was down in Cornwall trying to make sense of the fact that they appeared to own a whole village, and Aster was going to get her degree. Then if she wanted to, join the family firm. In a few years, they would have a better idea of what was what. In the meantime, however, Aster would attend all board meetings.

The next few months were going to throw up more questions than answers and, until they knew more, Ari didn't mean to impose anything hard and fast. But first things first, and that was to help those that had been abandoned by the family and, where possible, restore them to their previous positions. Nick was keen to stress that this might be a good opportunity to reassess everything and that each re-appointment should be looked at properly. After a while the conversation fell into minutiae and whilst Ari knew that the details were going to reign, she felt enough had been established for now.

"So, what next?" asked Nick. "What are you going to do about the road? Do we need the money? Most importantly, are you going to ask your neighbour out?"

Ari blushed in fury and confusion and was rescued from the teasing by Paddy, who had a heart as soft as a marshmallow. She reminded the others that Ari was only three months a widow and to knock it off. The salutary reminder made the sisters look guiltily towards their nephews who were now glued to episodes of their favourite cartoons and hadn't heard a thing. None of the girls had liked Greg and had a feeling that the marriage was heavily on the rocks, although Ari wouldn't say a word about it and would never have the subject discussed. No one was sad that he was dead, but in truth, they tended to forget him in all that had happened. They just wanted their beloved sister to be happy and have someone in her life to take care of her. Having lived with Ari and Greg the longest, Aster had the best insight into the relationship, but she was a closed book. If there was anyone more self-contained than Ari it was Aster. Whatever her feelings on the matter were, they were hers alone. The sisters had long since given up trying to guess what she was thinking.

Nick squeezed Ari's hand and apologised for being tactless.

"As I said yesterday, my gut instinct is to say no to the road," said Ari. I don't want to make any rushed decisions, especially on something that cuts into the estate. I also didn't like the developers, but I'm going to a site inspection tomorrow to see if there are genuine benefits for the community. What do you all think?"

"Go to the meeting, get a feel for it, and then we'll back you one hundred per cent, whatever you decide," suggested Clemmie. "You're the one living here and the one in overall control. Down to you, I reckon." The other girls agreed and finally it was time for them all to start heading home and continue with their new lives.

Standing on the steps as Ari waved them off, she had a deep urge to call them all back to her. She wanted to hug them so tightly and never let them go; life was lonely and scary at the moment, and she was fed up with doing it on her own.

Shouting out to the boys, she decided that she needed a bit of activity to shake off this melancholia. Boots and coats on, the little family headed off across the lawn towards the woods to see what they might discover. Leo thought there might be bears, so they all agreed to go on tiptoes until they were certain. Tiptoeing in wellies wasn't the easiest thing to do, and as they clattered their way through the trees, Ari felt her cares falling away from her until, exhausted and muddy, they all trooped back to the house, confident that all bears had been properly scared off and that the only ones remaining were the friendly ones, called

Boris. Just Boris. All friendly bears were called Boris apparently; on this Leo and William were agreed, and when Leo and William were agreed then it was a fact that could never be challenged.

15

The following morning Ari lay in bed snuggled under the duvet watching the clouds scud across the skies. Now that she had such wonderful views, she found it hard to ever close her curtains. As soon as she switched the bedroom light off, she opened the curtains and looked at the stars until she fell asleep. Like nearly everything about her new life, every aspect was a novelty, but the stars were something that she couldn't get enough of. Now it looked like it was going to be a sunny and blustery day. As she wandered downstairs, she heard voices in the kitchen and could hear the boys chatting excitedly to someone; maybe one of her sisters had returned? She walked into the kitchen and saw Dickie sitting at the table chatting to the boys as they ate their soldiers and eggs. The boys looked up and waved at her but returned to their food, clearly at ease with Dickie's arrival on the scene.

"Have I overslept?" asked Ari, surprised and happy that she had slept so deeply.

"Only a bit and I'm early. Wendy is coming shortly, to help me entertain the boys whilst you are out, and we'll get to work on deciding what needs to be ordered in. Any preferences for food?"

As Ari sat with the twins, she drank her coffee and was surprised by how good things looked after a decent night's sleep and someone else making the coffee. Whilst Ari was a bit nervous leaving the boys with a stranger, she felt reassured by Dickie. It was only a little over a month since Ari and the children had started their new lives in Norfolk, but it seemed, like most things, that they were adapting faster than she was. After giving her housekeeper a list of their regular foodstuffs, and reminding Leo and William to be on their best behaviour, she headed out to the car.

The gravel crunched under her shoes as she walked over to the garages. The wind picked at her hair, and she pulled a bobble out of her jacket pocket and looped her hair into a low ponytail. She had a headscarf in her pocket as well, so if it got worse later, she would whip that out too. She had picked out one of her aunt's suits, a tweed pair of trousers and a smart tweed jacket with a silk blouse beneath. As the eldest she'd always had the first crack at the second-hand clothes, so she was used to the concept of wearing someone else's things. That's all my life is she thought ruefully, this house isn't mine any more than it was my grandfather's or will be my sons', we are all just living here, taking care of it until we pass the house on to the next generation. Second-hand clothes, second-hand homes.

Driving along the country lanes, Ari was delighted with the scenery. She loved the way the countryside was laid out in front of her; big wide fields punctuated by the odd oak tree towering up into the sky. A few early poppies grew in the sandy verges adding splashes of red to the green edging, and ploughed fields were ready to burst into this year's crops. Driving past field after field, the satnav directed her towards the sea. The land grew even flatter and fell away as the sky loomed overhead. Wherever she looked the huge skies wrapped around her. She hadn't realised how calm she was until she saw a giant hoarding by the side of a small lane. It was full of happy couples, smiling down from the advertising boards. Confident in their brand-new cars and amazing looking homes, overlooking stunning seascapes. In fairness to the developers, it did look inviting. Seb's car was parked up alongside the hoarding. Feeling agitated, Ari took a deep breath and then, locking her car, she made her way over to Seb's.

"Nice hoarding! Just to let you know I have invited the developers to join us as well. I think it's important that I hear both sides. Is that okay?" Ari asked brightly.

Startled, Seb didn't think that was okay at all but he couldn't fault her reasoning. Before he could reply she continued, "So tell me what this development means from your point of view."

As they drove along Seb explained that all the land they were now driving through was bordered by his land and the sea. "My great-great-grandfather lost this patch of land, known as Hyssop Lakes, in a bet with a friend. Over the years the joke continued and was gradually forgotten or overlooked by subsequent generations. The estate continued to look after the land but crucially didn't own it. If I'm honest, I didn't even realise it wasn't our land until all this blew up."

Ari couldn't imagine owning so much land that you didn't even know what was yours and what wasn't. She grinned at her own high horse; at the moment she didn't have a clue what was hers when she looked about her. Was that her land, was that her mess? Was she responsible for those blocked streams? But still, surely, she had an excuse, she'd only just inherited. The Flint-Hyssops had always lived here, were they so complacent that they'd taken their eye off the ball?

"How do you not know you own somewhere?" Ari tried to keep the incredulity out of her voice but given Seb's rather defensive tone, it was clear that she hadn't quite managed it.

"I guess because I don't wake up every morning and read the title deeds, I get up and manage the problems and that includes the maintenance of this land. Our tenants have houses on here that we maintain, and we keep all the ditches clear and free-flowing. We farm the land and treat it exactly the same as every other part of our estate."

"So, you don't own your tenants' homes either?"

"No. It appears not."

Seb groaned, this girl was making his family sound like idiots. The defence of 'it's always been this way' fell apart with a few sharp observations from her.

"Who owns those houses?" Ari pointed to a row of four terraced houses sitting on a small ridge.

"They are part of the Hyssop Lake lands."

"And who lives in them?"

"Paul and Janet Burbidge. Jim Beam. Josie Lawrence and her four children and Edna and John Wheateaters."

"Janet Burbidge, she was the lady that had a go at me in the meeting room?"

"Yes."

"So, they are your tenants?"

"Yes."

"Living in someone else's house? Do they pay rent?"

"Yes, but it is subsidised."

"And who do they pay the money to?"

"Us. To the estate."

"Wow, so you are collecting rent on property you don't own. Nice gig!"

Oh, good grief. This wasn't going according to plan at all. This girl was ruthless and he had no defence. The whole situation was a shambles and now they were facing a mammoth development, in an area of outstanding natural beauty, simply to line some fat cats' pockets. And no doubt, this girl thought that's exactly what his own family had been doing for the past hundred years.

"It's not a gig. We pay for the upkeep of the houses. We replace bathrooms and kitchens when they need it. And, as I said, they live there for a subsidised rent."

"So, you are spending estate money on someone else's house? My plumbing's a bit dodgy. Can you come and fix that for me?"

Seb wondered if it was even worth replying. He was banged to rights and she wasn't having a bar of any excuses.

"If you have been taking care of these properties and all this land..."

"Yes, we're idiots. I get it..."

"That wasn't what I was going to say, I mean yes, but that's done. Do you have any grounds to own the land, based on the fact that you have always taken care of it? You know like people who adopt land by always using it?"

"Actually, we are pursuing that line through the courts but of course Shining Horizons are opposing us. It's a mess."

They drove on in silence for a bit and Ari felt that the atmosphere was awkward. She knew Seb was unimpressed with the grilling and with the invitation to the developers but she also thought that he was just sulking because she was proving harder to manipulate than he had anticipated.

"So, tell me," she asked, "what else have you been up to, or is this development all-consuming at the moment?"

Grateful for a change of conversation, Seb started to tell Ari about his friends' success at their stables. A mare that he part-owned had already become pregnant.

"This is her first season and she's already pregnant, obviously they're delighted but we aren't taking any chances. They are keeping her nice and quiet. If she's in a nice dark stable, she'll be more docile. Away from the other horses, she's less likely to be alarmed."

Ari looked across at him as he drove on, chatting about this horse. He was animated and smiling, happy in the face of his friends' success. The words nice, dark, quiet and docile rose up to mock her. She decided that if there was a bigger idiot on this planet, she was yet to meet her.

"Um. Look I think I owe you another apology."

Seb glanced at her quizzically and continued driving. "What for?"

"I think I've misjudged you. I overheard part of your phone call in Borough Market, and you were saying that she was docile and easily led and..."

"Yes?"

"And I thought you were talking about me," she said in an apologetic tone.

Seb looked over to her again this time incredulously. "You! Easily led? Docile! My God woman, have you not met yourself?"

"Oh God, I completely misread the conversation. I just seem to be having a hard time learning all the ropes and now here we are and there are the sodding developers. Oh, I am sorry."

Seb drew into the parking area, put on the handbrake and turned to face Ari properly.

"Honestly, I'm just glad that I hadn't done something to upset you. I was worried at the market but then I hardly know you or anything about you, and I thought I was probably being too forward. Instead, you thought I was playing the villain of the piece. Let's not say any more about it and, for the record," he said, nodding towards the developers, "it does make sense for you to hear from both sides at the same time. Come on, let's go and join them."

The road had petered out into a wide car park, edged with sand and marram grass and beyond the car park was a path leading down to the beach. There were gulls crying overhead and, along the shoreline, Ari could see a large pine forest. The whole scene was particularly beautiful and unspoilt by any buildings or caravan parks. The doors to a large fancy saloon car opened and Ari recognised some faces from the meeting.

"Lady Wiverton, so pleased you could make it, and Sir Sebastian, how pleasant," said Mr Bogett in a tone that barely concealed just how unpleasant it actually was.

"Hello, Mr Bogett," said Ari with a smile. "I was chatting to Lady Flint-Hyssop yesterday, trying to get directions and Sebastian overheard and offered to drive. Wasn't that kind of him? Shall we proceed?"

"And Sebastian?"

"He'll come with us of course. I'm the new girl on the block here and have no idea if half of what anyone tells me, is as accurate as they think it is. This way both parties can help ensure that I understand the situation properly. Yes?"

Despite the uncomfortable start, Gavin and his team explained their vision for this whole section of the coastline all the way up to the local town of Saxburgh. Ari was interested in the hospital, but Gavin was keen to stress that it wouldn't be a large general hospital but one with a small A&E and maternity clinic. Certainly, these would be important features for the local community but there were other plans, including an upgrade of the local library facilities from a mobile to a static one as well as an outdoor play park.

"We plan to build three hundred homes over two locations with the additional infrastructure to support them and the existing community."

"And what about here? I can see from your plans that you have lots of designs for the old cattle market but what about this end of the project? This beautiful remote wild beach?"

"Ah well, yes, this will be the crown jewel of the development. We will be building a collection of homes out here. We will ensure this area will be kept pristine as we will establish an area of privacy in order to protect the wildlife."

"You mean you are going to gate the beach," muttered Sebastian.

Ari looked confused. "I don't understand?"

"Sebastian's being a bit over dramatic. What we are going to do is restrict access to the beach in order to protect the breeding colonies of seals and rare seabirds. This stretch of coast will become a wildlife marine park. It will be exceptional."

"So, no one can use the beach?"

"Absolutely. Just the people that live here."

"Live where?"

"Here," said Mr Bogett. "We will be building a small environmental community out here. The rest of the development, closer to the town, will also be built along environmental lines."

Large white clouds were scudding overhead, and the waves were all topped with small white peaks. The air was clean and crisp, and Ari could imagine people paying an awful lot of money to live here. She would. In addition, the local community were about to get some impressive additions to their town. As a young mother, she knew the value of a local library, a good A&E and more play areas. Maybe Sebastian was just sore because he was about to lose land that he hadn't owned for a century but had still maintained. She looked over at him. He was looking out over the waves, his face tight and angry, his dark hair mussed up in the breeze. One strand kept getting caught in his eyes and he would tuck it behind his ear before the wind plucked it loose again. He was oblivious of Ari's observations, lost in dark thoughts.

When the time came to visit the next site, Ari sat in the developers' car as they set off towards the edge of town and the old cattle market. According to the developers, this was a run-down area that was going to benefit greatly from the improved infrastructure. Ari was torn. She knew what it meant to live with limited resources, and whilst she thought the area was beautiful, she wasn't blind to the fact that a lovely landscape didn't make up for a lack of facilities. Having a local A&E would be an incredible development but was it a genuine possibility or was it all smoke and mirrors just to get an exclusive gated beachside development?

"Do you have a timetable of works?" Ari decided she would look over the plans and see if anything else jumped out at her. They spent the next few hours driving around the town and there was no doubt about it, the area was down on its luck. There were lots of closed independents, a few mobile phone shops, some bookies and lots of charity shops. There was a locked chain on one of the playgrounds, with a faded council sign saying 'Closed for Repairs'. The local library was also closed, with the building standing empty. On the door was a laminated sign, listing the times that a mobile library would visit. Everything felt tired and dejected. A stiff North Sea breeze blew rubbish along the streets, and the party tugged their coats closer to their chests. Finally, despondent, Ari returned with the others to the cars. The developers were full of enthusiasm and Ari was impressed by their vision for rejuvenating this town. Despite their optimism though, she doubted their altruism. Maybe she was judging them unfairly? At least they had a plan.

As they got back to the cars, Ari thanked them for their visit and for taking the time to show her their proposals. She tried to be warm and encouraging and as she got into Seb's car they drove back in near silence to her own car. For his part, Seb had been shocked to discover how bad things had become in the town. Admittedly, he never visited as he had no call to, but he remembered going as a child to the local cinema—now closed like so much else. Was there more that he and his family could have been doing over the years? They were good employers and always took care of their tenants and workers, but could they have done more? His mind was full of the problems and he decided to speak to his parents as soon as he got in. Given Ariana's enthusiastic response to the developers, he was disappointed to realise that he may have to accept that the sale of her land would be going through. Maybe it was a done deal and the family would have to accept the loss of Hyssop Lakes, but they could still do something to help the town. He didn't believe for one minute that the proposed cottage hospital would materialise. Every time Peter had waxed on about the jobs it would create, and the regeneration of the local economy, it was all he could do to not actually snort with derision. Back at her car, Ari jumped out and thanked him for the lift. As they drove away, their minds were as one. Something had to be done.

16

As Ari drove home, she decided she was going to throw a party. She needed cheering up and it was about time that she said hello to the area properly. It was no good living in a place and not knowing who her neighbours were. In fact, it was weird how empty the countryside was. She still couldn't get her head around the fact that she could go a whole day outdoors and not see another living soul. She wondered if people in the countryside felt lonely or enjoyed the privacy? Either way, it was about time she said hello. Knocking on the door for a bowl of sugar was made impossible by the fact she'd have to walk miles before she ever got off her land and even then, she'd never be able to find all the little cottages tucked away down country lanes. So, a party it would be, and she was going to make it for everyone. She was going to ask Wendy and Dickie to help draw up a list of people to invite, then she would have a word with Lady Mary and get her to suggest a list of locals that had known her mother, and more importantly, liked her. Finally, she was going to call up her old friends and neighbours and invite them all up and of course, she'd get the girls involved. Although she knew they were all a bit overwhelmed as well, trying to adjust to their new lives.

Ari tried to imagine how well such an eclectic bunch of guests would get on with each other and decided that she had better get some entertainment laid on as well. And a big tent in case it rained. She wondered if Seb would come to the party; she'd have to invite him, but were parties his thing? He seemed so earnest and sometimes downright angry. Maybe inviting him was the wrong thing to do but it would look rude if she didn't; he'd probably say no anyway. For some reason, the idea disappointed her. She knew who she wasn't inviting though and that was anyone to do with the new development. This was for people who had helped her, and for people who the estate had helped in the past. Maybe she could start to right some of the wrongs her family had recently done to the neighbourhood. But this was going to be about having fun and saying hello, not saying sorry. This was going to be a party!

She headed into the kitchen, calling out, and soon her racket summoned Dickie, Wendy and the twins, appearing from various areas of the house, to be excitedly informed by Ari that they were going to have a party.

"We need jelly and a tent and a Batman outfit," shouted Leo and Wills.

"A Batman outfit?"

"Yes. I'm going to be Batman!"

"Will this be a fancy-dress party?" asked Dickie.

"God no," laughed Ari, wincing as she remembered her last attempt at fancy dress, "but if any child wants to dress up, they can. It's a no-rules party."

"No rules, no rules!" shouted the boys.

"Wendy, it looks like I have totally wound up the boys, do you think you could get the hose out and spray them down?"

Both boys screamed and laughed and ran off down the hallway with Wendy in pursuit, carrying a make-believe water hose.

"Now, Dickie, how about it? Can we manage it?"

Jane Dickens looked at the young lady of the manor, full of life and excitement, and could see her mother's love for life shining out through her eyes. As she listened to her plans, she loved the idea of it being a big event but decided that because there were so many differing groups of strangers that it might be easiest to run it like a fete with lots of diversions and attractions.

Ari interrupted her thoughts. "I suppose I'll have to have it in the house but I'm not sure if it can survive lots of excited children. What do you think? Or maybe rent a huge tent, like they have at weddings?"

Dickie thought with horror of a load of strangers all milling around the manor and proposed the pavilion instead.

Ari looked blankly at Dickie. "Pavilion?"

"Oh dear, yes, the cricket pavilion. Haven't you found that yet? Come on, get in the car. Let's explore."

With a shout to Wendy and the boys, Dickie was soon driving Ari along one of the estate lanes and after a few minutes they crested a small hill and swept around a large flat field. At the far end was an ornate building, in front of which Dickie pulled up. Ari stepped out and took in the large wooden structure.

It was two storeys high and whilst built in brick was adorned with lots of white picket fences around the perimeter of the building. These surrounded a large decked seating area. In front of the picket fence running the length of the building was a tiered stand of three benches leading down to a further paved area that was now overgrown with weeds and littered with the occasional empty can. Ornamental white posts rose up supporting the pavilion's balcony and upper level, which housed three further windows in the pantile roof, and the whole edifice was topped off with a small clock tower.

"This is the cricket pavilion, and this," announced Dickie with a sweep of her arm to the overgrown field, "is the cricket pitch."

"Oh dear, they normally look a little greener and shorter on the telly. Let me guess, Uncle David let it go..."

Looking at the cricket pitch it had clearly deteriorated faster than the building. Now, instead of a pristine sweep of green, a soft meadow of grasses and flowers swayed in the breeze. If she concentrated, she might be able to hear the echo of leather on willow, but it was hard over the buzz of the bees. Uncle Sammy from number eighty-one would be horrified, Ari thought with a laugh, if he could see a cricket pitch in this state.

Dickie nodded but unlocked the doors and Ari could instantly see the appeal of the venue. There was plenty of room; there was more space here than her old house for heaven's sake, and they'd had some great parties there. Until, of course, she got married. Despite her wishes, Ari and Greg hadn't held their reception at home. She had quickly learned that her in-laws were all about appearance, so a tacky local hotel and function room was hired instead. And Nigel and

Annette had reminded her at every opportunity of how large the bill was that they were picking up, on account of her having no parents to pay for the wedding. But they didn't want to make a thing of it. Of course.

Dickie saw Ari's face change from wonder to something that looked like anger or sadness and she stepped in quickly to reassure her that they could bring the old place back to life.

"Oh no, this is perfect!" Ari exclaimed, her face once more animated, whatever passing doubts she'd had disappearing. "How soon can we do this? Can you help? A lot? I don't want it to be fancy, but I want everyone to have a lovely time and to feel welcome. I guess we'd better add the local cricket team to the invite list. That is if they still exist? And get someone to mow the lawn?"

Dickie grinned; this was exactly what she had hoped for when she heard there was a new heir. Someone that wanted to breathe life back into the place, resurrecting the cricket fields for a party was a great start. She loved being at Wiverton. She had worked here ever since she left school and for the past thirty years had been its housekeeper. She knew exactly what was required. There was an awful lot she wasn't sure about, the London guests for example. How well would the old families as she liked to think of them, and the estate workers and villagers mix? But if Lady Wiverton thought it would be fine then it was Dickie's job to ensure that it was exactly what she hoped for.

#

The party had been planned for the second May bank holiday giving as many people as possible the chance to attend. The invitations had gone out and pretty much everyone had accepted, Dickie had been right to think of it in terms of a small fete, as at least a hundred people were going to show up at one point or another. The party was due to begin at two to allow the London contingent time to travel. Mama Vy was concerned about the food and had offered to cater, Dickie was concerned but Ari said the more the merrier and now Mr Kumar also wanted to cook. In the end, Ari told Dickie to hire some catering tents and they would provide the food and talent. She had had a long row on the phone with Mama Vy about accepting money for the food and she only relented when Ari told her how many bedrooms her new house had. At that point, Vy said she would be prepared to go halves. Ari decided that she would talk to Mama Vy's daughters. She had gone to school with them and knew that they would be less proud. Especially when they saw the size of her house. She didn't doubt she was going to receive a lot of good-natured ribbing when everyone turned up.

17

Finally, the day arrived, it was one of those perfect May days. The sun was warm, and the hedgerows were lush with growth. Hawthorn hedges were full of white blossoms, the cow parsley was waving in the warm breeze and everywhere was a sea of green and white. The late spring sun was waking up this season's butterflies and the bees were already busy harvesting all the new nectar. Best of all there was no rain forecast.

Ari's sisters had arrived the night before and were in high spirits. Listening to the laughter filling the rooms and corridors, Ari realised just how much she had missed this. The London contingent arrived around ten, in three minibuses. They piled out of the vans, in front of the house. Lots of the older generation were in their finest threads for a celebration, silks and waxed cottons, wrapped headscarves and brightly jewelled colours. Ari and her sisters' generation were in a range of outfits blending western and home, and their children all wore the customary uniform of jeans and hoodies, regardless of gender. Within seconds the sound levels went through the roof as everyone greeted each other with shouts of wonder at the size of Wiverton Manor and how good everyone looked. It had only been a few months but there was so much to catch up on. Ari selected two of the teenagers and told them they were in charge of the little ones. Having done a grand tour of the house, everyone then headed down to the pavilion and helped with the setting up and getting the pots and pans on.

Dickie had deliberately left things to be set up at the last minute. She thought if everyone was mucking in to help lend a hand, then they would all knit together that much quicker.

By two o'clock the party was in full swing and Ari was delighted to discover that she didn't have any nerves because the party had been slowly building around her for hours. It had sort of snuck up on her as she had been meeting new people in dribs and drabs. She was also thrilled to see how well her old and new lives were blending.

The little ones had grown into a tribe of superheroes, princesses, and every sort of fancy dress in between, several mothers were now keeping an eye on them and laughing together. Ari grinned when she realised that by the end of the day her old neighbours were going to know her new neighbours better than she did. The music played via the tannoy was an eclectic mix of old and new, and some of the teenagers had taken control and plugged their playlists in and were taking requests.

201

Ari turned towards the direction of the car park where a loud shout from the children went up. One of the fathers had also arrived in fancy dress. In a cape and a mask, he was pretending to be terrorising them as they ran around him shouting and poking him. He would spin around and lunge out but kept missing them, to their intense amusement.

Noticing that the Flint-Hyssops had also arrived she went over to greet them and said hello to the friends that they had brought along. Mary had promised that she would bring a few people that she thought Ari would like to meet and she was thrilled to discover that this rather nice couple were publishers and had two small children of their own.

Fabulous thought Ari, she could pick their brains about school in a bit. "You must bring them over to play with the boys. How old are they?"

Caroline smiled, "Six and four. They are here but they've already escaped to go and attack Seb." With that, she groaned as they all looked over to the lawn where the Monster was now on the floor and the children had turned into Lord of the Flies. They would jump on the father, children hanging off his limbs until he pretended to be overcome by them, falling to the ground. With a roar he would rise again, shaking them off and then they would bundle him down to the ground once more. Shouts and laughter drifted across the field.

Ari looked across the field in shock, was that Sebastian Flint-Hyssop rolling around in the grass with a tribe of children on top of him?

"Oh dear. I am sorry, Ariana. Sebastian does like to set things off. I think sometimes he prefers their company to ours!" Mary turned to Caroline's husband. "Andrew, be a dear, would you? Go and rescue your friend so that he can come and greet his host properly."

Turning to the others she excused herself and left with Andrew to go and rescue Seb. "I'm mortified, I'm so sorry. I'll have a word with my boys, I'm sure they started it."

Andrew laughed. "Not a bit of it. I know who started it. Sebastian one hundred per cent. He's godfather to both of ours and he spends most of the time playing with them when he comes to ours. If he comes over for supper they won't go to bed until he's read them both a story."

Ari was surprised, "Really? He strikes me as a bit formal and intense."

"Seb? Well, he does have a bit on his plate right now." That said, he bellowed out to the pack of children then greeted some of the mothers who had spent most of the display laughing, before introducing himself to the new faces.

Within seconds, the children began peeling off Seb, aware that this game was coming to an end. Ari looked down on him laughing, he'd looked so happy lying on his back with the children crawling and jumping on him as he roared and tickled them. Her face shone with astonishment and awe, that a man in his position could be so careless about his dignity and so relaxed in his own skin.

Seb realised that he had an audience and looked up at Ari, and as their eyes connected his face lit up with an enormous smile. It was silly, he had no idea why he was so happy but looking at Ari made him want to laugh as though he had just won the lottery. As they grinned at each other, the guests looked on with raised eyebrows and knowing nods of the head.

The moment was broken as Wills came yodelling in with a body slam for Seb. Unprepared, he oofed in a most uncivilised manner. Ari grabbed the twins and told them that food was ready then leant forward to offer Seb her hand. The minute his fingers wrapped around hers, Ari was overwhelmed by a sense of deep happiness. Her hand, in his, felt so perfect, his cool skin and solid grasp made her pause, she didn't want to pull him up, she wanted him to pull her down and with that realisation, her face blushed in embarrassment. She tugged at her hand to try and pull away. Seb didn't let go but did help lever himself up off the ground, holding her hand the whole time.

"Um, my hand, can I have it back? Please?"

Seb looked down in surprise, he hadn't realised he was still holding her hand. He had been thinking back a few seconds, when all he had wanted to do was pull her down beside him, and roll in the grass with her, like some overheated teenager.

"My apologies. It just felt right." And with that, he winked at her, released her hand and walked off towards the pavilion, leaving Ari staring after him like a fool. The boys tagged along beside him and he gave them his cloak and mask to play with.

As she walked back towards the pavilion, Nicoletta sidled up alongside her.

"Hello." Nick grinned at her, reminding Ari of the Cheshire Cat.

"Go away."

"Yeah, right. Ari and Sebster sitting in the tree..."

"Oh my God, stop it before he hears you," said Ari, her face going bright red and then she decided that surrender was the best strategy where her sisters and her love life were concerned. The two sisters walked arm in arm across the field, smiling and chatting to various groups as they wandered towards the pig roast. It looked popular and there was a bit of a queue forming. Ari and Nick greeted the various groups as they passed, both girls trying to guess which set of people the gathered strangers belonged to. They were getting pretty adept at spotting the three main types and figuring out what the tone of conversation would be. There was the county set or the "*Do you knows*" as Nick had dubbed them. They were keen to embrace Ari whilst being staggeringly curious about her. Some were, Ari felt, patronising, others were sympathetic; all tried to establish connections between her and themselves. She couldn't help feeling that if she didn't have a title or vast estates then they wouldn't be terribly interested in her at all. The second group belonged to local societies and the like, that had once used the hall and its grounds for various functions, and they were all equally unsubtle in lobbying her to reinstate their access. The final group were ex-employees that seemed to be holding their anger and resentment in check whilst seeing if they could get their old jobs back. The whole process was exhausting. Ari understood all their motivations but hardly anyone wanted to talk to her because of who she was.

"Do you know, I used to resent being the twins' mother, or Greg's wife, now I seem to have developed a new persona, Lady Wiverton. No one wants to know me. It's like I don't exist."

Nick squeezed her elbow. "We know you. We love you, and Mama Vy, who has cooked enough nyama choma for everyone here, she loves you too. You will never be so lah-di-dah that she won't call you out, down the high street, for wearing your skirt too short!"

"Oh my God, do you remember?"

Nick, in a savage mimicry, called out, "*Ariana Byrne! You go straight back in yo house and yo put some clothes on. Yo poor mother would be spinning in her grave God rest her soul if she saw what you looked like. Go on, git!!*"

As the girls approached the cooking area, they saw they weren't the only ones tempted by the smells. Lots of the *Do You Knows* were happily piling up their bowls, exclaiming how delicious it was, easily the tastiest food they had eaten since their service abroad or their foreign travels.

Mama Vy came out from behind the table and gave Ari a huge hug that completely engulfed her. "Child..." she didn't get much further before tears overwhelmed her and she hugged Ari again. Pushing

207

her away from her she looked Ari up and down once more, tutted over her skinny frame and called for a bowl of stew.

"Where are the children?" asked Ari, amused by the older woman's displeasure at her traitorous brood. She tutted and pointed towards the pig roast where a bunch of kids were hanging around for bits of crackle and apple sauce. Nick smiled, happy to see everyone mixing. There was food today from Africa, India, the Caribbean and Britain, and everyone was enjoying the variety.

Bhupi Aunty was laughing next to Mama Vy agreeing that the little ones had no appreciation for their traditional foods, preferring western junk. Ari grinned, she knew of old that this tirade was going to run and run. Both ladies were dressed in full traditional clothes, they weren't the only ones in saris and kitenges and some of the headdresses were outstanding. Ari and her sisters recognised an evangelical zeal when she saw it. These ladies had travelled to the wilds of Norfolk ready to face whatever the natives may throw at them. What they'd encountered were huge queues all lining up to eat their food and swap stories.

Nibbling on Bhupi Aunty's gulab jamun, she was convinced Aunty had a secret ingredient she never shared. Ari could never get hers to taste this moreish. Which given all the calories in it, was probably just as well.

Looking around she wondered where Paddy was. Aster was pouring drinks, Clem was chatting to some of the aunties, but there was no sign of Paddy.

"Just listen out for male laughter," said Nick, and sure enough over by the slippery pole, Paddy was astride the pole batting her opponents off with a pillow.

"Is that the entire cricket club calling out encouragement? At least she's wearing trousers I suppose," said Ari, as her sister fell off into the straw to a huge roar from the man who'd finally dislodged her.

"Excuse me, Aunty, Mama, I'm just going to have a word."

"Some things never change," laughed Mama Vy and she continued to serve the rest of the line. At the back of the queue, she saw a tall good-looking man watch Ari walk away. Too pretty for his own good was her assessment of him. As he got to the front of the line, he eyed each pot in a suspicious manner. Here we go thought Mama Vy. *Is it spicy? Is that actual goat? Have you got a korma?*

"I don't suppose you've got any irio?"

Mama Vy tipped her head down and raised her eyebrows and looked at him afresh.

"What do you know about irio? That's baby food."

"That's not baby food, it's one of the finest comfort foods known to mankind. Why should it only be for children?" he asked in a pleading manner. Vy laughed, true enough, it was a tasty treat but liable to put twenty pounds on your hips if you even so much as sniffed at it.

"Well then, tell me, where have you had irio?"

And Seb proceeded to explain how as a child he had spent a few years living in Kenya, while his father set up some schools and libraries. During the war, Lord Hyssop's life had been saved by a young Kenyan soldier and he had always wanted to say thank you in a proper manner. His wife had also felt that it would be beneficial for the children to spend a few years gaining a wider perspective of the world that they lived in. Especially as theirs was such a privileged background.

"There was a woman who lived with us, my ayah, and when we weren't running her ragged with our high jinks, she fed us the most amazing food. Her name was Ajuma and when we came back to the UK, she asked to join us, and we were thrilled to say yes."

"Is she here? I should love to swap recipes?"

Seb explained that she had died five years earlier and the whole village had come out for her funeral as she had been so well loved. "It's probably why you are so popular today. Everyone misses her food. My father especially."

"The gentleman sitting over there by the fire pits?"

Seb looked over to where his mother and father were sitting with friends, chatting and laughing.

"He's been up for seconds, thirds and, if your mother hadn't objected, he'd have been up for fourths as well," she laughed.

"That sounds about right!"

Warming to him, Mama Vy said, "I see you looking at our Ariana girl just then?"

Seb was a bit embarrassed to have been observed but decided to come clean. She had arrived out of the blue and no one had heard a thing about her or her mother in the past thirty years. People were bound to be curious.

"And that's all you're interested in, is it? Family history?"

Seb blushed a little harder and she laughed.

"I've known those girls all their lives When Lily and Michael first moved in, we didn't think they would last. She was such a fish out of water. From time to time you'd see a look on her sweet face of total bewilderment, like she had no idea how she had got there. Michael fitted in straightaway, but Lily never did. Oh, don't get me wrong. She was a lovely friendly girl and she would always muck in and help out. When she saw some of the other women scrubbing their front doorsteps, she went straight back inside and came out with a bowl of water and a scrubbing brush. I think those were her very first blisters. Every now and then, during a carnival, or a football match in the street, or when the bailiffs came to evict the Robinsons, Lily's face would close down a bit and if Michael was nearby, he'd give her a quick hug. I tell you those two were so devoted to each other, but they didn't have a penny to their name, and each time they had a child it just got worse. I told her once, that there were ways to stop all that, but she just smiled and said that they were a gift from God and who was she to say no? I told her that it would help if God could also send her the gift of money to look after them, but she laughed and said that they managed just fine. She'd had money and this was better."

Seb spooned some of the stew into his mouth, Mama Vy was on a roll and he was in no mood to interrupt. Making appreciative sounds at the delicious flavours he gestured for her to go on. "But I bet you helped out...?"

"Young family like that with no other family to help them, of course, we stepped in. What sort of people would we be? Every Monday morning, I would bring over the leftovers that I had made from church the day before. Every time I would say to Lily that I was going to throw it out unless she could make use of it. And every Monday she would say yes, with some excuse as to how helpful that would be, just this one time. I know for a fact that Lily and Michael didn't tend to eat much on the weekends when all the girls were at home, and I reckon as soon as that front door closed, she would help herself to a bowl straightaway. I always made sure they had enough to last two days."

Seb was savouring the food and said he couldn't believe that she ever had any leftovers, let alone enough to feed a family of seven for two days.

"Well, of course, there wasn't," she exclaimed, "Aren't I the best cook in the whole parish of St Bart's? Even Winifred has to concede that my matoke knocks hers into next week. No child, I would cook a fresh batch for them every Sunday evening as soon as Bert had gone out to play dominoes. Not that he objected mind you. Oh no, Bert saw it as our Christian duty to help our neighbours in any way that we could."

Pausing, Mama helped Bhupi serve more people, stirring the pots and ladling out deep rich spoons of stews and curries.

"So when did Lily die? What happened to Michael? I know it's impolite to ask but I can hardly ask Ariana."

The two women looked at each other in sorrow. Bhupi gestured at Vy to carry on, she wasn't a great one for talking and she carried on serving the food, nodding her head or tutting as one of Vy's tales brought back memories.

"Oh my Lord, what a terrible day that was. There was such weeping. I will never know what the good Lord had in mind that day. I know they say he works in mysterious ways but to my eyes, that was just cruel, leaving those five girls to fend for themselves. Michael and Lily were walking home when a lorry lost control and drove up onto the pavement, killing them and one other outright, and injuring lots of others. It was on the news and reporters were trying to make a story about how the children had been orphaned and had no family to come and take them."

Seb was baffled. They did have family? Had Lord Wiverton's rage been so great that he wouldn't step forward?

"Michael was Irish and had spent most of his life in care homes and Lily had never spoken of her family. I asked Ari if she knew them, but apparently, they had written back to her requesting that she leave them alone! I ask you, what sort of monster leaves five children to the care of social services?"

Seb was appalled. He knew there had been bad blood in the family, but this was beyond the pale. "So, what happened to the children?"

"Well now, Ariana was eighteen, so she applied for legal custody of her sisters. It was quite a battle, but she had the support of all of us, and a caseworker that thought the girls would be better off together. Ari had been planning to go to university but she gave it up and started working to bring in money. Clementine failed her A-levels which wasn't a surprise given how tough the first two years were for the girls, so she went out and got a job as well. The twins did okay in their exams, but they also left school and went to work straight away, but young Aster proved to be as bright as Ari and she went on to take up the Cambridge dream that Ariana couldn't. And, of course, a few years back Ariana met and married Greg and they had those two little angels. Then he drowned one night in the canal on his way back from the pub. And then finally this!"

Vy waved her hands around the field. "And this, as they say, is a whole new chapter. God willing, a happier and easier one. Although how anyone who had all this, couldn't find some room for five grieving children is beyond me. I don't want to speak ill of the dead but her grandpappy must have been an extremely wicked man."

Seb looked over to Ari where she seemed to be talking to John Eyres on the cider stall. He wasn't sure but by the body language, it looked like he was building up a full head of steam about workers' rights and the evils of the upper classes. He couldn't disagree with the two women, what a terrible thing to do to flesh and blood. But it certainly gave a massive insight into this grieving widow that had spent her whole life fighting in poverty. He was oddly relieved to hear that Ariana's husband was dead. Did that make him a monster to wish such grief on her and her sons? And to have endured so many hardships in such a young life explained her reserve and her determination. Feeling ashamed of himself he thanked the women for the backstory. As he went to go and intercept Ari, Mama Vy had a final word.

"Just take care and don't mess her around. And remember, I'm only telling you this so you understand why sometimes, you might catch her mother's bewildered look on her face, as she looks around at this new life of hers."

18

Having had a quiet word with her sister, Ari wandered over to the cider stall as the queue had finally thinned out and she fancied seeing what all the fuss was about. There was a group of people standing around, one man was pontificating, but no one seemed to be serving. Ari turned to one of the women and asked if it was self-service or were they waiting for the stall holder? A man interrupted by pouring her a glass, declaring it the finest in the county and continued with his sermon.

"I'm telling you, this is all for show. She wants everyone back and we'll be so bloody grateful, tugging our forelocks, that we won't blink a bloody eye when she cuts our wages and ups our rents!"

"Problems?" murmured Ariana sympathetically.

"Problems alright. The new bloody Countess, swanning in here with her high and mighty ways, thinking she can fix all the trouble she's caused by throwing a stupid party."

"I thought it was a nice idea," said Ari.

"See, see you've already been sucked in but mark my words this is a ploy, I know her sort.

Complete waste of space, bleeding us dry whilst partying their lives away."

Oh, you've met her then? I beg your pardon."

"No. I never said that." The man looked at Ari suspiciously, "I suppose you're on her side then? You lot all stick together, same as her father before her."

Ari prickled, she shouldn't, and she knew this oaf wasn't referring to her father, but any perceived insult always brought out the worst in her. "Her father? I think the previous lord was her uncle?"

"Makes no difference, girl. These lot are all the same. You mark my words I know exactly what she's thinking."

"How impressive you are to claim to know the inside thoughts of anyone other than yourself!" Just as Ari was building up a full head of steam, she was cut off by a familiar voice as Wendy came over to join them. Prior to the party, Ari and Wendy had agreed to use her title at all times to help people learn who she was, without having to do constant formal introductions. Ari thought it seemed a bit pompous and silly, but Wendy had pointed out that there was never an occasion that the previous earl had ventured out without his full title firmly attached, so to speak. Plus, it would speed up the process, before Ari formally welcomed her guests. And most importantly thought Wendy, privately, it would help to continue to acclimatise Ari to her new way of life.

"Your Ladyship, the priest and vicar have just arrived together. I thought you would like to meet them."

"A double act! That sounds like fun." Smiling at the group suddenly made awkward, she apologised that she hadn't had a chance to introduce herself properly and have a chat. "By the way, who makes the cider? It's excellent."

"I do," snapped the man she had just been talking to, his stance tight, radiating anger and embarrassment in equal measure.

"Well, nice to see you're not a total waste of space either then." And Ari left the group to join Wendy and the local clergy. As she left, the voices around the cider table rose as the cider maker was mocked. She wasn't sure if that encounter had been a successful one or not but there was no point trying to suck up to people that were prepared to dismiss her before even meeting her. Crossing the field, Ari was struck by how people seemed to be having a good time, the kids had all teamed up and were mucking around with some bats and balls and soon the leather was flying. Some of the fathers had joined in and moved the action away from the other guests.

"Looks like your guests are showing the local boys a thing or two about cricket," said Wendy. "That'll smart. Jim's boy over there is considered a local rising star, but that pair seem to be toying with him."

Ari watched the Shanti brothers as they showed off but from the look of it, the tall blond boy was enjoying himself. He seemed to be throwing his arms up in mock horror and grinning widely, then leaning back into the ball as it was bowled to him at a vicious speed. He stepped into it and sent it soaring over towards the trees with a pack of the smaller children running off after it.

"He seems to have risen to the challenge!" laughed Ari. By now they had reached the two men of God who were also avidly watching the cricket.

"Those two lads are jolly good. Are they part of your crowd?"

Ari smiled; she liked the idea of having a 'crowd'. "Yep, but I can't take any credit for their genes. We have Pakistan and India's finest out there, and stepping up to bat now is Aleesha, West Indies' golden girl. I do hope the boys underestimate her, that's always fun and it makes her day."

Both the vicar and priest were male and in their middle years. The C of E priest seemed to have the benevolent warmth of trifle and custard. He was plump and jolly and seemed the absolute archetypal village vicar. She found herself looking at his ankles for the cycle clips.

"He doesn't ride a bike," drawled the priest, reading her mind, "he has a little Fiat 500 in which he visits his flock."

Ari grinned at the priest; she liked an observant eye. Unlike his colleague, he was dressed head to toe in black and was tall and skinny. His hair had been shaved at some point but was currently growing back in strange lumps. A cigarette trailed between two fingers, dropping ash on his rosary. "And do you visit your flock, Father?"

"If they're dying or something similar. Say a new delivery of Jameson's. Otherwise, no one needs a busy-body priest, least of all me."

Ari smiled inwardly at the friendly bantering between the two men of the cloth.

"Did I hear someone mention Jameson's?" Ari turned around to find Sebastian standing beside her. He still had bits of grass in his jumper and she felt an overwhelming need to remove the grass just so that she had an excuse to stand a little closer to him. Embarrassed by her thoughts she stepped away as if to make room for him in the group, but her eyes kept flicking to the little bits of grass.

"Hello, Sebastian. Have you been rolling around in the hay with the village maids?" asked Father Michael, his eyes twinkling as he lent forward to remove the strands from Seb's jumper. "You know they frown on that sort of thing these days."

"Hello, Father. I was ambushed by some scurvy knaves who mistook me for an ogre, but I was happily rescued by a fair maiden."

Ari blushed to her roots, tickled pink and mortified.

"I do like a twist on the traditional fairy tale," grinned Wendy, "but your princess left you looking like a tramp."

"Better than a frog I suppose."

"Oh, I don't know, you have the features..."

Everyone laughed and Ari guessed from their relaxed ribbing that Wendy and Sebastian had known each other for years. She stood listening to the banter but unable to join in.

"But on to more serious matters, Father Michael," said Sebastian, changing the topic. "Father has received a bottle of Islay as a thank you for some help he provided to an old friend. It's a sixty-three and he feels it needs to be drunk in the company of a higher power." Seb turned to the vicar, "Father John, you are also most welcome. There would be no finer way to break your vow of abstinence?"

"Satan get behind me! I'm quite happy with my Lapsang but please pass on my thanks to your father. Michael, I'm concerned that you haven't taught Master Seb better than to tease his elders."

"Ah, John, what can I say? The youth of today are beyond me. Even as a lad this one here was wild and ungovernable."

Seb exclaimed harshly that he was being unfairly victimised by the whole group. "Our beautiful host appears to be the only one with any kindness! She has no hard words for me." He smiled again at Ari and once more she felt an amazing sense of sheer happiness spilling out of her as she grinned back at him.

"That's only because I don't know you yet," she teased, and everyone laughed. The talk gradually moved on to the agricultural show taking place the following week.

Ari stood and listened; it was clearly a big deal. The closest large community gathering she could compare it to was the Brixton Festival, but she had a feeling that there was absolutely no similarity. She tried to keep her mind on the conversation, but it sounded like a foreign language and all she wanted to do was loop her arm through Seb's and lean against him. This was ridiculous but she was so aware of his presence. She loved the sound of his voice and as he was illustrating a point, she watched how expressively his arms moved, the blond hairs on the back of his tanned hands showing a life lived outdoors. It gave a different impression to the tired, angry businessman she had first met at The Bull. Then he had only looked at her in disgust, now he smiled and joked with her. This was no good, she didn't know how she felt, and she had no idea who the real Sebastian was. Sometimes she thought she viewed him as a friend, but she honestly couldn't imagine touching a friend's face the way she wanted to touch Seb's. Sometimes she thought he was a total snob and a lazy over-privileged rich boy, one that was only now flirting with her, because she was one of his sort of people. In fairness, she also wasn't drunkenly shouting in his face. Overwhelmed with confusion, Ari brought her attention back to the conversation and when she realised that they were still talking about yields and heifers and the main ring, she coughed and said she had better leave them to it and go and mingle.

Heading back to the pavilion she was aware that someone had caught up with her and in delight, she saw it was Seb. Instantly she reigned back her grin but appeared to turn it into a scowl as he paused, uncertain, before speaking.

"Ariana, Ari, I wonder, if you haven't been to a county show before, would you like to come with me? I can show you and the boys around? It's quite a large site and it would be a shame to miss anything. And I can answer any questions you have. Of course, you don't have to, I just thought it would be neighbourly to offer." Seb seemed to garble his words in an effort to get them out. Ari was surprised, if she didn't know better, she'd assume he was nervous. She didn't want to sound too enthusiastic but equally, she couldn't think of anything she'd rather do. Ari couldn't think of a reasonable excuse to say no and was surprised by how pleased Seb seemed when she said yes. As they walked off towards the pavilion together, the sounds of the party continued on into the early evening. The fireworks exploded in the night sky drawing an end to a wonderful day.

ELIZABETH HURLEY

19

The next few days settled into a pattern as Ari got to grips with running the estate. The party had been excellent in terms of her getting to meet people and she was being regularly approached now to re-instate various activities that had been allowed to slide. All requests and suggestions were being added to the considerations list and she had assembled a core team to discuss each appeal. Daily she would meet with Wendy, who was now acting as something of a personal assistant, Dickie, the housekeeper, and Mr Billinge, her re-instated Estate Manager. Whilst Ari had the final say on all decisions, she was grateful for their insights. She had decided that in the first year she would simply observe how the estate worked, or didn't, and any changes or new directions she would implement after that time. The others had left, and she was sitting at her desk in the study trying to understand the importance of arable yield and wondering if it was too soon to admit defeat and go and play with the boys before lunch. They should have come back in from their explorations with Wendy and she could examine all their treasures. As she leaned back from the paperwork there was a knock on the door and Dickie entered.

"Ma'am. You have visitors, a Mr and Mrs Paxton. I've put them in the blue room." Her face was clearly disapproving of the guests, but Ari didn't have time for that. What the hell were her in-laws doing here? And then she groaned. Of course, the party! Clearly, the jungle drums had beaten far and wide. She doubted anyone had been malicious or gossipy, someone says something to someone, and then they happen to mention it to so and so, and suddenly it's up and running and screeching to a halt at the porcelain bulldogs at the front of her in-law's house. She had sincerely hoped that when they had collected Greg's belongings that would be the last time she ever saw them. Remembering their harsh words, Ari straightened herself up and looked at Dickie.

"Which is the blue room?"

"Don't worry, ma'am. I'll announce you," and she headed off to the front of the house. In a second, Ari realised she was heading towards the uncomfortable and imposing sitting room. The views outside weren't impressive but the walls were lined with paintings and antiques. It was a room to remind visitors to the estate of its wealth. It was not welcoming. Ari grinned, they clearly hadn't impressed Dickie, who last week had been on her hands and knees playing Hunt the Ant, with some of the children from her old estate. Dickie didn't care a jot about money or background, she went straight to a person's character and these two were lacking. With a start, she realised that it was also the first time that she had called Ari 'Ma'am'. Ari didn't care for that much but realised that it was a sort of armour and Dickie was making sure that Ari was properly dressed. As they got to the door, she told Ari that she had set a bell by her chair and that she should ring if Ari needed anything, and with that, she opened the door and announced her.

"The Countess Wiverton."

Ari smiled inwardly and thanking her she asked for a pot of tea to be brought and then faced Nigel and Annette. As she entered the room, Nigel was examining the bottom of a vase, Annette peering at the signature on one of the larger portraits. Both now stared at her warily and sat on the slightly lower sofa opposite the armchair where she took a seat. The bell was by her side on a small table and between them sat an ottoman table with a few piles of magazines and books; no doubt in which the estate featured. Ari was silent as the couple gabbled on about how they were sorry to have missed the party, but no one had sent them an invitation.

"You've got to keep on top of your staff," boomed Nigel, full of false cheer, "tell them who's boss right from the start. You know me, I've been in management long enough to know how to lead a team. You've got to keep them on their toes. Threaten redundancies and you'll soon see an improvement in their work ethic! It's a big job for a young girl, but I'm here now and I'll show you how it's done. Best to keep stuff like this in the family, eh? That way you know who you can trust."

Ari's stunned silence was less to do with thinking what to say but simply in having to listen to this tripe spewing from Nigel's mouth. Where did he get off suggesting that he have anything to do with her life? Annette took the silence as a good sign because as ever, she was completely incapable of reading a face, and ploughed on.

"And I'll be here to look after little Toby and Liam. They need their nanny around at a time like this. Family need to stick together, love. But don't worry, we're here now."

Again, Ari was spared from replying as Wendy came in with a tea tray, poured a cup for everyone and then quietly left again. A perfect example of the perfect servant from the Edwardian era. Ari would have laughed if she wasn't currently so angry. She took a sip of tea, noticing that it was the Lapsang. An acquired taste and probably not one that her guests would like. She wondered if that too had been

Dickie's idea. Clearing her throat, she addressed her visitors.

"You didn't receive an invitation because you weren't invited. My sons' names are Leo and William, not Toby and Liam but then, as you remember when we last met, you told me they weren't Greg's anyway, so I suppose you can't be expected to know their names. So, why are you here?" She looked at them enquiringly while she sipped her tea and leant back in her chair.

Annette paused and looked at Ariana, feeling a huge hatred for the girl sitting smugly in her chair sipping at her revolting tea, like she was better than them.

"Why you little—"

"Come on, Ari," Nigel interrupted his wife, sensing she was about to explode and spoil all their plans. "It was poor Greg's funeral. We were all upset, and people say things they don't mean in the heat of the moment. Of course, little Leo and William are Greg's, and our beloved grandchildren. Kiddies need their family at a difficult time like this."

"And what time is this?" asked Ariana coolly.

"Grieving for their daddy of course," replied Nigel.

"Their 'daddy' has been dead for four months. We haven't seen or heard from you once. I sent you our forwarding address. Did it make it past the bin? My number is still the same, but I haven't noticed any calls from you. During this 'difficult time', you and the rest of your family have been invisible. Your sons have not been in touch with their nephews, no doubt because they also thought I was some, what did you say, Annette? 'Some cheap slapper that tricked Greg into supporting her after someone else knocked her up.' Those were the words you used weren't they, Annette?" Before she could jump in, Ari continued, "And as for missing their father, yes the boys have been upset in an abstract sort of way but then they barely saw him. As you recall he moved out twice and whenever his affairs failed, he returned, all piss and vinegar, blaming me for his cheating. And then, when I'd insisted that he came to see his sons, I was to blame for the affair ending! When he was home, he would come back from work and go straight out again and on the weekends, he'd be out playing football, watching TV, or explaining himself to the local police. He did nothing with his children except to shout at them when they made too much noise or mess. So, do they miss him? No, not so that you'd notice."

Any attempt at civility was now long gone as far as Ari was concerned. In fact, until she had spoken those words, she didn't realise quite how much she had been holding them in; releasing them felt powerful.

"Well," Nigel cleared his throat, "the fact of the matter is that they are our flesh and blood. And we have a duty and a right to see them. In law. We may have made mistakes in the past, but you can't deny us now."

Not now that I've got all this money thought Ari. She'd be blowed if these venal pieces of carrion were going to feature another second in her life. Let alone in that of her children's. She looked at Annette, who could barely keep the hatred off her face. Ari looked at her bright red lipstick on the rim of the cup, remembering the time when Annette had advised Ari to make herself look more presentable. This was shortly after the first time Greg had moved out. The boys were nine months old and Ariana was exhausted; frankly, she didn't know how she would have managed without Aster to help her. Aster may have not been a doting maternal aunt being just fourteen, but she loved her sister and regularly looked after the children so that Ari could get out of the house for a quick half hour. She drew the line at nappies though, so any fresh air Ari had got was quickly expelled as she walked back into the house. It wasn't just the nappies, she was convinced that everything smelt funny, housework had gone out the window, mealtimes were strange haphazard affairs. When Greg had walked out, Annette had visited and visibly recoiled at the state of the house, blaming Ari for her poor hygiene driving Greg out of his own home. Ari had wanted to point out that he had actually moved into her home but was too exhausted to start a fight. In fact, Ari was so tired and dejected that when Annette suggested she start wearing make-up, Ari asked her for advice. God knows the woman wore enough. Maybe they could go to town together and she could show her what to do? At that moment she felt that she had hit rock bottom, turning to her mother-in-law for help and support. But of course, rock bottom can always sink, the rock can turn to stinking slimy mud and Annette had looked at her with incredulity. She'd rejected Ari's suggestion, saying she barely wanted to spend these few moments here with her, let alone go into town and pretend to play mother and daughter. If her own mother hadn't been able to show Ari how to look after herself and keep a man, then it certainly wasn't her job. As she left, she'd reminded Ari that she had told her to get an abortion when they first mct and that she had made her bed and now had to lie in it. Annette then left the house without even asking after the babies or looking in on them as they slept on the sofa, in the front room.

Annette spoke, snapping Ari back to the present. "Nigel's right. We've spoken to a lawyer and when you inherited you were married to Greg which means that he gained the title, not you. And when he died it passed to his eldest son. Not you. None of this is yours. And we are their grandparents." With a triumphant smirk, she challenged Ari to contradict her.

Oh wow, thought Ari, they weren't after some money, they were after all of it. The gloves were off but that was okay, she knew she had the knockout punch.

"Did you tell your lawyer which title it was?" She looked at them with a sharp smile, "I mean you do know this is a female peerage, don't you? You do understand what that means don't you?" She silently examined their blank expressions enjoying their confusion. "The title of Wiverton was created for a woman and as such avoids male primogeniture, it can move through the female line. Which means that if she marries, her titles remain hers and do not pass to her husband. So yes, all of this, is still mine. But I'll tell you what, if you can tell me the date that the boys were born on, I'll give it all to you now, as the doting grandparents you so clearly are."

Nigel looked at Annette, but Annette simply continued to glare silently at Ari.

"No? Okay then. How about this? How much money do you want to walk out the door and never

ever return or contact the boys in any way, shape or form?" Endgame thought Ari, she had had enough of them sitting in her home spreading their poison through her life.

There was barely a pause and then like glass shattering, both voices jumped in, Nigel said, "Half a million" and Annette said, "Twenty thousand!"

"Which is it?"

"Twenty thousand," said Nigel realising that he might have a greater chance if Ari thought he was being reasonable.

"And if I refuse?"

"Then we will make your life hell. We will take you to court and insist on visiting rights to the boys and every time we see them, we will tell them what their mother really is and how she broke their poor beloved father's heart and every time we see them, they will begin to hate and resent you just a little bit more. And there won't be a thing you can do to stop it happening. Or, you can pay us now and never hear from us again." It was Nigel's turn to lean back with a smug look, his trump card had been played and he knew he was going to win.

Ari looked at them and then put her teacup down; now came the real gamble. "I also have a lawyer, in fact, I have lots, and they warned me about scenarios like this and they advised me to record all conversations. You know, just so that my back is covered and that I can't be blackmailed or threatened. So, of course, I am recording this conversation. And of course, I also have your written letter disavowing yourself of any biological links to my children. So here is my counteroffer. Leave this house now. Never again approach me or the children. Should there be any contact between you or any part of your family towards me or the boys I shall have my lawyers go straight to the police and have them issue a restraining order against you." With that Ariana stood up and rang the bell. The door opened instantly, and Dickie entered.

"Dickie, my guests are leaving. Please see them out. Right away."

"You fucking jumped up bitch!" shouted Annette lunging at Ari. Ari recoiled, stumbling over the side table. Falling saved her from Annette's fist. Nigel having some semblance of common sense grabbed at his wife, realising that he had just lost any and all hope of getting his hands on the money. Pulling his snarling wife by the arm, he followed Dickie out of the house. As he turned to speak to Dickie, he was greeted by the door slamming firmly in his face.

20

Shaking, Ari picked herself up and righted the little side table. Her tea had spilt across the rug and was going to need cleaning up. She headed to the kitchen for a cloth and met Dickie who had run back from the main door having first locked it.

"Ariana! Are you okay?" Her genuine concern for Ari was so touching and it was all she could do to stop the tears welling up.

"Yes. Absolutely fine. Well, that was all a bit unpleasant and I've spilt the tea, so I was just going to get a cloth. Oh, and throw the tea set away," she said, looking at the bright red smear of lipstick, "I don't want that in the house anymore."

"The Sevres tea set?" Dickie looked dismayed.

"Yes. Is it expensive? Stupid question. Fine, send it to auction, let me know how much it makes and we'll work out what charity to send it to."

"But it's been in the family for centuries," pleaded Dickie.

"Well, now it's not," snapped Ari. And if she could burn down the entire blue room as well, she would.

Loud voices from the corridor told Ari that the boys were back and would be ready for lunch. Realising she had lost her temper with the wrong person she took a deep breath. "Sorry, Dickie. When I'm calmer, explain the significance of the tea set. In the meantime, I'm going to have lunch with the boys."

Heading through to the kitchen she found one end of the table covered with bits of twigs, stones and a few feathers. Ever since they had made their art entry for the County Fair, they had been fascinated with going out and exploring. Whilst the twins proudly displayed all their exciting finds to their mother, Wendy rustled up some stew that had been merrily simmering in the Aga, awaiting the explorers' return.

"Shall we put them in the display cabinet after lunch?" asked Ari.

Ari had cleared out one of the curio cabinets, from the library's side room. Moving fascinating headdresses, stone figurines and other, no doubt, priceless objects into other cabinets. Now the boys would come in and fill up their case with wonders. With the afternoon activity sorted, they tucked into lunch dipping their bread into the juices and happily dripping it everywhere. Ari couldn't imagine ever being so grand or so grown up that this wouldn't feature in her top ten of favourite meals.

As she was finishing, Dickie came in with a smile on her face. A delivery had arrived for the three of them. Intrigued, Ari and the boys went out to the front drive and waiting for them on the driveway were three brand new bikes.

"They've arrived!" exclaimed Ari. "Look boys, I figured we all should learn to ride a bike now that we have all this space."

When Ari had ordered them, she had asked if the local company could deliver them fully built, including stabilisers for the boys. She had been too embarrassed to ask if adult bikes could be fitted with them and now she looked at her bike a little daunted. Leaving the staff to carry on, Ari and the children went out on to the front lawn and tried out their bikes. The boys mastered them straightaway. It took Ari a bit longer as she tried to work out how to make it move forward whilst not falling over. In the beginning, she could only manage one rotation of the wheels before she keeled over, left or right. She became good at putting her foot down to stop the fall but slowly, as the boys trundled up and down, she realised that if she kept pedalling it was easier; if she went too slowly, she was liable to fall over. Gradually she got it and was laughing and wobbling with the boys when they heard a car coming down the drive. Looking up, Ari recognised Seb's Range Rover and in her excitement, she tried to wave at him. As she took her hand off the handlebar, she wobbled wildly. Grabbing both bars again she lurched in the opposite direction and before she knew it, the bike shot off the lawn and onto the gravel driveway. She was aware of a screech of tyres at about the same time that she completely lost control of the bike, and then she and the bike were skidding along the gravel.

For a second, she thought she was going to be sick and then she became aware of a lot of people rushing towards her. Seb was kneeling by her side and had his arms around her, reassuring the two little boys that Mummy was fine. Feeling bruised and foolish, Ari agreed and looked about her. Her bike seemed undamaged and she appeared to have nothing more than a sore shoulder and a grazed leg, which was beginning to bleed nicely through the gravel dust.

"Does it hurt, Mummy?" asked Leo, full of concern.

"Well, just a little, I think I should master going forwards next time, before tackling tricky manoeuvres like waving." She grinned weakly at the boys, reassuring them that she was okay. In reality, it bloody stung and she wanted to cry.

"Come on," said Seb, "let's get this sorted, "Boys, you and I will take the bikes back to their shed and we'll join Mummy in the kitchen where she can get a plaster on those cuts."

Ari made to stand up but wobbled on her feet.

"Change of plan," said Seb and the next thing she knew, Seb had scooped her up and was walking towards the front of the house with her in his arms. As much as Ari protested, he refused to put her down.

"Make way for the wounded soldier," he called, and the boys took up his herald, shouting that a wounded soldier was coming through. By the time they made it to the kitchen Ari's mortification was complete as Dickie, Wendy, and Tom Billinge had all rushed in alarm to see what had happened. Only when Seb had told Dickie that Ari had nearly fainted and needed a strong tea to go with the plasters, would he leave her side. Wendy got the TCP out and the boys looked on in concern, they knew just how much this was going to sting—no matter how much people told them it wouldn't hurt a bit!

"Right, boys, let's go and sort out the bikes and when we get back Mummy will be right as rain. Tom, can you show me where the boys store their bikes?" As the four of them left, Ari could hear Seb and Mr B explaining about the proper care of bikes. In turn, the boys were explaining that they had never had bikes before and that they could already ride and that they

hadn't even fallen off once. William pointed out that
Mummy didn't have stabilisers. As they moved out of
earshot, Ari finally moaned, swearing a bit and
shedding a few tears, as she tried to help Wendy
remove bits of gravel from the cuts. Half an hour later
she was curled up on the sofa with the boys watching
Harry Potter, drinking hot chocolate, and sporting
some nifty Thomas the Tank Engine plasters. Seb sat
in an armchair watching the group and sipping on a
glass of water. They made a lovely sight and he
enjoyed just being in their presence. For a family of
strangers he already felt remarkably protective of
them. Maybe because they didn't seem to have anyone
else looking over them.

"Is your car alright? I forgot to ask." Ari had
been mortified to see it up on the lawn, as he had
skidded to miss her.

"It's survived worse." Seb grinned. "I just
popped over to sort out arrangements for tomorrow. If
you still feel up to it?"

As if a tumble off her bike was going to stop
her. She had learnt over the past few weeks how
important the show was. Lots of her tenant farmers
would be present and it was a great time for
neighbours and friends to catch up, apparently. And
the children had entered two competitions, the
flavoured fudge, and the wild art and they were keen

245

to see how they had done. This was her home and her life now; Greg and his family were behind her and she had to learn how to be a country girl and leave the poor city girl behind her. The boys would grow up with this as normal and she needed to make sure she understood everything and ran it properly for them.

Having arranged an early start, Seb left the family on the sofa, insisting that Ari stay put. He could see that the boys were already falling asleep and that Ari wouldn't be far behind them. Smiling he popped into the kitchen and told Wendy that they were all asleep in the front room and that he would be back again for an early start. As he walked out of the house, Wendy smiled to herself, she liked how things seemed to be shaping up.

21

"Blimey, it's massive! Children, do not let go of my hands. At all. Seb, you never said it was going to be so busy!"

Ari looked around the car park, there were cars in every field she could see. The Royal Norfolk Show itself must be enormous.

"Come on, boys, let's go get a programme and decide what to look at first."

Seb had parked in the exhibitors' car park so they were quickly onto the site and Ari finally got her first sense of an agricultural fair, and her first sense was one of noise, bodies, and lots of various smells all at once. Looking at the guide she saw there was a big ring where various displays would take place and marquees featuring floral and vegetable displays. There were steam engines powering funfair rides, livestock sheds, and the list went on. For the first time since she had moved to Norfolk, she felt at home. Whilst it was clearly nothing like the city, it also was in so many ways. For months she had lived in a huge home, often not seeing or hearing anyone for hours. When she went out for a walk, there was no one there either, fields and forest all utterly devoid of humans. Some days she wondered if there had been a plague and everyone had died. How would she know? The landscape was so vast and so empty. Now it was full. Everywhere she looked she could see people. In some directions, all she could see were people, large groups flocking around particular pens or exhibits. Everywhere there was noise, certainly not the noise of shops and traffic, underground announcements, street preachers warning of the end of the world, buskers, and market traders exhorting you to buy the very thing that they happened to have for sale. The sounds may not be the same but the volume was; there was a group performing a dance routine which appeared to involve wheelbarrows, in the distance the music from the carnival floated across the fields, the overhead tannoy was announcing something about to start in the main ring and everywhere there was the hubbub of people chatting and laughing.

"Overwhelming isn't it?"

"It's fabulous," exclaimed Ari, and indeed it was. To a girl who had spent months trailing around a silent house looking for echoes of her mother and trying to work out how to fit into her new life, this was wondrous.

"How are we going to do all this in a day?"

"Perfect planning. Shall we start in the animal pens so the boys get to see the nitty-gritty of what it's all about?"

It sounded like a good plan, but Sebastian soon discovered that everything would take second place to seeing how the boys did in their entries. Even if that meant dashing from marquee to marquee in different areas of the showground. Seb had a quick look at the plan to see where all the competitions were being displayed. He explained to the boys that running from display to display would be inefficient. It would be better if they moved around the fair in a clockwise manner. He got halfway through his explanation before the boys tugged their mother towards the Women's Institute tent.

By the time they got to lunch, they were all shattered. Seb had grabbed a table in the National Farmers Union food hall. The boys started tucking into crisps and a bowl of stew. After lunch, they headed out again. This time they headed towards the farm animals in the massive livestock sheds.

Walking into the vast buildings, Ari was a bit overwhelmed by the noise and smell. The giant barns were permanent structures and the air was oppressive, the heat had built up and there was no breeze at all. Walking down the aisles between the livestock pens, people had to squeeze past each other, rather than stepping into the open animal pens. There were rows of goats and sheep, another shed with a variety of rare breeds. Ari was amazed by the size of the pigs and given the amazement on the boys' faces, so were they. Finally, they made it to the cattle shed and Seb introduced her to a farmer that he knew was one of her tenants.

"Oh, a silver," said Ari, pointing to a rosette pinned to the side of the pen. "Congratulations!"

"That's my first silver in twelve years," glared the farmer. Ari wasn't sure about the hostile tone but plunged on regardless.

"But that's even better. You must be so happy?"

"The other eleven were gold."

"Ah, Ted. Well, oh dear, it does seem odd sympathising with someone for getting a silver." Ari felt a fool but was also aware that the farmer somehow seemed to be holding her accountable for the second place.

"Ever since Lord Wiverton told us to get the cattle out of the lower field, we have noticed a clear decline in their form!"

Oh, so it was her fault. Sort of. God, how long was this to go on for?

Spotting her distress, Seb scowled at the farmer and pointed out that it was hardly the Countess' fault. It was rare for Seb to pull the title card, but she had noticed at the fair he had been using her title a few times. As they left the shed, Ari asked him about it.

"This is your base. This is the centre of your new world; everything will network through here. You need to be known for what you are, then people can learn who you are later. Sometimes it's easier to lean on a title in the beginning. Think of it like when you hear nurse or officer. You instantly have an expectation of what they will do and how they will behave, and how you should respond."

"But I don't want anyone to think that I'm better than them!"

"That's not what I meant. I mean they hear the title and they remember your power and your influence. Some will remember you are their boss. Others will remember that you are their landlord. You don't want them to see a small nervous city girl. You need them to see the estate. You embody vast acreage, properties across the land, a huge portfolio, and a lineage that goes back many centuries. When you talk, they need to see all of that."

251

Ari was quickly realising that not only was Seb right, he was also the wrong person to be with. Not that she wasn't loving his easy-going company and the fact that the boys had taken to him. But this wasn't the jolly she'd thought this was going to be. This was work.

She got on the phone to her estate manager and discovered that he too was at the show. She asked him if he could free tomorrow up and take the time to introduce her properly to all her tenants and to anyone that her estate had business arrangements with or potential opportunities. Nick kept saying that the estate needed to keep its eyes and ears open to new commercial avenues. She was regularly sending out texts to the sisters pointing out grants and subsidies that were available for various ventures. Clem had sent a rather snippy reply saying that she was fresh out of Fishing Quotas and maybe Nick could stop wasting her time. A few more messages went back and forth, and Nick calmed down on the daily 'pep talks'. However, she wasn't wrong, and all the sisters were trying to think of things to do to improve their fortunes.

The rest of the day proceeded with the boys pulling them in every direction. Seb also introduced her to so many people that she wondered if it would be out of order to take photos of everyone and add their names to them, but sighed, smiled and moved on to the next stand. She knew she was going to have to come back again the following day.

#

The farmer smiled and nodded at what Mr Billinge was saying and then turned to Ari, "There you go, ma'am, just you do as he suggests, and you won't go far wrong."

Ari bristled at the patronising tone. Day two at the fair was proving to be much harder than day one. Back in London no one would have spoken to her like an idiot or suggested she couldn't do something based on her gender. Maybe the country was just behind the city in this, as in so many other things. Or maybe, reasoned another calmer voice, they just didn't know her? In London, she had had to prove herself time and time again. Then, it was her youth fighting against her, certainly not her gender, as she fought the custody case to look after her sisters. Even so, she had to remember who she was, and as Seb had made clear the day before, she wasn't just Ariana but also Countess Wiverton.

Summoning up a smile she replied, "I shall, of course, pay very close attention to Mr Billinge. The man's an absolute genius when it comes to estate management. And to yourself, of course, I doubt there is a soul alive that knows your herd better than you do." She paused scratching the ear of a particularly tousled cow and then returned her gaze to the farmer, "But ultimately I am responsible for the welfare and continuation of the entire Wiverton estates and we will do whatever it is that I decide."

Ari wished she could see Mr Billinge's face, standing beside her, but the farmer's was a picture. "Now, that said, I appreciate that you have suffered from recent estate decisions and I'd like to put that right. Could we arrange a time for me to come and visit and you could show me around your farm?"

It was clear that the farmer was wrong-footed but he wasn't sure how to respond. In the end, a date was fixed, and he decided he would talk to his wife about the countess before he made up his mind. She always had a better understanding of the mysterious ways of the female mind.

As they left the pen, Mr Billinge gave Ari a small nod. "Nicely done, ma'am. Now can I suggest we visit the Hayholt Farm next? I think you'll find them more enjoyable."

Ari walked away thrilled that she had managed to remember a group of cows was called a herd; she didn't think her authority would have been improved by calling them a flock. She still wasn't certain what a load of pigs was called and as for crops she couldn't tell them apart. The only one she had nailed so far was rapeseed and only when it was in bloom. Its vivid yellow flowers painted huge swathes across the countryside and whilst it felt weird to hear the boys shouting rape from the back of the car, there apparently wasn't any other name for it. The faster they all learnt to recognise the other crops, the better. As they approached the Hayholt stand, Ari saw two ridiculously glamorous girls rocking their tweed outfits, perfectly made-up with fabulous hairstyles. Even their wellies looked cool. Ari instantly felt self-conscious but also happy to see the effort that these two had gone to, to look so impressive. As Mr B introduced them, Ari enthusiastically burst out, "You two look terrific! I was beginning to think it was all mud and straw in the country!"

The two girls laughed and looking Ari up and down commented that she was also looking very retro dapper.

"Lolz, no, not retro, this is original, all I have is hand-me-downs at the moment. Mind you I don't think Coco Chanel ever had a county show in mind when she designed these trews and they were the only thing I could find to go with the wellies. I don't think my aunt or grandma did trousers!"

All three laughed and the taller of the two introduced herself as Heidi and the girl beside her as Honey.

"It's actually Heulwen, my folks are Welsh, but no one seems to know how to spell or pronounce Heulwen. It means 'sunshine', so I used to be nicknamed Sunny and then it became Honey, and Honey stuck. So to speak. Which is apt."

The girls went on to explain that as well as running a pig farm they had several apiaries and were building up that side of the business. At this point Mr B interrupted her.

"As promised, I would like to introduce you to the new owner of Wiverton."

The pair blinked and looked visibly startled and then started laughing at each other. "You're Countess Wiverton? We pictured someone shorter."

"And wider."

"And older."

"With a good set of facial hair."

Ari grinned, "You thought I was a bloke?"

"Oh no, we knew you were female, everyone's been talking about you. We just expected, well, something else." Honey grinned again. "Well it's a pleasure to meet you, even if I've lost my bet. I had you accompanied by aggressive Jack Russells. Heidi had the beard."

Ari stroked her face quickly and decided that Heidi had also lost her bet, so it was even-stevens.

Mr B interrupted the laughter and reminded the girls that they had a specific reason for the introduction. The girls looked embarrassed and glanced down muttering about it not being relevant now. Ari had wanted to help this friendly pair and was sorry that for whatever reason they had now changed their mind. What was it about her that had put them off? She didn't want to press the issue, but Mr Billinge was less reserved. He'd known Heidi and Honey for a few years now and was greatly impressed by their work ethic and entrepreneurial skills. Heidi had taken on an ailing pig farm from her parents and had proceeded to revolutionise it, bringing in rare breeds, higher welfare standards, open days, and some clever sidelines. A few years after taking over, Honey had arrived to help her cultivate an apple orchard and had stayed on, moving in with Heidi. Since then the partnership had begun to thrive. One of their schemes was 'clean' honey; they had begun setting up beehives miles from any nearby busy roads. They had been approaching large landowners for permission to site their hives on the land. Mr B wasn't sure if the scheme would work but if anyone could make a go of it, it would be these two. Which was why he was surprised that they had baulked now, there was nothing to lose by asking and privately he thought Ariana would jump at the opportunity.

"Well it doesn't matter now that you're definitely putting the road in. It will be too close to the hives, so it makes it a bit of a non-starter."

"We haven't made a decision on the road?" Ari looked confused. "Who told you it was going ahead?"

Heidi and Honey exchanged glances again. Had they misunderstood? But no, the chap from Shining Horizons had been quite emphatic, explained Heidi. In fact, it was all anyone had been talking about this morning as the news spread across the showground.

"The bloody bastards! Where are they? Mr B, we need to go and find them now and put a stop to this straight away." Turning to the girls, Ari apologised for her abrupt departure. "I haven't made my mind up about the road yet, please can you tell that to everyone you meet, and if I don't accept the road then please come and use my lands for your bees. It would give me great pleasure."

As they walked towards Shining Horizon's stand, Ari called up Peter Ghrab and expressed her displeasure in the strongest of terms. Stopping him halfway through his apologies she hung up and then turned to her estate manager.

"Right, I've torn a strip off him, would you mind having a word with whatever idiot salesman is putting out this nonsense."

Mr Billinge nodded solemnly and thought this was smart, she looked close to losing her temper and he wasn't sure if that was a wise move on her first outing to the County Show. As they approached a large sales tent with fancy banners flanking each side, a young man in patent brogues and a blue suit was just hanging up from a call and looking pale-faced. Mr B headed straight for him, whilst Ari stood back and watched as he loomed over him, standing closely so that no one else could hear what was being said. By the time he had finished, the chap, looking even paler, picked up his clipboard and shot out of the marquee into the crowds.

"Bloody hell! What did you say to him?"

Billinge pretended to act reserved but Ari could see that he had enjoyed himself as he recounted how he'd told the salesman that it might be appropriate, very appropriate, if he went to visit every stall and explain how he had made a mistake.

"That was all you said?"

Mr Billinge looked upwards and rocked on his feet. He confessed that he may have used other words and may have emphasised various words but other than that, yes, more or less. In fact, Mr Billinge had had a great time of it. He hated these jumped-up city boy estate agents. They came in, swanning around with lots of fresh money, acting like anyone who chose to live in the country was an idiot, and if they had actually been born there, then an inbred idiot. Plus he liked Heidi and Honey and wanted them to succeed. Finally, he was growing to like his new employer and was beginning to see a long future ahead for him. The last few years had been getting more and more precarious and the idea of leaving his job had filled him with despair. Focusing on future and happier thoughts, he suggested they stop for lunch and for the second day, Ari found herself tucking into a hearty meal in the NFU marquee.

For the rest of the day, Ari was introduced to tenants and a whole range of other people and organisations. Each time, she took notes, trying to keep everything clear in her mind. She knew that otherwise she would be overwhelmed by all the information. Finally, she also made appointments to visit people or arranged for them to call on her. And all day long she canvassed opinions on the road. Views were mixed, but the overwhelming tone was of disapproval, albeit politely put. Exhausted, the day came to an end, but Ari realised that she probably needed to come again tomorrow with just the boys so the three of them could just mooch about incognito.

22

Finally, the weekend arrived, and Ari would have given anything for a lie-in. She couldn't remember being more tired, it was a happy tired, but it didn't stop it from being tired, nonetheless. The third day at the show had been just herself and the boys. It had been wonderful, and she realised with a start that it had been quite a while since the three of them had done something together without anyone else. She'd also forgotten just how exhausting it could be trying to keep an eye on them both at the same time, especially with so many incredible diversions. They were still a little skittish of some of the larger animals up close, but they had fallen in love with the miniature Shetlands and the massive shire horses, that played together in the exhibition ring. They were also entranced by the quad bike jumping and suggested that they could do that next year. Ari was smiling sleepily at the memory, when the boys ran into her room, jumping on the bed and telling her that Seb was downstairs. That was enough to startle her awake and the boys were soon followed by an apologetic knock from Dickie. So much for a lie-in! Then she saw with horror that it was already ten o' clock, a perfectly reasonable time for someone to come calling. Damn them.

Grabbing her clothes, she came downstairs running her fingers through her hair in an attempt to tidy it; hopefully, it wouldn't look like she had been asleep just five minutes earlier. From the twitch in Sebastian's face, she wasn't fooling anyone, and her facade was further ruined by a massive yawn and the boys announcing that Mummy had only just got up! Admitting defeat, she smiled sheepishly at Seb and invited him to join her for a coffee. As she walked towards the kitchen, she suddenly felt wide awake and was grinning at what the day may bring. Both boys were jumping around everyone's feet so Seb bet them they couldn't find him ten different types of leaf from the garden and soon peace was restored.

"That was nicely done," said Ari.

"Funny isn't it, it just came back to me. I remember Mother constantly finding things like that for me and Geoffrey to do. I imagine we were just as loud and noisy. Although twins, talk about it all being doubled! Anyway, the reason I've come is I have a bit of a surprise treat for you and the boys today. I noticed they were a little shy around the animals at the show. Do you remember my friends that have just had a foal? I thought the boys would like to come and say hello?"

Ari was touched by his thoughtfulness; fancy noticing the children's reluctance to approach the animals. She fully understood it and in fact a healthy respect for these massive beasts seemed well placed, but this was their world now and big hairy creatures were an integral part of it. She was surprised that Seb had noticed as well though, and that he had thought of a nice solution.

"That sounds like a lovely plan. When are we expected? Do I have time to actually brush my hair?"

Seb laughed, "You can even have a shower."

Groaning, Ari scowled at him and then warned him that he was in charge of the children and not to allow them to fob him off with ten leaves from the same tree.

Half an hour later they were driving along, heading west to a large stables near Cambridge. The surrounding soft flat land was perfect for racehorses and the place they were heading to was well known for turning out champions. Ari was intrigued, she had never been to a professional equestrian centre before and when they arrived, she was surprised by the obvious security fences and state-of-the-art gates. Sensing her surprise, Seb commented that there was an awful lot of money in racehorses. He laughed that they had more money spent on them than he had. Ari smiled but inwardly winced, the easiness with which some people lived their lives constantly surprised her. She doubted that these racehorses had more money spent on them than Seb had, but she didn't doubt for one second that they were better cared for than many of the children that she had grown up with.

The car pulled up in front of a large modern house and it seemed that the house had been built at the same time as the stables. No doubt security cameras had announced their presence because as soon as the car pulled to a stop, the front door flew open and a small woman came running out and threw herself up into Seb's arms. Following behind her was a great big bear of a man who was pretending to do the same, Seb put the woman back on the ground and attempted to run away. Clearly, Seb was amongst friends and calling to Ari and the boys he introduced them to his old school friend Toggles and his wife, ex-jockey and now head trainer, Minty. As Ari shook hands with both she wondered if anyone was called John and Jane anymore.

"So, are you an Araminta as well?" asked Minty as they headed towards a nearby stable block. Well, that explains the Minty, thought Ari and declared herself an Ariana.

"Parents can be such rotters, can't they? Have you ever seen anyone less like an Araminta than me? There was I trying to convince everyone that I was going to be a great jockey. And there was Mummy shouting out to me *'Araminta, poppet, darling!'* God, it was excruciating. The stable boys took to calling me Minty and I was tickled pink. Out on the paddocks, the name stuck. Everyone assumed it was down to the polos I kept in my pockets for the horses."

Braying like one of her horses, she led the party towards the stables and explained to the boys how to approach the mare and her week-old foal.

They walked along a line of stables and several horses popped their heads over the half doors, curious that it might be feeding time. Minty introduced each in turn to the boys, telling them all about their form. Each horse had its own personality, which made some more trainable than others. One horse was a proper escape artist, and needed clips constantly on her stable door, whilst the gorgeous looking Black Bess, was prone to sulking for days on end. Finally, they came to a separate block.

"We've got the mare and foal in here; I give them a bit of peace and quiet from the other noisy lot. The foal needs a lot more sleep than the others."

The mare was clearly relaxed with Minty and gave a little whinny as she entered the stable. At that moment the foal stood up and sauntered over for a feed from mum. Ari and the boys were transfixed by the foal's awkwardness and vulnerability. He seemed to be all legs and hadn't yet worked out how to use them. Minty explained how important it was to handle foals from day one. It all added to their future development and trust with humans.

After much awe and gentle stroking, Toggles decided that it was time to give mother and foal a bit of space.

"Right now, boys, I think now is the time to go and meet the main attraction."

As they left the stables he turned to the boys with a big excited smile on his face.

"How do you feel about puppies?"

And with a big grin, he walked towards the house, the boys in tow, jumping up and down and asking a thousand questions.

"Puppies?" hissed Ariana to Seb. "What were you thinking? Hasn't it occurred to you that the boys might see one and want to take one home?"

Seb was taken back by her annoyance. To him, it had seemed like the obvious idea. The boys needed a pet, the house needed dogs, and Ari needed... Seb groaned, Ari needed another responsibility like a hole in the head. It had seemed like such a good idea at the time, all he had seen were the positives but he had blissfully ignored the fact that Ari had never had a dog, was recently widowed, had a huge estate to get to grips with, and two little boys that were clearly a complete handful. What on earth was she supposed to do with a demanding puppy?

As they walked into a large kitchen, Ari could see that a section had been penned off, and a run for mother and pups had been set up. Currently, the pups were out and bouncing about, both boys were sat cross-legged in the middle being very still, giggling nervously as the puppies ran over them and jumped and yipped excitedly. As she watched, one little puppy climbed into Leo's lap and promptly fell asleep. Leo and William gingerly stroked him following Toggles' instructions. The boys looked up at their mother with large beseeching eyes and then back carefully, to their tiny sleeping charge.

Debate at this point seemed futile and an hour later Ari found herself being driven home with a tiny bundle of fur sleeping on her lap, the only signs of life an occasional wag and a snuffle.

"So, tell me? Do all puppies have this built-in melt factor or is it just this breed?"

"It's a safe bet that any puppy is irresistible, but springer spaniels are particularly special. Once

you've got to grips with this little girl, you'll wonder
how you ever managed without her."

23

Daphne Albright was enjoying her morning stroll with her menagerie in tow. What dew there was had now dried off the short grass and Joy padded alongside Daphne, her old legs making her a welcome companion. The other dogs were darting back and forth across the path, rummaging in the hedgerow, and bothering the rabbits in the field. Normally Daphne had this walk to herself but today she noticed that she wasn't alone. Heading towards her she spotted a young mother with two small boys and a puppy; all three seemed to be equally excited, bouncing, jumping and leaping at butterflies; it was a merry scene if unexpected. As she approached, she noticed with approval that the mother called all her charges to attention with a call of 'heel' and 'single file'. She was only moderately successful but at least the intention was there.

"Morning! You've got your hands full!" said Daphne.

Ari laughed, "Somewhat. I found myself calling the boys to heel the other day. I swear someone is going to hear me soon and report me to social services."

"Nonsense, children are like puppies they need to know what the rules are and who's boss."

Ari eyed Daphne's pack of dogs that had now gathered around her feet, there were two Labs, the yellow one slow and lumbering in contrast to a sleek younger black Lab, a cocker sniffed the ground around him, and a Jack Russell sat looking glad of the rest.

"So, who's in charge of this bunch?" asked Ari, expecting the lady to introduce herself.

"Shere Khan"

"Sorry?"

"Shere Khan, he'll turn up in a minute when he notices that we have fallen behind." And on cue, an enormous spotted cat walked along the path towards them. Ignoring the boys' outstretched palms, it glided past them, glared at the puppy, allowed the other dogs to sniff him and then sat in front of Daphne, looking out towards the field. Here was a cat that knew all eyes were on him and was regally ignoring everyone, happily the king of all he surveyed.

"Is that your cat?! Do you live nearby?" Ari asked in astonishment.

"Yes, he's mine and no I don't live nearby. Khan just likes to come out for walks with us. Every day three or four miles, he walks along and makes sure we all behave and get safely home. Isn't he magnificent?"

Ari agreed that this was indeed the case. The idea of going for a walk with a cat filled her with delight; it seemed so odd to her but from what Daphne told her this had been Shere Khan's way ever since he was a kitten—he was a Bengal apparently and this sort of behaviour was entirely normal for them. He was also a prodigious hunter. Daphne related with pride and embarrassment the time he had dragged home a bittern. Ari's blank look then elicited an explanation of the size and secrecy of this large, elusive wading bird.

"Although if I'm honest it has landed me in a spot of bother, what with bitterns being a protected species and all that. My friend, Mary, has a bit of a bee in her bonnet about bitterns and protecting them."

"Well, surely she'll understand," said Ari, " I mean for a cat to kill a bird of that size must be pretty unusual?"

"It was a young 'un. I mean it was still twice his size..."

"Oh dear, yes, how many chicks are in a nest?"

"One."

"Ah."

"Ah, indeed. In fact, the whole incident has become a bit of a bother. I felt so guilty that I have started buying RSPB subscriptions for all my nieces and nephews and godchildren, and keep buying Mary bird related gifts and now all we talk about is blasted birds. I know I'm overcompensating and quite frankly I'm becoming a bit of a bore but I'm not sure how to stop!"

At that moment Will, who had been waiting patiently, decided that now was the perfect moment to try to stroke the cat. The puppy had been having similar thoughts and as one, they both moved on the apparently unsuspecting cat. In a rush to get to the cat, the puppy stumbled over the yellow Lab's tail who jumped to her feet disturbing the rest of the pack. In alarm, the puppy retreated with his lead now wrapped around Will's feet who promptly fell over. The little boy was now lost in a sea of excited fur and paws, there was a lot of barking, and a rather alarmed call for Mummy. Ari rushed forward to reassure Will that everything was okay as did Daphne, who called all the excited dogs to order. This was exactly the sort of incident that could set off a lifelong fear of dogs if not handled properly. Reaching into her pocket she pulled out a handful of treats for each of the dogs who were now sitting as if nothing had happened, all eyes paying close attention to Daphne's hand as she fed each dog. To try and make the little boy smile, she pretended he was also one of the dogs and handed him a biscuit as well. With a laugh, he told her he was a boy, not a dog! Daphne asked him what dog he would be if he could choose and he decided he would be a flying dog. All agreed a flying dog would be a marvellous thing.

"But not when they go for a wee," giggled Will. Leo watched all this from behind his mother's legs and then decided that if treats were being handed out, he wasn't going to miss out, and he came forward to join the pack. In the interests of fair play, Leo also pointed out that the puppy should have a treat as well.

The boys were then formally introduced to each dog and Daphne told the boys all their high and low points, making the boys laugh. From the large black Lab who was abandoned as a puppy, and the little Jack Russell that got stuck in a rabbit hole and everyone thought he was lost forever. Ariana watched on in masked concern, all she wanted to do was grab the boys to her side and not let go of them. However, she took her cue from the older lady, grateful for her calm approach. Gradually the boys went from reserved and cautious to lifelong best friends with the four hairy hounds.

Whilst all this was going on, Shere Khan watched in disgust from the side of the grass verge, and then wandered off, no doubt to find his own treat, currently leading a peaceful existence running through the long grasses.

Taking their cue from Shere Khan both women smiled and continued their walks. As she ambled off, Daphne could hear the mother chatting to her boys about what an adventure they'd all just had. The boys laughing and retelling the epic battle of dog biscuit lane.

#

Mary Flint-Hyssop got up as she heard the door knocker followed by a 'hello' and Daphne walked through to the morning room. The two ladies were old friends going back more decades than either cared to admit and were easy in each other's company, both at ease in each other's home and relaxed in their opinions, especially when they deviated from what was considered acceptable. Given how lovely the weather was they decided to have coffee outside and enjoy the warm sun. A bird started singing nearby and Mary wondered if once more Daphne was going to start going on about bloody birds again. This whole situation was getting silly. God knows Mary loved birds, but Daphne had gone from being a polite listener to occasional rants about climate change and habitat loss, to some sort of zealot. She had heard less boring born-again Christians.

"Oh hark, hark the lark!" cried Daphne.

"Blackbird, actually. Now tell me, how did little Edward do in his tests?" What grandmother could resist the siren call of family pride?

"Wonderfully, apparently. He had to do an oral presentation and he gave it on the plight of wildfowl in the Fens of England." Daphne beamed with a slightly panicked air. "So that was good. We are all so proud, I think he must have got the idea from the latest RSPB magazine I sent him. Did I mention I got him a subscription?"

Mary nodded glumly and sipped her coffee. This was getting ridiculous and frankly exasperating. All they talked about these days was birds and she was sick of it, where had the gossip gone, the speculations, the political debates? Quite honestly, Mary missed putting the world to rights with Daphne. If this was how it was going to be, then so be it, but she missed her old friend and wondered if it was worth one last gambit to try and bring her back to the light.

"Nice walk this morning?"

"Actually, we had quite an adventure. I met a lovely family walking on the Wiverton estate."

"A mother and two small boys?"

"Yes, that's them. Do you know them then?"

"I suspect that was the new Countess Wiverton."

"The new heir? Oh, I'm glad I didn't mention it was private land!"

"Well no, that would have drawn attention as to who was the actual trespasser!"

"Oh stop," laughed Daphne, "but damn it, I shall have to avoid that walk until I next meet her to ask fresh permission."

"I don't think it will be a problem," said Mary, "she comes across as welcoming if a little out of her depth at the moment."

"Out of her depth?" And at length, the two ladies relived the scandals and tragedies of the de Foix family. More coffee was consumed and as lunch approached Mary suggested that Daphne stayed for a bite to eat. Both ladies were laughing and relaxed. The sounds of the birdsong giving way to bees and crickets as the heat of the sun warmed up the insect life and the birds retreated to the shade of the trees. Cathcart brought out some salad and quiche for the friends and was happy to see that both ladies were once more their old selves, reminiscing and righting each other's memories about past events. Recent visits had been friendly but awkward and now normality seemed to have been restored. Even to the extent that Mary brought out the crib board and offered Daphne a glass of wine. The afternoon wore on and the conversation meandered between beloved family members, interesting books, clever performances, interminable sermons and so on.

"I have a confession," said Daphne, "I have missed our chats terribly, and I am completely to blame, I think it's time to come clean."

Mary raised an eyebrow but let her friend continue; was it possible that she was also aware of how incredibly boring she had become?

"I was talking about you this morning to Lady Wiverton. About your love of birds."

Mary inwardly died. "Yes?"

"Well I was out with the dogs and Shere Khan, and I was talking about some of Khan's more impressive achievements and I happened to mention his most impressive, and worst achievement ever."

Daphne fell silent, then taking a gulp of wine, proceeded in a rush of dread and embarrassment.

"A few years back Shere Khan killed and dragged home a bittern."

"A bittern! An adult bittern!! My God, they're huge."

"No," wailed Daphne, "a fledgeling!"

"Oh no, not nest thirty-nine?" Nest 39 had been watched with great excitement, the chick was thriving and there were hopes that it would help re-populate the area.

Daphne nodded miserably and confessed to how awful she had felt at the time and had then spent the past year trying to make amends. As she looked up from her wine glass, she was confused to see a huge grin plastered across Mary's face.

"Do you remember my lurcher, Tickles?"

"Gosh that's going back a bit but yes of course, never forget a dog."

"And do you remember that year when we were visited by the Siberian snowy owl and all the UK went wild and news crews came down and we were in all the papers."

"And on TV as well if I remember correctly."

"Yes, there was a huge fuss about it. And then remember that it left, presumably back to Siberia?"

"Yes?"

Daphne picked up her tea cup, grinning. "Remember Tickles?"

"No!"

"Yes! And shortly after that, I started to take a more active interest in the preservation of birds and their environment."

"Tickles killed the Siberian owl?"

"Yes!" By now both ladies were howling with laughter, tears streaming down their eyes.

"Oh my God, Mary, that's priceless, this past year I have been beside myself with mortification and there's you, covering up the slaughter of a rare visitor."

"At least my massacre wasn't on the protected species list!"

And in a gale of laughter, they picked up their cards again, chortling now and then about the plight of the other, both agreeing that bird welfare was frightfully important but no longer needed to dominate their conversations. In fact, it would be a while before either could mention birds in the presence of the other without them both falling into fits of giggles.

24

Ari and the boys were playing in the rose garden when Dickie announced Sir Sebastian who promptly followed her out into the warm sunshine. This whole announcing people made Ari smile. Certainly, in a house this big she would never hear the doorbell ring. But there were a few people she had no objection to just wandering in; her sisters obviously. And she could imagine a time when she wouldn't mind Seb either. Mind you, it was also unhelpful to allow them to just wander around for hours shouting Hello. She guessed announcing people did make sense and of course, as with the incident with her in-laws, it was a nice weapon to have in your arsenal. No, the upper classes definitely knew all the tricks of living in large properties. Making room on the rug, Seb settled down beside her and was immediately assailed by the boys and the puppy.

"This is a lovely surprise. Have you come to check on Dragon?"

"Dragon?"

"Yes, the boys have named the puppy Dragon." Ari explained that as they had already agreed that the house was called George, it seemed only fitting in their eyes that the puppy should be called Dragon. But George had killed the dragon, Ari pointed out. The boys explained that this time Dragon was going to be nice and it would give him a chance to do the right thing.

"Atonement for the Saint, eh?" asked Seb. The boys didn't have a clue what 'atonement' meant but it sounded good, so they agreed. Plus, they pointed out, George was their friend and so was Dragon and friends should play nicely together. Seb couldn't fault their logic.

"Well I think it's a great name, my first dog was called Perseus, it was a fabulous name but I could barely say it and I could never remember how to spell it, so we tended to shorten it to Percy."

"What's a Persusus?" asked Leo.

"Perseus was a great hero from Ancient Greece, who slew a fearsome gorgon. Do you know the story?" Leo said he did but he was happy to hear it again. William said Leo was fibbing and before it got out of hand, Seb quickly plunged in. As he told the tale to an audience of two enthralled boys and a bouncy puppy, Ari got up and went to get some drinks for everyone. In the kitchen, Wendy had already had the same thought and a tray had been made up. Carrying the pitchers of water, she and Wendy headed back to the garden and set up under the gazebo. It was a pretty little building in a sheltered corner of the garden, with a beautiful view looking back towards the house. The thatched roof of the gazebo protected those sitting beneath and was a welcome pool of shade.

Calling the boys over she could see that the children had found a new area of exploration, Greek myths. Well, that should last them a few years she thought. Gulping down their water and grumbling as Ari reapplied the sun cream, they ran off again exploring the back of the tall herbaceous border. Every so often a group of delphiniums rustled as the boys no doubt tried to find their way out of the Minotaur's layer. A few minutes later she heard some giggling and they ran into the house with Dragon in pursuit.

"Dickie? Did you know that Dragon is a bitch?" Both boys sniggered and then tried to look innocent.

"Yes, dears, and her mother was a bitch as well. Now run along and make sure there's some water for Dragon, she looks thirsty."

Disappointed that they had failed to shock Dickie they discovered that no one else they told seemed remotely interested either, so after all three had some water they went back outside to play.

Ari wondered what they had been up to but decided that as she hadn't heard anything actually breaking, she wouldn't investigate. Her attention returned to Seb, who had cleared his throat.

"Geoffrey, my brother, is home next weekend and we're having a dinner party. He's secured some massive deal which is going to be an enormous boost for the estate, and he wants to celebrate. I wondered if you would like to be my guest? Before you say yes, I have to warn you, it's going to be white tie; he's terribly pompous and lots of his friends are either total bores or crass idiots."

Ari laughed. "Well how can I decline such an enticing invitation? But seriously I've never been to a dinner party before. What does white tie mean?"

Seb went onto explain the level of formality involved but he promised he wouldn't abandon her. "If anything, I'm hoping that you'll say yes so that I have someone I actually like to talk to all evening."

Ari was delighted that he'd said he liked her and said yes straight away. As he left, she headed to the kitchens to see if Dickie could help her with what was involved in a dinner party.

Dickie smiled at her as she walked into the kitchen.

"I see the boys have learnt a new word today. They came in here and tried to shock anyone they could find by saying 'bitch'. It was all we could do to keep our faces straight, dear things."

The boys were clearly loved among the staff, but everyone was mindful of how much trouble two little boys could stir up if given half a chance and the rule was always to encourage but not indulge, prevent but not chastise. Except, of course, when chastisement was required. Like the time Wendy found them on a chair eating the biscuit mixture from out of the bowl.

Ari pulled up a chair and explained her invitation; that she had said yes but now she was at a loss as to what to wear. Dickie for once looked bothered.

"What's wrong? Should I have declined?"

"Oh no, it's not that, but this is a bit out of my comfort zone and it's essential that you present well. This is going to be your first formal outing. We need to start on a high."

Ari's heart sank; this sounded even worse than Seb had made out. Dickie blanched when she heard the invitation was for the following weekend but told Ari to leave it with her. As soon as Ari returned to

play with the boys, Dickie got on the phone to Mrs
Cathcart, the Flint-Hyssop housekeeper, and it became
clear that this was going to be a no-holds-barred event,
the only thing missing from the invitation was
decorations. Dickie gulped, there was no way Ari was
ready for this and she wondered what had possessed
Sir Sebastian, why did men never think? There hadn't
been a lady's maid in the house since Lady Wiverton
died as Jacinta just made use of local beauty salons.
Well, Dickie had misgivings, but she wasn't sure what
else to do, and so she rang around a few parlours until
she booked the services of a team of beauty specialists
that would come out to prepare Ariana. It was short
notice but when Dickie named the client the salon was
miraculously able to rearrange some bookings and
would come out the next day to do a trial run.

       The minute the cars arrived the following day,
Dickie knew that she had made a mistake. The team
consisted of a hairdresser, a make-up artist, a stylist, a
manicurist, a spray tan specialist, and an
empowerment coach. Both Ari and Dickie raised their
eyebrows at the last job title, but Ari chose to keep
faith with Dickie and not say anything. All six gushed
around Ari and soon heated tongs and brushes were
being plugged in and palettes of colour were being
laid out. Dickie watched in dismay as her mistress

looked steadily more and more concerned. Dickie explained what was required, Ari needed to look like the Countess Wiverton, she was to look young, beautiful and powerful. Ari sniggered. Dickie gave her a quick glare and continued. The nails were to have a French polish only, Ari didn't know what that meant but the manicurist looked disappointed as she closed the lid on the diamanté. There were going to be no haircuts or dyes, just dressed, and the spray tan was going to be nothing beyond a healthy glow. Confident that she had left clear instructions she then left with the stylist to go through Jacinta and Cecily's wardrobes to find something suitable to wear. It was clear that the stylist didn't understand the term 'white tie' and it had taken some while to convince the girl that she wasn't joking about a full-length gown and elbow length gloves. In turn, the girl despaired of Dickie's suggestions, promising Dickie that times had moved on and that Ari would look a laughingstock in some of her choices. As the stylist had banned any outfit older than ten years and Dickie had banned anything that wasn't full length and jumpsuits—that had been a tussle—they narrowed down the choices to three of Jacinta's evening gowns. Dickie felt uncomfortable with the raciness, but they were full length, so she was prepared to let Ari decide. As she and the stylist walked back into the living room, the sight that greeted Dickie left her speechless. Ari took one look at Dickie's face and her shoulders slumped.

"I don't have a mirror. What do you think?"

Dickie knew it was Ari because that's where she had left her, and it certainly sounded like her, but what the hell had they done to her?

"What have you done to her hair? And her face, my God, what is that?"

Ari's dark hair seemed to have grown and was now twice the length and standing out in a huge plume. It was incredibly dramatic, making her small face look odd and a bit nightmarish. This was not helped by the startled looking eyebrows and dark pouting lipstick. The pout was emphasised by an incredibly chiselled jaw and cheekbones. The effect was certainly powerful, but it was also terribly, terribly Hollywood.

"Don't you like it? I said no to the tan, I hope you don't mind but apparently, I had to wear a set of paper knickers whilst I stood naked and someone sprayed paint on me. I didn't fancy that. But look I got my nails done like you suggested."

Ari wiggled ten long plastic pink and white shellacked blobs at her. Trying to make her smile. She knew this was a big deal and wanted to get it right and she hadn't wanted to let Dickie down. The whole experience had been a nightmare with all these gossipy gushing strangers pulling her about, but she was conscious that as lady of the manor she had a role to play. But now looking at Dickie's horrified face she was aware that she had somehow failed.

Conscious of Ari's body language, Dickie felt deeply ashamed. She knew the girl was depending on her and desperate not to let anyone down. So far she had borne up under the constant, gentle tutelage, she had learned who the staff were, she had got people back into their homes, and Dickie knew she was burning the candle at both ends trying to get up to speed, all whilst grieving for a lost husband. Now Dickie had failed her by asking her to look like some sort of carnival clown. She cleared her throat and turned to the team of beauticians.

"Thank you, everyone. You have been splendid, but this isn't quite the look that we were after, please send us your invoice and we will be sure to recommend you for your prompt service."

Politely Ari thanked them for their efforts and confided to loving the nails and being pampered. She hated her nails they felt like someone had glued a shovel to the tips of her fingers, but she was so sorry for the team, you could see they were offended and disappointed that their best efforts had failed to make the grade.

When Dickie came back into the room Ari hadn't moved, she sat on the stool, tears dribbling through the acres of mascara and foundation.

"Just how bad do I look?" mumbled Ari.

"Oh, honestly you don't look bad at all, just not right. I am so incredibly sorry; I've overreached and let you down."

"You think you've let me down? I think I've let you down, I've just never much bothered with make-up and hairstyles and we could never afford to go out anywhere and then I got pregnant and what was the point after that?"

Dickie felt even more ashamed of herself, heaping so many pressures on Ari's shoulders, although once more she silently cursed Sebastian.

"Okay, you need a laugh. Let's look in a mirror, we'll have a laugh and then we'll put on a pot of tea."

Dickie led Ari to the front hall and Ari stood peering into the full-length mirror, her shoulders twitching and jerking until she could no longer hold back and roared with laughter, calling for the boys and chuckling with Dickie.

"Holy crap. Who is that!? Where's my phone I have to take a picture."

When they arrived both boys solemnly declared that Mummy looked beautiful but were a bit worried about hugging her, the hair looked like it might attack at any minute. Having been pulled away from their games to look at Mummy looking pretty and scary, they asked if they could go back to their trains. Ari wondered how she had ever managed before Brio.

After a cup of tea, Ari decided to call Clemmie and see if she could help. Her sister had a stunning eye for design and fashion, and she had made lots of contacts in the industry, maybe she could think of a solution. She sent Clemmie a text with the word, HELP and attached the photo of herself.

Five minutes later the phone rang.

"What did you let the boys do to you!!!" screeched Clemmie, and so Ari poured out the whole sorry tale. A few minutes later Clemmie hung up promising her sister that she would be back in touch, she had someone in mind but needed to check if they were in the country or if they would be able to fly back. Soon the phone rang again.

"Hi, I've spoken to Rafe. He's on his way, can you put him up? He'll be there tomorrow, him and his dog, she's a poppet. I showed him your photo and he said to '*leave the hair and nails alone, he'll fix them, wash your face and smile. You're too pretty not to.*' You're going to love him. Or not. But you can trust him, he's so talented, his client list is uber elite. Trust me, you can trust him. Now look, I must run, it's sodding chaos up here. Let's catch up soon, we all need to get together."

And in a flurry of bye byes and love yous she hung up leaving Ari remembering what a whirlwind Clemmie could be when she had the bit between her teeth.

25

The following day Ari returned from her morning bike ride with the boys to find a Volvo estate in the drive. Wondering who was calling on her now she walked in through the back hallway and heard a lively conversation taking place in the kitchen; it was the morning coffee break, and everyone seemed to be enjoying the laugh. Ari was always a bit uncertain about breaking up these moments, she felt a bit awkward, but it got easier every time she stuck her head around the door, so she kept at it. This time she was surprised to see that all the staff were present and laughing at something a young man sat at the table was saying. As soon as he saw her, he jumped up.

"Countess Wiverton, I presume. I can see your sister in you. Making you look beautiful is going to be the easiest job I have ever had." And with a flourish, he handed her his card.

"Rafe Jones & Delilah"

Ari turned the card over; it was blank on the other side. She raised an eyebrow at him.

"I don't need a sales pitch; my work speaks for me."

"There are no contact details?"

"No, I know. It's wildly affectatious, isn't it?" he said with a twinkle.

"And Delilah?"

As she said the name, a large ugly mongrel shuffled out from under the table, wagging her tail and hitting it against the table leg.

"Another affectation I'm afraid but she goes where I go, she's too old for kennels. It's rather meant I'm only working in the UK for now, but quite frankly a year of Hollywood and the White House is enough for a poor country boy like me to cope with."

He was clearly comfortable with his own talents and seemed to have been regaling everyone with tales of the rich and famous before she arrived. All she cared about was his kindness to his dog. He might have joked, but he was young to turn his back on a market as lucrative as America, especially as he had already clearly achieved a dizzying level of success.

"Right," said Ari, smiling, "would you like to follow me and let's see what you can do. Wendy can you bring me a coffee and another drink for Rafe. Dickie, will you join us? We're going through to the conservatory to talk. Delilah?"

As she walked along the corridor Rafe watched how she moved and silently worked out her measurements. He hadn't been joking, she was going to be easy, the only trick was going to be balancing her youth against her title.

They sat down and Ari and Dickie began to fire questions at him, he in return reassuring them explaining some of the previous events that he had worked on and the names of some of his clients.

"So, if we engage you," asked Ari, already confident that she would, "how long would it take you to assemble your team?"

"No team. Just me. Well just me and Delilah, but her contributions tend to be an enthusiastic wag. In the past, people didn't need a huge entourage unless they wanted to show off. In a house like this, you'd have had what they called a lady's maid and she'd have taken care of the whole shebang. Consider me your lady's maid. I can do it all."

Clemmie was right, she did love him, and she also liked Dickie's approving smile.

"Right then, "said Ari, "that's settled, if you want this gig it's yours. We'll pay you for the dry run today and then for the actual event. Is that acceptable?"

Rafe grinned. Clemmie had warned him she could be forthright, but he just saw it as someone that knew how they wanted things to pan out. After her last disaster with make-up artists, he couldn't blame her for being cautious. He'd seen the photo after all.

He put his hand out; Rafe liked to shake on a deal, lots of women weren't great at it but soon he would be manhandling them into dresses and sorting out their bodies. They needed to get comfortable with him quickly, plus he liked to judge people on their shake. Ari didn't surprise or disappoint, and given the glint in her eye, she knew she was being tested.

"So where do we start? Please God let it be with my hair and nails!"

After a close inspection, Rafe said he would remove the nails and patch things over, they would look fine at the party but then he recommended leaving them a bit scruffy whilst the nail bed recovered. The hair was a different matter and he wanted to leave the extensions in, just in case removing them caused a problem prior to the engagement.

"I promise I will do everything to calm it down, you might even end up liking it." Personally, Rafe thought the hairdresser had done a good job putting them in, but an awful job styling them, and they seemed woefully inappropriate for someone who by her own words liked climbing trees with her boys, cycling around the estate, and swimming in the rivers.

297

"The trick is to make you feel as comfortable as possible—the happier you are, the more that will shine through, regardless of hair, make-up or outfit. Speaking of which, what are you wearing? That will be critical."

Ari and Dickie looked at each other and then him.

"We haven't decided yet, would you like to have a look and see what you think?" said Dickie. "Lady Wiverton hasn't had time to buy herself any new clothes and so she's living out of the family wardrobes at the moment."

"Wardrobes plural? Oh, I do like the sound of that. Come on, let's go and rummage."

As they entered Jacinta's bedroom Dickie showed him the three gowns that the previous stylist had thought might be appropriate.

Rafe looked at the dresses in disgust, "We are NOT putting her in black. Oh, dear God is that Lycra! To a white tie? No, no, no." He flicked quickly through the large wardrobe, looked Ari up and down and looking at Dickie he said "Next." So, they all traipsed off down the corridors to Cecily's dressing room.

"God, was your aunt a nun or just dead? The seventies were so cruel. What is this fabric? No don't even touch it, your nails might ignite." Having dismissed everything in the wardrobe, Rafe turned back to Ari. "Okay, you seriously do not have anything to wear. But don't worry I can have something couriered up in the morning, you have an easy figure to fit so we won't need to make many alterations to anything that gets sent up."

Dickie decided to trust her instincts, she liked this lad and despite his youth, he certainly seemed to talk a good talk. "What about something older?"

"Older. Dear lady, don't tease, what do you have in mind?"

"Well, we still have Ariana's grandmother's clothes from the fifties. They are up in the attic rooms but in perfect condition. The previous stylist said no one wore old clothes, but it's just that the previous Lady Wiverton had such beautiful taste?"

"Well let's go and have a look then. I could spend all day looking through old clothes." He smiled reassuringly at Ari, "Don't worry, even if there's nothing here you are going to look fabulous."

By now the boys had got bored and looking forward to an opportunity to explore the top floor joined the adults.

Dickie led the party upstairs and unlocked a door into a long room full of trunks and wardrobes.

There were piles of boxes on side tables and a long mirror at one end.

"This was the children's dressing-up room, no one ever seems to throw clothes away in this family, so they gradually drift up here. Your mother and David used to play in here dressing up and wearing hats and playing make-believe. The only things they weren't allowed to touch were the clothes in boxes."

Rafe looked around and saw a whole stack of dress boxes. He knew on sight that these were made by design houses to keep their most special garments safe.

Gulping he asked, "Did Ariana's grandmother use a lot of couture houses?"

"I believe so. She even modelled for Dior once or twice, which created a huge scandal. Her parents were furious with her, but she thought it was fun. It was just after the war and life had been sombre for a long time. The balls had started up again and she just wanted to be young and happy."

Rafe lifted the lid of a box and gently pulled back the tissue paper protecting the fabric beneath. "Oh, my, God." Gently lifting the heavy dress out, he gave it a gentle shake and showed it to the women. The pink satin shone in the light, a soft fur trim around the neck lent a dreamy quality to the small sleeveless bodice that tapered down into a full tailored skirt.

"Wow, Cinderella. This is your dress!"

Ari looked at it in alarm, unconvinced she could carry off anything so beautiful.

"Don't panic. Let's see what else there is. We'll put this to one side for now, but in my eyes, this is a front-runner.

As the day wore on, more and more beautiful gowns were pulled out and Rafe commented that many were of museum quality, freaking Ariana out even more.

Pulling one cloak towards her she was marvelling at the intricate embroidery. The entire garment was covered in flowers and insects with the odd bird, the shining threads weaving in and out of the shimmering fabric. The edge of the cloak was trimmed in a fringe and she waved it towards Rafe.

"This one has been spoilt, I think. Looks like someone stitched on curtain tassels for a fancy-dress look."

Rafe looked over and screeched at her, reverentially removing the cape from Ari's undeserving hands. "That is a signature feature of Balmain, you wretched heathen!"

301

Balmain, Dior, Balenciaga, Fath; these were simply words to her, she was certain that if Clemmie were here she would know exactly what she was looking at and not mistake anything for upholstery.

She sat back on the bare wooden floorboards and looked at all the silks and velvets around her. She need never go clothes shopping again, so long as she never did anything but attend balls and red-carpet events. Nothing seemed particularly functional; maybe when she next walked the dog she could step out in Dior. Cycling might be out of the question though. Maybe she would just stick to feeding the chickens in it?

The small attic windows cast a soft light over the room and reminded her that the day was passing and no decision had been made. Whilst Rafe was in his element she was impatient to get on with it. This was fun but it wasn't achieving anything. Picking up the pink gown and ignoring Rafe's wince at her rough treatment she stripped down to her underwear and with the help of Rafe and Dickie, she wiggled and shuffled into the dress. There was then some more shuffling as she removed her bra, grey straps didn't really go with the soft bodice.

"Well, what do you think?"

Rafe sighed, "You need new underwear," and scowled at Dickie as though it were her fault that the mistress of the house was wandering around in holey, discoloured supermarket knickers and bras.

"Focus, Rafe, no one is looking at my knickers. Dickie, what do you think?"

So far Dickie had been silent and Ari was terrified that this was going to be another clown moment. It was essential that she looked the part, even if she didn't feel it and at the moment she felt that the dress was overwhelming her. A long mirror stood in the corner of the eaves and scooping up her massive skirt, she went to have a look. In front of her stood a tall, slim girl standing in the most glorious dress. Her bare arms and shoulders were framed by a sumptuous pink satin that came to life against her skin. Leading down from the small, boned bodice the fabric started to pleat out in larger and larger folds flowing down the front of the skirt. The reverse of the pleat was in a darker berry colour, providing a vivid contrast to the soft pink and peeping in and out until the outer skirt reached the floor. The darker colour of the lining could now be fully seen. This voluminous open skirt was now the foil for a slimmer full-length skirt, emphasising her height. Stunned and with a small smile on her face she turned to look at the other two.

"This is okay, isn't it?" But she didn't need to see the happy tears in Dickie's eyes or the excited gleam in Rafe's to know that she did indeed look very okay.

From the age of eighteen when she had to plead her case to take care of her sisters and keep the family together, she had understood the need to project confidence and assurance. It was irrelevant that she was a grieving teenager who was crying every night into her sodden pillow. All she wanted was to see her parents just one more time, to say goodbye properly or to tell them that she loved them, or to cling on to them so tightly that they never walked out of the front door. It didn't matter that she was an A-level student with three straight As and a place at Cambridge waiting for her. None of that had mattered, her past and her future were irrelevant. Standing in the family court, all she had to do was show them the present. That she was capable of taking charge of the family. Image was everything.

Looking back into the mirror she thought she could see the beginnings of the Countess Wiverton. She still had a long way to go, but she knew she had lots of people who were going to help her. Plus Seb had promised to not leave her side all evening. Just thinking about Seb made her happy, she couldn't wait to see his face, she was going to blow his socks off.

26

Seb had spent most of the day once more poring through the archives, looking at old maps and ledgers, looking for a miracle to untangle this sorry mess. His sense of failure was all the more acute in the light of his brother's phenomenal success in securing a deal between two international banks. Geoffrey had asked earlier if he could lend a hand and the suggestion had filled Seb with horror. Most of his life he had spent his time in the wake of his big brother's path saying, 'He didn't actually mean that' or 'What he meant to say was'. County planners and town councillors were touchy souls and Seb could only imagine in horror the things that Geoffrey might say in an effort to help move the situation along. Seb was certain that Geoffrey's intervention would indeed move the situation along, to a crashing resolution and closure. Tonight was going to be all about showing off and underlining how fabulous Geoffrey was. He was proud of his brother and of his achievements but it just cast his own failures in a greater relief. Why in the name of God hadn't previous generations bought the land back? Why the hell had no one paid attention to the problems that were being stored up? The only saving grace of tonight's event was going to be Ariana. He had originally admired her attitude but as he had got to know her, he realised that whilst she was genuinely insightful, much of her confidence was a mask and every so often he would see her laughter as she mocked herself. He had begun to think that tonight's do was a big mistake for her to attend. She was still far too new to this life and was bound to come a cropper. He couldn't bear to see her fragile confidence knocked and had told his mother that it was essential that he be seated beside her. It didn't matter what she wore or how she behaved, but he knew that a girl who grew up living in a three-bed terrace in the East End of London, did not have any experience of white tie occasions. He berated himself for not inviting her over to dinner or taking her out to get her more used to fine dining. When he had invited her, she had asked if they would be eating tea off the good trays and then laughed at him when he had thought she was serious. The fact remained though, and as she herself said, if there was more than one fork by her plate then it was going to be one fork too many. But despite his worries, he was looking forward to seeing her, and he was planning on catching up and finding out how life with Dragon was coming along. With some Vivaldi playing through the car speaker he felt upbeat even if he wasn't driving his favourite car. On the way out the door, his mother had stopped him and suggested that he take the Range Rover instead.

"No one in a full-length gown wants to try and get in and out of a low-slung sports car."

As he pulled up in the drive, he wondered exactly what sort of a gown Ariana had managed to find. She had told him that she didn't own any long skirts or dresses but that she would sort something out. He wondered if she had been to any of the local charity shops. He had been amazed when she told him how much she and her sisters had shopped there. Her sister Clemmie, apparently was a whizz with the sewing machine and could fashion anything into something that a teenage girl was happy to be seen in, in public. Before leaving he'd asked his mother to lend him one of her cloaks just in case Ari needed one, but his mother refused, saying that Ariana had a full outfit. Clearly, the wires had been buzzing between the two houses and if his mother was relaxed then he should be too.

Dickie opened the door and welcomed him into the hallway. A fire was roaring in the hearth and the house had the feeling of a welcoming home. There was a loud cry from the top of the staircase and two boys and a puppy all came running down to greet him, the boys shouting 'bundles' ready for another game.

He was about to swing them off their feet when Dickie
stepped in front of him and warned the two boys not to
mess him up. In a pact of manly solidarity, Seb rolled
his eyes and the boys giggled, all of them used to
being told off by women who expected them to stay
clean and tidy. All the time. Only Dragon hadn't
received the message and jumped up excitedly until
Dickie also shooed her away. In all the excitement Seb
had taken his eyes of the staircase but now, walking
slowly down to meet him, was a figure from another
era. The Countess Wiverton moved down the staircase
towards him. Her gown was breathtaking and set off
by long white gloves, one hand resting on the curved
wooden banister. She wore a large ruby and diamond
necklace with matching drop earrings. Her hair had
been swept up into a large tower of tresses that had
been pinned in place with diamond hairpins. As she
approached him her painted lips twitched, and Ari
grinned out at him from under the elegant make-up.

"You'll catch flies," she said and softly placed
one gloved finger under his chin.

Looking at her in amazement he turned to the
boys, "Did you know your mummy was a princess?"

Both boys thought this was very funny and
Dragon who once more wanted to join in the laughter
came bounding up again. This time everyone reacted,

with Ari recoiling into Seb in an attempt to avoid the puppy attacking the Dior.

Wrapping his arm around Ari, Seb was steering her towards the car when Dickie came out with a large, embroidered satin cape.

Ari thanked her and whispered to Seb that it was a stupid coat, it had no pockets and apparently couldn't be allowed to get wet either as it was too precious.

"I'm going to be upstaged by a cape of all things. Look at it, it is both glorious and yet utterly useless at the same time."

Seb gave her a quick squeeze and told her that nothing and no one was going to upstage her tonight. Eventually, Dickie and Wendy got Ari into the car, with as few creases as possible, and after gently kissing the boys goodnight and telling them to behave themselves, they drove off. As they left Wendy thought how incredibly good they looked together. In his long black tails and crisp, white shirt and waistcoat he was the perfect foil for her exuberant soft pink gown. Grinning to Dickie the pair of them returned to the house, herding the excited children back to their tea.

Keeping his eyes on the road Seb couldn't get over the fact that the glorious creature beside him had yesterday been learning how to milk a cow. As she chatted on it was clear that she was enjoying learning about her farms and how the estate worked, but the more she chatted, the more he realised that she was nervous. When she asked him halfway through a conversation about crop yield if he thought she was overdressed, he berated himself for a fool for not thinking about how this must feel to her.

"Trust me," he said, giving her hand a quick squeeze, "you look perfect and will fit right in."

She wasn't going to fit in, she was going to shine and eclipse every other person in the room, but he suspected that that was not what she wanted to hear right at this moment.

Clarice Kendrick had been having a bad night. She had been looking forward to this party for months, she'd convinced Jasper to bring her as his plus one to Geoffrey Flint-Hyssop's party. She knew Jasper wouldn't have a date, being besotted as he was, with Geoffrey. There would be no way he'd bring one of his many boyfriends to a do like this in case it spoilt his career chances. Clarry thought that was a bloody laugh, half the men she met were gay, they just pretended they were straight to their families and then had outrageous affairs while away on business trips. Not that Clarry cared, she had her eye on a bigger goal. She knew Sebastian, Geoffrey's younger brother would be present, and she was certain that she had caught his eye last time they met. She'd tagged him on a few photos, and he'd liked them, but nothing recently. Still, that was one of the reasons she had her eye on him, he was more serious than the other guys she hooked up with, he wasn't fake, and wasn't all about himself or looking good on social media. She was fed up dating men who took longer than her to get ready to go out. Plus, by all accounts, the family was loaded and, most importantly, he had a title and she fancied a bit of that for herself. Last year she'd been out with friends and one of them had made a joke about the fact you couldn't call anyone over thirty a 'trophy wife'. At thirty-five, Clarry easily passed for twenty-eight in a good light but that one snide comment had been preying on her mind. She didn't plan on being a trophy anything, she would be in charge. That said, playing the field, as fun as it had been, had become dull recently and time was running out. She needed a marriage and a good one at that. Old, rich, gay, ugly; she didn't care but young, handsome and titled would be even better.

However, things had been going wrong from the start, she'd called Rebecca who was also attending the party, to discuss outfits. They both agreed that cocktail wear would be fine but when she arrived, Rebecca and every other woman present was in a floor length skirt and she was certain Rebecca was laughing at her. No doubt revenge for the last time they'd met and Clarry had gone home with Becca's date. She'd known when she arrived that she had looked amazing and against the other women she stood out a mile. Half the men couldn't take their eyes off her legs or the way the skirt clung to her arse, which, along with her bare legs, was also perfectly toned. Geoffrey had walked up to her with a welcoming smile and commented on how breathtaking she looked. Then things began to fall apart.

Realising that she had probably made a dramatic misstep, she begged him to introduce her to his mother to apologise for her attire. She would play the American card if she needed to. His mother might be a pushover, in which case she wouldn't bother but it always proved smart to butter up potential in-laws first, to smooth her path to Sebastian. When she approached Lady Flint-Hyssop, she instantly knew she had made a colossal error, strong English men tended to have formidable mothers and this small woman in front of her was radiating disapproval. God knows there was nothing about her smile or her handshake that seemed cold but Clarry knew when she had been assessed and found wanting. What was it about the

English? You could never tell where you stood with them, the more they liked each other the ruder they were, they didn't call for months and then turned up and stayed for the night. They invited you to drop by and if you did, they would look appalled. Her ability to sum people up was why she was so successful; she could quickly assess who was a manipulative pushover and who was going to play hardball. In front of her stood a bloody howitzer. The final nail came when she apologised for her dress, playing up the American farmgirl, bright lights, big city routine. Lady Flint-Hyssop had nodded sympathetically and then kindly enquired if she would like to borrow a skirt to go with her top. It sounded polite, even helpful, but everyone present knew it for the put down it was and, thankfully, Geoffrey whisked her away to introduce her to some of the new investors. Clarry had never thrown a drink in the face of the landed gentry before and she suspected that it wouldn't have gone down well, but boy was she tempted. Excusing herself for a moment she was even more determined to land Seb; that would beat any glass of wine in the face. She walked across the lawn, her stilettos puncturing through the grass as she went; why on earth were they having drinks outside? Her satin heels were unlikely to survive the evening.

Sneaking into the dining room she saw that Seb had been placed next to some old dowager. That didn't suit her plans at all, so she swapped place names ensuring he was by her side. When she walked back onto the terrace Sebastian had arrived and was standing next to some young-looking girl wearing the most extravagant outfit, who seemed to be the centre of a small group of people. Clarry wasn't an idiot, standing next to a girl that looked ten years her junior would not do anything for her. Instead, she got chatting to some of the men who were more than willing to listen and laugh along with her. Soon she realised she had her own little coterie, most of whom were Geoffrey's new investors from work. Malcolm was happily leering over her and normally she'd oblige by leaning that little bit closer to him—his bonus last year had been eye-watering and worth the sweaty gropes—but she had her eye on the main prize, Lady Clarice had just the right ring to it.

Lady Flint-Hyssop took one final glance around the dining room before her guests made their way to dinner. The room was magnificent, Mary had pulled no punches and everything shone and glittered, the candelabras had been lit with actual candles making the lighting in the room warm and flickery. Candlelight was much kinder to older skin levelling the playing field as it did and casting everyone into a smudgy soft focus. The crystal glittered and the flowers leant a soft blossomed perfume to the room. The table was laid for forty and each chair was attended by a liveried member of staff. The effect was absolutely dazzling, a reminder to some of Geoffrey's investors what a safe, solid, and powerful pair of hands they had placed their money in. Lady Flint-Hyssop knew that what impressed people who lived in glass and steel skyscrapers, was not the obvious show and tell of money. It was the sense of stability. In a business where companies could crash and burn in a single marketplace fluctuation, stability was king. This solidity that went back centuries was designed to remind them gently but forcefully what they had invested in and what it stood for. As she made one final sweep of the table, she noticed that someone had swapped over the place cards and that Ariana had been moved to the other end of the table. Crossly, she picked up the card and swapped it back with the person who had clearly made the switch. After tonight she would quietly ask Geoffrey to ensure that that particular young woman was not invited again. She didn't care how she dressed but she would not stand for someone messing with her seating plan. Especially as it might have upset Sebastian, or even worse, Ariana. Satisfied that all was now in order she allowed the butler to announce dinner.

As the courses were brought in and out Ari was relieved to have Seb by her side. The room was overwhelming and she couldn't believe her mother had grown up accustomed to occasions like this. She felt utterly out of her depth, but she was enjoying herself. This was something new and challenging. When she'd arrived, she'd decided that the only way to survive the evening was to pretend to be David Attenborough, observing some strange new indigenous species. The women glittered in beautiful gowns and jewels, the men were glorious in their uniform long black tails and sharp white shirts and bow ties. She had thought people were joking about the concept of the correct fork but as she sat down, she saw in front of her a whole plethora of knives, forks, spoons and God knows what else. She didn't know if this was a campaign of shock and awe but Seb had warned her that his mother was pulling out all the guns. As each new course arrived, Seb simply placed his hand on the next fork never once making eye contact with Ari, but quietly and covertly, she followed his every signal. She was also feeling bolstered by the occasional reassuring smiles from his mother and father. Everyone was so kind, but as Mary had pointed out earlier in the evening, Ari outranked everyone in the room. Had she chosen to drink her soup through a straw everyone would have gamely followed suit.

In fact, when the soup had arrived, Ari glanced up to find Mary looking at her with a smile and a raised eyebrow. She laughed and picked up her soup spoon at which point Mary pretended to pull a face and Ari laughed out loud, causing the men on either side to look at her curiously. She made some excuse about a silly memory and silently smiled into her soup. As the evening progressed, she relaxed, pleased that she hadn't let the side down, then Geoffrey stood up and proposed to break with tradition. Instead of the men moving two to the right the ladies would instead. This was met with general laughter and approval, especially from some of the louder men, and Ari heard someone mention that it was about time he got to see those lovely legs again. She guessed that was a reference to the amazing redhead that had arrived looking like she had been poured out of liquid gold. She was certainly the most stunning lady in the room, but Ari thought it was a bit rude of whoever it was, to draw attention to her outfit. No doubt she was feeling mortified. Looking across to the woman to try to give her a supportive smile she noticed that far from being uncomfortable, she was positively preening under the attention. At that moment the woman looked in her direction and Ari's smile died on her lips as the redhead looked her up and down, and then gave her a most dismissive sneer.

318

Discomfited, Ari then realised that she was going to have to stand up and move. What stupid idea was this? Her outfit was incredibly heavy and unwieldy. Similarly, those of most of the other women were cumbersome to stand up and sit down in. She liked the notion of moving the guests around, but in her mind, there was a good reason why the tradition was that it was the men who moved. She also realised with dismay that she was now nowhere near Seb and, in fact, she was sitting between two total strangers who seemed to have been having an enjoyable time with the wine.

She knew she was probably being rude, but she didn't feel comfortable about starting a conversation. She didn't want to risk making a fool of herself or somehow putting her foot in it. She would hate to do anything that might take the shine off this spectacle. It seemed it wasn't going to be a problem as the man to her left launched into a loud introduction, which basically seemed designed to let her know that he was rich and clever, as well as being the main mover in this deal and that without him it wouldn't have happened. He had also rather impressively managed to shoehorn in the fact that he had a yacht, a flat in Monaco, and had some sort of car on a waiting list. She only knew it was a car because the man on her other side started asking impressed questions about it. As far as she could tell the older gentleman to her right might be a neighbour of hers while the younger man was an American and was involved in the deal. The older chap was near deaf and kept shouting across her to the man on her other side. In fact, he didn't seem to be speaking to her much at all as she clearly didn't know anything about cars. God this was tedious.

"Tell me, which one's the merry widow?" The American interrupted her thoughts and looking up, she realised the old boy had returned to shouting at the woman on his other side and the American had switched his attention back to her.

"Oh, I'm sorry, I don't actually know many people here," said Ari. "Who were you looking for?"

"The Merry Widow! Apparently, according to Geoffrey's little brother, one of the guests here is recently widowed and absolutely loaded. I thought I might introduce myself over coffee. See if I can't beat Seb to the finish line," he said, and laughed loudly.

Ari's heart thumped in her chest; the evening lost its sparkle and the food sat like a heavy lump in her stomach. Falling back on David Attenborough she decided to pretend she was once more observing, not actually taking part.

"What does she look like? Shall we try to guess which one she might be?"

It felt odd to pretend to be looking for herself and whilst her companion was a drunken idiot, he was nevertheless entertaining. Over their puddings and cheese, they studied each guest. Which one of the other ladies was out dancing on her husband's grave? Merrily squandering his ill-gotten gains. By the end of the meal they had established that her husband must have made his money by international smuggling, that she was in her sixties but had had countless facelifts, so now looked at least, what? Sixty? Both laughed again as Jim had explained that a few of Geoffrey's guests had been planning to introduce themselves as well but that no one had caught her name.

Ari commiserated but promised solemnly to let him know if she worked out who this gangster's moll was. Finally, Mary stood up and invited whoever wished, to join her in the Ming room, whilst the smokers stayed behind for cigars. Ari was happy to see that this wasn't a traditional male-female split and several of the ladies stayed behind, including the redhead who had already accepted a massive cigar from the man seated at her side. Given the way that she was leaning into him, they were clearly well acquainted. Or about to be. Following behind Mary, Ari was preparing to make her excuses when the older lady looked at her tired face and instantly assessed the situation.

"Was it too much? Come with me."

Leading her into a quiet hallway, Mary nodded sympathetically about Ari's headache but when she suggested she get Seb to drive her home, Ari was firm. She had no wish to bother him. Mary frowned inwardly. They had seemed to be enjoying each other's company during dinner, maybe something had happened when she changed partners? It had been lovely to watch her son, relaxed and happy. It was no secret that she was hoping that Lily's charming daughter was going to be the one that Seb fell in love with. In fact, she thought he might have already. However, the poor girl was recently widowed, so maybe Mary had misread the depth of her grief. This evening may have been too tiring for her. Disappointed that Ari was overwhelmed she called for one of the drivers to take her home.

As Ari sat in the back of the car, tears poured miserably down her face. She hadn't thought that Seb was only interested in her for her money but what did she expect? She knew nothing about his sort. The idea that he had nicknamed her the Merry Widow and was bragging about her to his brother and friends horrified her. She was reminded of the night when she had first gone looking for Greg in the pub. He was drunk and a girl was sitting on his lap. Loudly he'd announced to the table that, before them stood his ball and chain, and warned them all that they didn't have to marry the first girl they knocked up. Ari had run out of the pub in tears and had never again gone looking for him when he was late coming home. Now, as she sat surrounded by yards of crushed silk billowing out on either side of her, tiny in the darkness, out of her depth and feeling ridiculously let down, she felt even worse than she had then. Previously when she had mistaken his conversation about the horse she had been embarrassed. Now she was heartbroken at her foolishness.

Mercifully the house was quiet as she slipped inside. Heading upstairs she peeled off all the trappings of her new persona. Lying down on her large cool bed, she was once more Ariana, alone.

27

The following morning Ari woke up slow and sluggish, remnants of last night's clothes and jewellery lay scattered across the floor, but for once she didn't care about the mess. She dragged on a pair of trackies and a warm dressing gown and headed downstairs. Flicking on the kettle, she realised she was up before anyone else and looking at the clock she realised that she was up ahead of most people. Although probably not the dairymen. Farms had to be run, animals to be milked and fed, bakers had to have their ovens hot and running to provide everyone with their daily bread. Nurses were wandering through the wards ensuring that patients had slept comfortably through the night. There was a whole raft of people getting up early to look after others. And this was her as well. Last night may have been work, but it was the easy comfortable sort of work, eating good food, drinking fine wine, chatting in pleasant company. Oh well, maybe not. But here at five am, here when the world was silent and still, here was where the real work started, here was where she took care of others.

Grabbing her coffee and a hot water bottle she headed off to the study and began pulling out plans and ledgers.

The day passed in a paperchain of appointments made, documents read, and notes scribbled. Thank God for Wendy, mused Ari. Only breaking the day to eat with the children she spent the rest of it working, happy with how well the boys had taken to their new life. By the end of the day she had a plan of action and a busy week ahead of her. Sitting down with the boys she explained that she was going to have a lot of work on over the next few weeks and she wouldn't see them much. Unfortunately, she'd chosen to tell them this devastating piece of news whilst they were watching their favourite TV show and their fragile spirits took this blow with a shrug and a quick return to the screen. Suitably chastened, Ari returned to the study, only pausing to sweep Dragon off the sofa.

Over the next few weeks, Ari walked the length of the proposed route and explored the beach and land for the new eco-village. She spent every day popping into the local town asking questions at the mobile library, doctors' surgery and playgroups. She chatted to managers, shop owners, and the general public to get a feel for what the genuine opinion was about the suggested development. Everything was informal but slowly she built up a picture of life in the town. Having come from London she was staggered to discover that buses stopped after six and shops and libraries also closed early. She had had an idea in her head about how lovely life in the countryside was, but she was beginning to spot that as usual, the grass was absolutely not greener. Although in fairness, they did actually have grass in the countryside. There was very little grass where she'd grown up.

After her informal conversations she then started speaking to other people, off the record, but in a more formal manner. Having got a few things clear in her head she rang Sebastian and suggested a meeting. He had called her the night after the dinner party, but she had put him off. She was angry with herself and with him and would have preferred to have nothing to do with him. However, the unpleasant fact was that she needed his help if her scheme was to work, and he needed hers if he was to beat the developers.

Finally, the morning of the planning meeting arrived. It had rained all night and the morning arrived wet and gloomy but nothing was going to dampen Ari's spirits. The rest of her sisters had all turned up over the past forty-eight hours ready to back her scheme and their roles within it. Arriving at the council offices they splashed in through wet puddles and shook off coats that steamed in the stuffy offices. Given the importance of the hearing, they were in the largest room and Ari saw lots of familiar faces from the town and neighbouring villages, as well as local farms. Sebastian and his family were also present and although she briefly waved and smiled at Mary she didn't go over.

"Ariana, my dear, could I have a moment of your time?" Even without turning around Ari knew the sound of Peter Ghrab's oily voice. Looking up, she smiled politely.

"Mr Ghrab, how pleasant. Can we talk after the meeting, I'm trying to concentrate on my notes?"

Peter looked put out, "Actually, it is rather urgent, you haven't signed the transfer of sale documents yet..."

At that moment the clerk called the meeting to order and Ari was reprieved from making a reply.

Having called the meeting to order the council began to run through various smaller issues and the afternoon wore on. God how she wanted to be back at home, listening to the birds singing and the wind blowing through the trees and, startled, Ari realised that here in this horrible stuffy room was the first time that she had truly thought of Wiverton as home.

"We now come to planning application XRG/124-7865."

The proposal was put forward and Shining Horizons were offered the chance to say a few words in support of their application. They had clearly hired a planning consultant who knew all the right buzzwords. Ari sat patiently, waiting for the right one and then stood up asking if she might make a point of order?

The clerk smiled at her, "This isn't a courtroom, we don't make points of order."

"Oh, my apologies," Ari blushed furiously, "I didn't mean to be rude or interrupt but something he just said was factually inaccurate. Should I wait until later?"

The speaker coughed and frowning at Ari assured her and the assembled room that nothing he had said was inaccurate.

Ari looked back to the clerk for guidance.

"Well, briefly if you will, miss. For the record if you could just give your name and what you think is inaccurate and we shall let him proceed. Yes?"

"Of course, Your Honour, thank you."

"Well, this still isn't a court and I'm not a judge but thank you for the pay rise." There was a general murmur of amusement, the meeting had been long and boring and any excuse for a little bit of light relief was welcome. People leant forward to see what the young woman had to say; it was always fun to watch stuffed shirts get knocked off their perch and they hoped this girl had something good up her sleeve.

Ari cleared her throat. "Thank you. My name is Ariana de Foix, and I am The Countess Wiverton. The representative for Shining Horizons just stated that they own the land on which they will build a feeder road to the development. I own that land, I haven't sold it to them and, after much consultation with my family and people in the surrounding area," Ari paused for effect, "I will never sell it to them."

The room erupted to cheers and jeers, the local journalist got on his phone to call for a photographer, and the clerk had to keep shouting for everyone to be quiet. Ari didn't dare look over at Ghrab but given the pinpricks she was feeling all over her skin, she knew that he was giving her daggers. She kept her face calm and kept looking at the clerk who was now looking back at her with a curious smile. He knew she had twisted proceedings to make a dramatic impact and now he had to decide if he was going to slap her down or allow her to continue, though in light of what she had just said, it did rather stop the entire proceedings in their tracks. Amused and a little admiringly he decided to give her the benefit of the doubt.

"Good afternoon, Countess, you appear to have caught a few people on the hop. Might it not have been a good idea to tell Shining Horizons that you weren't planning on selling them the land."

Ari smiled, "Well I think they rather assumed and forgot to ask me if I was okay with that."

From the side, Ari heard Peter Ghrab cry out that she was lying and that everything had been arranged with her uncle, "It was a gentleman's agreement!"

Ari coughed and looked back to the clerk and then looking herself up and down she said, "Well, I'm afraid, as is probably obvious, I am not a gentleman."

There was more laughter now and whilst Ari thought she might have the crowd on her side, she knew they only supported the team that gave the best showing. What she needed was the council's support and she was desperately willing the clerk to ask her one key question.

"This proposal will bring much-needed jobs and facilities into the area. A hospital would have been wonderful. Did you have something else in mind?" he asked, and Ari relaxed.

"I do." Ari waited for the room to quieten down and then she outlined what she had been working on over the past few weeks. "In the first place, I have recently been speaking to government officials, and it appears they have no plans to fund any new, what they term cottage hospitals. So Shining Horizons may well build the hospital but there will be no money to actually run it. At best it will become a private hospital."

There were mutters around the room, but Ari rushed on, she needed to keep the momentum going.

"That said, the town of Saxburgh is in a difficult position finding itself the victim of council cuts imposed by the necessity of an economic downturn and, also, in some small part, by the downturn in fortunes of my own family. Through no fault of their own, the lives of people living in Saxburgh have been curtailed and hampered over the past few years and I plan to do something about that. This morning, I submitted plans to the planning offices downstairs to build a new community centre on land owned by the estate on the edge of the town. It will house a new doctors' surgery, a library, and a citizen's advice centre. This advice centre will be a small practice, but it will be open seven days a week nine am to seven pm. It will be run by trained professionals and will be fully funded by the Wiverton

Estate. It will also be free to any resident of Saxburgh and neighbouring villages. We are also refurbishing our vacant houses in the town and will be offering them at affordable rents to those that need a home. Previous tenants will be getting first refusal. Work started on these this morning. We know we have got a lot wrong in the past few years, but we hope to start putting things right again. In addition to this, we will build a cycleway and footpath leading from the new community centre over our land and towards the land by the Flint-Hyssop estate and down toward the beach."

With that, she sat down and the room once more exploded. Her eyes closed. Ari waited for the next move, hoping that everyone would play their part, even if it was unwittingly.

"Let me speak, let me speak!" roared Peter Ghrab at the clerk.

The clerk finally got the room back in order again. "Countess Wiverton, thank you for your astonishing and generous comments." He was interrupted once more by Peter, demanding to speak.

The clerk glared at him. All along, this man and his minions had bullied and sneered at the council staff, accusing them of incompetency when things didn't run fast enough and of bias when it looked like things weren't going their way. "If you would avoid interrupting me, Mr Ghrab, I was just thanking the Countess for her comments and generous donation to the town and was then about to give you a chance to reply. Please proceed."

Ari sat still and silent praying that the final pincer was about to close.

"We applaud the Countess's offer of a little drop-in centre. I'm sure everyone will be delighted and of course, new wallpaper is always a welcome sight in a slum tenancy, but Shining Horizons are also talking about building state-of-the-art homes on land that she seems to have forgotten she doesn't actually own!"

He waited for a laugh but was only greeted by stony silence. No one had liked the comment about slums. He went to clear his throat but as he did a clear deep voice interrupted.

"No, she doesn't own it," Sebastian came to his feet, "but I do."

This time the clerk had to threaten to empty the public gallery if they didn't pipe down.

Seb continued, "This morning I bought Hyssop Lakes back from the current owner and am delighted that it is back within my family's holdings. We will be ensuring that the cycle and footpath lead all the way to the beach, and we will be building hides and will continue to treasure the area as a nature reserve available to everyone. We are also looking at ways to ensure that Saxburgh town once again recovers its spirit and returns to the thriving hub it once was. The first of which is that we will be working in partnership with the Wiverton Estate to deliver a working business hub for start-ups and those who want to get back into work, or need help growing their businesses. We are sorry that it took the greed of external property developers to open our eyes to our own neglect, but we have learnt our lessons and I hope that we will all benefit from that."

And with that, Peter Ghrab and the staff of Shining Horizons stood up and walked out of the chambers.

28

"Motion dismissed!" shouted Tony, and the champagne corks flew.

After the planning officers had dismissed the case, Seb invited everyone concerned back to the house. Having watched the plans Ari had put in place develop over the past few weeks Seb had been convinced she was going to win, more importantly so was the then owner of Hyssop Lakes who had agreed on the price that Seb had offered originally. It was less than the developer's offer, but Ari's proposal had made it increasingly unlikely that they would ever get those plans passed. Instead, he had settled this morning for a guaranteed sum rather than a speculative deal with Shining Horizons. The minute the money and deeds had transferred, Seb had gone shopping and filled the house up with drinks and snacks. It was an altogether less formal affair than his brother's previous party, but no less a celebration and the champagne was now flowing freely. The only dampener to the entire event had been Ariana's change in demeanour towards him. He had been enjoying her company over the past few months and he had begun to feel that it might be reciprocated. He had gone slowly, respectful of her recent loss and, even if nothing romantic happened, he had hoped they might become friends. They had had a lovely evening or at least he had, Ari had looked beautiful and she was so funny and clever that he'd felt that he was falling hopelessly head over heels in love with her. And then nothing. Door slam, cold shoulder, thank you and goodnight. He had no idea what he had done but suddenly, Ari could barely look him in the eye and would only talk to him about her plans for the estate. Even while she was shutting him out, he was in awe of her ideas and her work ethic, she was dynamite and if it was possible, he fell for her just a little bit more. Now he stood chatting to others celebrating their change in fortunes and kept glancing over at Ari at the other side of the room.

She was laughing with Janet Burbidge who had just asked her to forgive her for the umpteenth time, for calling her names the first time they met. Her glass was empty and just as she was looking for a top-up, Geoffrey turned up with a bottle and a little bow. Janet sloped away; Geoffrey wasn't her cup of tea at all. Ari smiled up at him, she wasn't sure about him either, he seemed basically nice but also somewhat reserved and maybe a bit intimidating. Currently, he also looked a little damaged.

"What happened to your eye?" she asked, thanking him for her refill.

Oddly he laughed and then looked a little shamefaced. "Hmm, I got that over you, to be honest. I goofed a bit. I do that sometimes, goof things up. I'm brilliant at figures, I mean actually brilliant, but human beings? Well, then I slip up a bit."

Ari looked puzzled, "Over me?"

"Hmm, yes, the other week at the dinner party I was chatting to some of the team and mentioned who would be there and I mentioned you and referred to you as 'a widow as wealthy as you were merry'." Seeing Ari hitch her breath he rushed to say, "I hadn't meant to be rude. I guess I just didn't think. However, when Seb heard about it last week, he lost his temper and pointed out with his fists just how rude I was. So. Sorry. More fizz?" he said as Ari knocked her glass back.

"No thanks. Can you excuse me?" said Ari, her heart thumping, as she headed towards where Seb was standing by himself watching the room. She leant on the sideboard beside him. Both stood side by side looking out over the party.

She cleared her throat, "I heard something that someone said about me, and I took it the wrong way. And I thought it was you that had said it. And I was upset, and I took it out on you. Sorry. In the words of your brother. I goofed."

Seb groaned, "Merry Widow?"

"Yep, when that idiot, Jim, said Flint-Hyssop was after the rich merry widow. I got the names confused and thought he meant you. Sorry." Ari finished her glass and continued to look across the room. Refusing any chance of eye contact with Seb.

"God, please don't apologise," he said.

For a few moments, they both continued to lean against the sideboard, their hands almost touching. Ari felt remarkably happy and she realised it had nothing to do with the successful hearing. As she stood there, her heart softly pounding, Seb hooked his little finger over hers. Saying nothing and not looking at each other they continued to stand side by side, neither prepared to break the moment, and Ari knew that she was in trouble.

Tilting his head towards her he suggested they pop outside to chat properly. Out on the patio, Seb led her away from the smokers and they sat in the shadows watching the insects flitting in and out of the nightlights scattered around the borders.

Seb cleared his throat. "This has been a good day."

Ari laughed, "You have no idea. It's silly but I've hated the idea that you called me a merry widow.

And now I hate the fact that I could have thought that of you."

"Ariana, what you have gone through over the past few months has been incredible, and I've only witnessed a glimpse of it. I am in awe of you and can hardly take offence if you believed something when you are feeling so unsure of yourself. I've watched you arrive; grieving, terrified, brittle and vulnerable, and you have been thrown into a world that not only are you expected to understand but also to lead and, remarkably, despite all the crap thrown at you, you have risen to the top. Seriously, you are completely amazing, and I am sorry that my family gave you even a moment of grief, let alone weeks of disappointment."

Ari sat still beside him, unable to reply. He made her sound like some sort of superhero, when she was just doing what had to be done. She was never usually at a loss for words but now she was utterly adrift; what did this glorious man want? She was desperate not to throw herself at his feet which she knew she would do in a heartbeat. She had the boys to think of and her new life, she couldn't go around just having random flings with the first handsome man that looked her way. Instead of words, she leant against him and placed her head on his shoulder. Seb twisted his body slightly and wrapped his arm around her, his hand resting on her waist, tenderly pulling her closer towards him, sheltered and warm.

Seb sat there and realised that he never wanted this moment to end but was also aware that Ari had buried her husband less than a year ago. He couldn't rush things, God she was probably still in love with him, it was such a young marriage. Convinced that he was probably going to lose Ari, he was also determined that he wouldn't scare her off.

"Tomorrow, shall we go out for the day? With the boys or by ourselves?"

"What do you have in mind?" she smiled, enjoying the warmth of his body and the mundanity of the conversation. Nothing felt pressurised, she was so giddy sitting beside him like this but also totally panicking.

"Shopping, sightseeing, bike ride, funfair? We still have the infamous Mustard Museum to explore?" said Seb, his suggestions getting sillier and sillier as they looked at the rain now falling beyond the lip of the gazebo roof.

"Okay, just us," decided Ari, "the girls can look after Leo and William. Come round in the morning and tell me what you have in mind. It will be lovely to not have to make a single decision."

"It's a date! Now the only decision you have to make is, do we walk or run back to the house?" And grabbing her hand he pulled her to her feet and they ran laughing across the lawn and burst into the party through the patio doors. Everyone turned at the noisy entrance as both Seb and Ari were soaking wet and laughing. Realising he had an audience, Seb picked up a spare glass of champagne and stepping away from Ari raised his glass and toasted her.

"Ladies and gentlemen, the Countess Wiverton, without whom today wouldn't have happened. Ariana!" And as Ari blushed, the assembled party laughed and cheered and saluted her. Ariana wasn't sure she'd ever been happier.

29

The following morning started slow and late, with lots of people padding around the manor in various states of pyjamas and baggies, knocking back Alka-Seltzers and black coffee. Wendy had rustled up a late fried breakfast and gradually the sisters were beginning to wake up. The night before over at Hyssop Hall had been great fun with everyone letting their hair down.

"Ariana, I can't find the children. Do you know where they are?"

All five heads snapped around to look at Wendy, standing by the door. Ari jumped out of her seat.

"What do you mean? When did you last see them?"

"About an hour ago, I left them sleeping in the playroom while I went to prepare their lunch. When I got back, they were gone."

"And Dragon?"

"Also gone."

Ari looked out the window and whilst it had finally stopped raining, the sky seemed to suggest it was a short reprieve.

"Okay. I'm sure it's nothing but let's split up. Wendy continue to search the house in case they are hiding, call for Dragon she's more likely to come running." Seeing that Aster and Pads were still in their pyjamas she told them to also join the indoor search party. "The rest of us let's head outside."

Shouting for Dickie, she explained what had happened and asked her to gather all the estate hands and start looking in the outlying sheds that the boys may be using as a den, again suggesting that calling for Dragon might help. She had the best hearing and wouldn't appreciate that she was in any sort of trouble.

Mr Billinge pulled up to the front of the house on his quad bike. "Here," he said handing out some walkie-talkies, "Wendy just told me the boys have gone AWOL. I've checked the shed and their bikes are gone too." He then suggested that everyone used them to keep in touch. "Now they think they are on a big adventure no doubt and having the time of their lives and haven't even given a thought to how much they're scaring their mummy. Your boys are perfectly fine, hen. Don't you worry. Now let's go find them."

Ari listened to Mr Billinge and felt her rising panic steadily calming down again. He was right of course; she knew she was overreacting but her children weren't with her and she didn't know where they were. It was hard to stay calm.

Just as the party was preparing to split up, Wendy came running down the front steps, all sense of decorum gone.

"Ari. The film on TV, they were watching Indiana Jones. The scene with the rushing river and they were talking how cool it was, not like their river, and then I said that our river looks a bit like that when it rains."

Before Wendy had even got to the end of her sentence Ari felt her heart freeze. Her panic didn't so much rise as explode as she realised that that was exactly where her two adventurous little boys had gone. They had seen it had stopped raining and had decided to go and see if their little river was also a raging torrent.

There was no need for words. In fact, Ariana wasn't certain if she could even manage them as, jumping on the back of the quad, she and Mr Billinge raced off down to the closest point of the river whilst the others ran towards the estate Land Rover. As she bounced across the field, she noted another Landy coming up the drive. In front Mr B had opened up his walkie-talkie, "Dickie, love, looks like Sir Sebastian is arriving at the house. If he has news of the boys let us know, otherwise send him down to us at the river."

Ari continued shouting the boys' names, although she wasn't sure if they could hear her over the wind in the trees. Before they even reached the river, it started raining again. As they sped down the field, along the mown path toward the riverbank, Ari saw two brightly coloured bikes, dumped in the short grass. Mr B shot past them and right down to the river's edge. Ari jumped off and started screaming for the boys.

The river in front of her was a nightmare. Gone was the shallow beach where golden lights had played on the small pebbles below. Usually, the river gently flowed under the willows on the other side, creating a deep still pool, perfect for a little swim. Now it was a violent and angry swirling mess of black and white water. Bits of branches rushed past, and it was higher and wider than she had ever seen it leaving her immobilised with horror.

"There!" bellowed Mr B, over the roar of the river. Further down the bank a tree had fallen and was lying in the river. On its trunk clung two small terrified boys. As the twins saw her, they started screaming her name, panic breaking their voices, as they sobbed and howled for their mummy.

Ari overtook Mr B as they ran to the tree. The trunk was only about two-foot-wide and she was uncertain if it would take her weight or if climbing on

345

to it, might loosen it from its precarious mooring, sending it tumbling along the river and taking her children with it. Holding onto its roots she lowered herself into the river but was instantly aware that it was far deeper than she had realised, and that the force of the water was too much for her.

"It's too strong," she shouted at Mr B as he helped her back up onto her feet. "I'm going out onto the trunk."

"Ariana! Wait. The others will be here shortly."

Ari ignored him and began crawling out along the tree, inching her way towards the children. The trunk at this section was smooth and Ari had to move carefully to maintain her balance as the water below tugged at her legs as they straddled the trunk. Every so often a shift in the river meant a wave of water would surge around her hips. Further along the tree, she could see that the boys were getting more buffeted. Leo was closest and had his arms and legs wrapped around a branch, his body between the flow of the river and the branch. The slowness of her progress killed her, but eventually, she edged towards Leo and finally wrapped her arms around him.

"Hang on, Will. I'm coming. I'll have you in a minute as well." Assessing the situation, Will seemed to be better wedged amongst ivy and branches but he was also sitting in the fastest part of the river and was getting knocked about by white water and other debris. As she watched, a large plank of wood sped past, hitting the tree and then, swirling on, was sucked back down under the water and rushed out of sight.

Over the noise of the river Ari heard shouting and looking back towards the bank, she saw Aster inching along the slender tree trunk towards her, a rope tucked under her arm. At the edge of the river, a group of people stood, including a white-faced Seb. Lying forward on the tree Aster took the rope and held it as far forward to Ari as she could. The trunk where Ari and Leo were wedged was now narrow enough that Ari could wrap her legs around it and lock her ankles together. Leaning forward she grabbed the rope and pulled it towards her. Over the rain and the river, she could hear the cheer from the bank.

"Now, Leo, this is going to be really challenging but I know you can do it because you are so big and brave. I need you to hold onto this rope and don't let go of it until you are back on dry land. You need to shuffle along the tree, never letting go of the rope and get to Aunty Aster. Then she'll help you get back to the bank." Waiting for him to understand what was happening she yelled to Aster, "When you get

Leo, both of you get back to the bank. I'll hold the rope at this end."

She saw now that some of the men, including Seb, were standing downstream on the riverbank with extra ropes. Presumably to try and catch anyone that slipped off the trunk.

With infinite slowness Ari and Leo swapped places and then Leo, shaking and sobbing, inched towards Aster keeping the rope tucked under his arm. As he reached Aster they both slowly moved back to the bank. Looking towards them, Ari could see that the level of the river had risen some more and the trunk was now almost underwater. Feeling sick she looked back at Will and gave him a big smile and a thumbs up. At that moment she heard another cheer and looked back to see Leo on the bank being surrounded by hugs and blankets.

Knotting the rope around her waist, Ari left the safety of the branch and edged toward Will. The power of the water was terrifying, but she wasn't going to leave her son. If they were going to die, they were going to die together. Crying, she inched further. Her weight was making the now slender trunk bounce but it didn't seem to be any greater an issue than the brute force of the river, which was savage, tearing at everything, sheer force breaking and pulling things down in its path. One small tree would soon be dispatched, wrenched along by the deadly current.

There was, at least, now more to cling on to. The ivy was thicker here and there were lots of branches. Ari could see that Will was firmly embedded and as she got closer, she realised that Dragon was also beside him looking just as worried as he did.

"Dragon ran on to the tree and got scared so I went to get her but then I got scared and Leo came to get me, but the river kept getting bigger." Will was clearly trying to sound brave and reasonable, but his voice was shaking the whole time and he kept sobbing between pauses.

Shouts from the bank alerted Ari and as she looked, they were all pointing upstream. Heading towards them was a large bush, it seemed to rise out of the water and then be pulled down again, it was turning constantly so one minute she saw flowers the next, splintered roots. Shouting at Will to hang on she tightened her grip around him and Dragon and braced both legs around the tree trunk. The bush hit them, and Ari felt her clothing being tugged and torn as the bush tried to continue past. "I love you, William. You and Leo are the best things in the whole universe. Do not let go of the rope!" She would not cry, she would not let Will see how scared she was, she'd be damned if his last impressions of life were of fear and panic. "We'll be home soon. Don't worry. And you can have as many marshmallows in your hot chocolate as you want, okay."

Will tried a weak smile at his mother but all he could see was twigs and leaves tearing at her hair. It looked like the trees and bushes had risen out of the riverbed and were trying to eat her and drag her back down under the water. With a wrench, Ari felt her hair released and the bush finally found passage underneath the tree and shot away, bobbing up twenty metres further along the river.

"And a flake?"

"As many as you want," sobbed Ari.

She knew time was running out; the river was still rising, they were now up to their waists in water, and the river was becoming faster and deadlier. They could no longer wait for rescue, they were going to have to try to make their way back along the tree.

"Listen, Will, the rescue team will be here any minute now but if they don't get here soon, we'll have to try and make it back along the tree ourselves. Can you do that?"

As she spoke a large piece of wood popped up in front of the tree. Thinking she saw a way out, Dragon leapt onto it, the river whisked her away, and

Will, trying to save his dog, lurched after her. Ari lunged for Will and in a moment of horror found herself dragged under the icy water.

30

The shock of the cold was nothing to the sudden tumbling buffeting feeling. One hand was still on Will and with the other, she tried to swim up to the surface whilst pulling him towards her. She felt a great tug on her waist where the rope was tied and then her head broke the surface. She took a giant gulp of air, dragging Will up out of the water, screaming his name. Spluttering, he started shouting for Dragon, but Ari gripped him tightly towards her. With one arm wrapped around him and the other holding on to the rope, she prayed to every God that she had ever heard of, that the team on the riverbank would be able to pull them to the side.

Slowly she felt herself being dragged sideways as she gripped the rope and Will. With each passing second the force of the river lessened until they reached the bank. Hands stretched down grabbing them both and dragged them out. Slowly someone managed to remove the rope from her grip but nothing would dislodge her hand from Will's jumper. As they were lying on the wet verge, Leo broke free of his blankets and came running towards them. For a moment the three of them just lay there coughing and crying and hugging.

"How are they, John?" asked Sebastian. "Do they need to go to hospital?"

Dr John Cooper had been the local doctor for many decades but had never seen Seb so distressed.

"They're all fine. The sisters are all up there and I think the three of them will soon be asleep. I'll come back in the morning with a shot against Weil's disease. They also need to keep an eye on any persistent coughs in case they inhaled water, but that's pretty unlikely, even in cases like this. I think in a few days' time they will be as if it never happened. Although I think it will take a while longer for them to get over the loss of the dog."

At that moment the door opened and Clementine stormed in.

"What the hell are you still here for?" she snarled at Seb. "The boys upstairs are hysterical. It's been less than a year since their da died and now they must face the fact that their dog, that they probably loved even more than him, is dead. Jesus Christ, they nearly died. We almost lost our sister and nephews because some stupid jumped up prat wanted to play at happy families and thought it would be a good idea to give them a dog whilst he cosied up to their mother. You total useless waste of space."

Seb recoiled from the sheer fury on Clementine's face. He tried to defend himself but realised he was without any counter-argument, he had barged into their lives and it had nearly killed them.

"Now my dear..." began the doctor, but Clem cut him off.

"Don't make excuses for him, Doctor. Ari's started vomiting, can you come and check her over again?" Swinging back to Seb as she got to the door, "And you! Get out of the house right now, and don't you ever come back."

John gave Seb an apologetic smile and followed Clem up the staircase. Shaken, Seb stood up and quietly let himself out the front door. Opening his phone, he started ringing everyone he knew that lived near the river and asked them to keep an eye out for the body of a little dog. Firing up the Landy he drove down to the next spot along the riverbank, swinging his torch and calling out, in the vain hope that somehow Dragon had managed to swim for the edge. The wind pulled at his clothes, his shoes were caked in mud, and he was soaked through. For hours Seb checked the riverbank, walking a stretch and then going back to the car to drive on to the next section. The branches of the trees swung above his head in the dark and occasionally he would be hit by twigs and leaves. He was immune to the external nightmare

unfolding around him as the storm continued to pick
up force. Clem's words rang in his ears and he kept
seeing that horrific moment when both Will and Ari
seemed to slip and disappear under the frothing water,
the rope pulled down beneath the branches. He was
just heading back to the car for another section when
his phone rang.

"Seb darling, Dai the vet has just rung. The Pig
and Whistle said that one of their patrons just found a
little, wet spaniel in the car park, they think it's been
in the river. They called Dai and he knew you were
out looking."

The Pig and Whistle was miles away right by
the river's edge. Surely it wasn't possible that more
than one spaniel had fallen in the river tonight.
Thanking his mother, he jumped into the car and
headed towards the pub. As he arrived, he heard the
barman call time. He was surprised by how late it was
but then he saw Dai over by the fire holding a small
bundle in a towel, surrounded by a group of people.

Dai the Vet was a well-loved local vet who had
transferred to his Norfolk practice years ago. When
he'd arrived, people had asked what to call him. Back
home he was known as Dai the Vet, in his hometown
back in Wales lots of people had similar names, so to
stop any confusions people picked up descriptions to
go with their names, and the habit grew. The librarian

was Ken the Books, there was Dai the milk, but the best was Jones the Bill. Paul Jones was a town dentist who had switched from the NHS to private. He had desperately tried to get people to revert to Jones the Drill, which he had never much cared for either, but Jones the Bill bothered him. His wife told him to stop mentioning it. Not because she thought the name might change back but she was fed up of his explaining to her every evening, the actual costs involved in an implant. And so Dai the Vet arrived in Norfolk and brought his name with him. He loved living here but sometimes he missed the mountains. A few years back he'd heard that a gorgeous Welsh woman had moved onto Hayholt Farm. Fooling no one, in his role of the local vet, he went to make a routine call but was disappointed to discover that whilst she was indeed gorgeous, she was half his age and even worse she was utterly immune to his charms. She was clearly besotted with her new boss, and when he heard that she and Heidi had set up home together a few months later he didn't blink an eye. He still hadn't met anyone he hoped might become Mrs Dai the Vet, but he had settled into the community and was well known and liked. Best yet, he could be relied on to come out to a call at any hour of the day. Like now, sitting in a pub, warming up a little dog. As the bar door swung open everyone looked up to see a wild-eyed dishevelled man. It took a moment before Dai recognised him, he looked so different from his normal style.

"My God, boy. Look at the state of you! Did you go in as well? Now, do you recognise this little girl?"

Removing the towel from its head Seb saw two dark appealing eyes look around and as soon as they saw Seb, the young dog wriggled in the vet's arms. Putting her gently on the floor, Dragon ran straight towards Seb, licking his face and wagging her tail as Seb held her aloft.

"Well, I guess that's a yes then. Where did you say she went in?" When Seb told him, Dai and the others whistled in amazement; that little dog sure had a powerful guardian angel. With Dragon back in her blanket and stowed in a cardboard box, Seb headed back to the manor. If he could do nothing else right, at least he could make sure that when the boys woke up, their beloved pet would be back in their arms.

When he got to the hall, he could see that the lights were still on thankfully. He'd have woken the house if he had to, to reunite the boys with Dragon but happily he only had to knock. He was just letting himself in when Clementine walked into the hall.

"You just let yourself in then?" The hostility in her voice hadn't dropped a single degree. "I thought I made it clear earlier on. You are not welcome. Ari never wants to see you again."

Seb bore the brunt of her tirade, the thought that Ari never wanted to see him again churning him up inside but completely understandable. Without speaking he unzipped his wax jacket and lifted Dragon out. Clemmie stared in wonder.

"Is that Dragon?!"

"Yes, she was found a few miles downstream. I thought it would be good for the boys to wake up and find her in bed with them?"

Clemmie was beside herself. "Oh my God, that's incredible. I'll take her up straight away."

As Seb passed the puppy over, Clem gave Dragon a massive cuddle, nuzzling her face into her coat, her eyes wet with unshed tears.

Looking back up at Seb she said, "This doesn't change anything you know." Her voice was no longer angry but no less sincere. "Thanks for returning Dragon but they don't need you. You got what you wanted, the planning decision has been rejected, so it's best if, you know, just leave them to get on with it. The boys have only just lost their father, they don't need a string of uncles in their lives, do they? And think what it would do to Ari? Best you bugger off now before you cause any more harm. I'm sorry if I sound harsh but she's my sister and we would all do anything to protect each other."

Giving Dragon a final little pat on the head, Seb turned and left the house. Clem's earlier attack on him and her measured words just now, helped him see the light. Ari was a grieving widow and, in his enthusiasm, and feelings for her, he just hadn't stopped to think of her emotional state. The idea that she might have been politely bearing his visits was appalling to him. How could he have been so blind?

As Ari slowly woke up, she was aware of the snuggly duvet over her. She opened her eyes and realised that both boys were to one side of her and soundly asleep. Gently stroking their hair, she relaxed again, the bed was soft and warm and whilst it was light outside, she was in no hurry to get up. As she drifted off again, she realised that one of the girls must have put a hot water bottle in the bed, there was a warm little lump by her foot. She moved away from the warmth and was startled when it moved. Peering over the top of her duvet was a brown little nose and the happy waggy face of Dragon. Amazed, she sat bolt upright and as the puppy tumbled down through the covers, she bounced back up and jumped between Ari and the boys. The kerfuffle disturbed the twins and chaos ensued, their bleary eyes wide and wet within seconds as they hugged and wept over the little dog with Ari also hugging and crying happy tears all over them. There was a knock at the door and Paddy poked her head around, beaming at the little group.

"Who's up for breakfast? I've made pancakes." The boys and Dragon tumbled out of bed and went running downstairs, and Ari smiled as the noise downstairs increased as the boys bounded around with their aunts.

"Who found Dragon?"

Smiling, Paddy told her how Seb had apparently turned up last night soaked to the skin. "He's pretty fabulous, isn't he?"

All Ari could do was grin back in return. "What do you think I should do?"

"How about going over and saying thank you?"

Ari rolled her eyes at her sister, "Well obviously, but I think I ought to let him wake up first!"

Paddy walked over to the window and drew back the heavy curtains letting bright daylight into the room. "It's two o'clock in the afternoon. I imagine he's awake."

"Well, I'd better get over there right away before he thinks I'm being rude."

"Sure," drawled Paddy, "that's why you're rushing over. So you don't look rude."

Ari was going to dash straight out but Paddy pointed out that she hadn't had a shower or bath after her river dunking and that she wasn't sure how appealing Seb would find Eau de River Mud. An hour later, all nice and clean, if somewhat grazed and bruised, she was pulling up in front of Seb's. As she entered the house Mary came down to meet her and offered her some tea. She appeared uncomfortable and Ari was disappointed not to find Seb. However, she didn't want to seem rude and joined Mary in her lovely sitting room. The large windows all looked out over parkland that stretched out into the distance.

There was an awkward silence and then Mary seemed to recollect herself. "How are the boys? Tony and I were so upset when Seb told us what had happened. It's incredible that nothing worse happened and dear Dragon survived!"

Placing her teacup down Ari beamed at Mary, "Yes I know, that's why I came over, to thank Seb in person and invite him over for supper."

Mary paused and took another sip of tea. The room was silent except for a grandfather clock ticking.

Then as she put her cup and saucer down on the table, she looked at Ari with concern, her eyebrows knitted together and her lips pursed as though she couldn't think how to say what was needed.

"I'm afraid you've just missed him. His flight left at noon."

"Flight?" Ari was confused, she certainly didn't know much about Seb's life, but she was sure that if he had mentioned he was going abroad she would have remembered.

Mary looked at Ari with pity and in-built fury at her son, she had no idea why he had announced this morning that he was flying out to the Bahamas. He'd made up some nonsense about needing to catch up with work, that he'd been letting things slip and he wanted to work without distraction. In fact, it rather left a massive workload on Tony's shoulders. All the plans that he and his father had made yesterday after the court decision would now have to be done by Anthony alone. At first, Mary assumed he must have had a massive row with Ari. It was clear to her that her youngest son had fallen hopelessly in love. Every conversation led back to Ariana, every observation someway linked back to her estate and he talked about the boys incessantly. She didn't think he was fully aware of his feelings yet, but both Mary and Anthony were certain, and quite frankly she couldn't have been happier. Ariana was a wonderful girl who she had been looking forward to welcoming into the family. And the thought of having two little grandsons living nearby filled her with joy. But here was Ari, clearly eager to see Seb. Whatever his problem was, Ari knew nothing about it.

"Yes. Well, you know what a workaholic he is. Now that the planning application has been settled, he's decided to get away from it all and catch up on the backlog of other business matters that he's been putting on hold." Mary could barely bring herself to look at Ari's crushed expression.

"Oh yes, of course," said Ari with an unconvincing laugh. "There's no rest for the wicked is there? Well, please thank him on our behalf when you next speak to him."

Brushing imaginary crumbs off her lap, Ari stood up and made her excuses. Mary felt wretched and reminded Ari that she and the boys were most welcome to pop in anytime. From Ari's polite agreement she knew that she never would.

Driving home Ari berated herself as an utter fool. Seb was a lovely person that had helped her find her feet and had worked alongside her towards a common goal in improving the lives of the locals. Her stomach lurched; God was it all a ruse? Had he played her for a fool just so that she would stop the building of the road across her land? As terrified as she was, her heart told her that wasn't the case, Seb was a genuinely nice person, he had even brought back Dragon. He wouldn't have bothered if all he had been after was a victory in the planning department. This whole mess was her own silly fault for falling in love with the first man that had been kind to her. And she had fallen for him. Sitting drinking tea with Mary she'd realised that she was hopelessly in love with Sebastian and that she was an idiot. Why the hell did she think he would want to lumber himself with a widow and two children. Hardly what you would expect from your blushing bride.

By the time she returned to the manor she had managed to convince herself that it would be fine and breezed into the kitchen laughing and asking if there were any pancakes left. When the others asked when Seb was coming over she told them she was a wally and had forgotten that he was flying off to clear a whole backlog of work. The boys were disappointed but quickly diverted with the promise of another chocolate spread pancake. Of the sisters, only Clem seemed unconcerned, simply shrugging her shoulders, when the others looked at her with worried expressions. Finally, the day came to an end and Ari could stop smiling; curled up in bed with the boys for a second night, the little family fell asleep in each other's arms. As the morning came and her sisters gradually departed, the house became steadily quieter as each car crunched away down the gravel drive. When they had all gone Ari told Dickie and Wendy to take the next two days off and, in total privacy, Ari began to rebuild her carapace so that no one could see how broken she was.

31

September merged into October and then into November. Ari and the boys had attended bonfire parties but ignored Hallowe'en. The boys were still occasionally spooked by things and Ari felt that they had had enough terror recently. She also felt that they were less settled than they had been before the storm and their near drowning. From time to time they asked when Seb would be coming back and in desperation, Ari bought some kittens and another puppy, although Dragon was hardly a puppy now, more a boisterous teenager. The new animals kept everyone busy and whilst the dogs had to sleep downstairs, the two kittens had instantly claimed the bedrooms as their own domain. Ari still hadn't enrolled the boys into school, they would be five in January so, in theory, they should be in by now, but it wasn't yet mandatory. It was a decision that seemed too big for her to deal with for now.

Last month she had finally received the date for Greg's inquest, and she was surprised at how relieved she felt. That chapter in her life was nearly finally over and she hadn't realised until she saw the letter how much it had still been holding on to her.

Now she was sitting in the inquest courtroom. It was a large featureless box of a room, fluorescent lamps overhead lighting up the long rows of seats facing a large table. Presumably, this was where the coroner sat. Anyone making a statement would simply come to the front of the room. There were no podiums or boxes. The whole arrangement was plain and dull. Nothing to intimidate or overwhelm. Just a simple space to announce a ruling on how someone had come to meet their untimely death. No one was with her; she hadn't told her sisters and wondered if they were even aware of it. There was no Aster of course, as Ari hadn't told the police she had been there that night. No need to drag her into it as well. She looked up from her book as she became aware of someone walking towards her. Smiling she recognised PC Meg Lindon from all those months ago; she had two cups of coffee in her hand and offered one to Ari.

"This should be just a formality. It's pretty open and closed. Did you read the report?"

When Ari shook her head she continued, "I don't blame you, it can always be unnerving. It's rather clinical and not many people want to read about their loved ones like that. Anyway, like I said, I reckon the coroner will have us out of here in under an hour."

Ari thanked her and sipping her coffee she was relieved that it wasn't going to be a long drawn out affair, no fuss, no drama. At that moment the door opened, and Annette and Nigel walked in. Ari groaned. Mercifully as soon as they saw her, they walked to the other side of the room and sat down in silence. With a huge sigh of relief, Ari returned to her book, a brilliant piece of science fiction where the main protagonist loved tea as much as she did. Tea from a vending machine was akin to drinking out of a puddle.

There was some movement from the front of the room and the coroner called the inquest to account. Ari was asked to recount her last few moments with Greg and she replayed the row that they had had. She had already relived it for the police, but she thought with discomfort that it was probably the first time that his parents had heard it. She then sat in silence and heard from others how he had gone to the pub and had a good time. It was agreed that he was considerably drunk when he left the pub but not so inebriated that he couldn't walk. He had left alone. Listening to the story unfold, Ari found herself desperately sad for the young man that had made her laugh when they first met. He had changed from a happy, cocky Jack the Lad, into an embittered and aggressive young man and now she was listening to the final hours of his life as it came to an end. A policeman now stood up to explain how he had been called to the scene when a young couple had seen something suspicious in the canal. The doctor who carried out the post-mortem confirmed that Greg had died by drowning, a blow to the front of his head was evidence that he had slipped and fallen into the canal hitting his head on a submerged shopping trolley. It was this trolley that his small backpack had got snagged up in preventing him from rising back to the surface. The coroner said there was no evidence of him struggling and that he was likely unconscious from either the blow to the head or the alcohol. The report was read in silence broken only by a sob from Annette.

Nigel jumped up, "And what about her!" he shouted pointing to Ari. "She murdered my son and you're all sitting here pretending that she had nothing to do with it. My God. You heard her confess as much, they had had a row earlier in the evening. She followed him and shoved him in the river!"

The coroner asked for silence and when Nigel had settled down, he called PC Lindon and PC Moore for their testimony. The blood in Ari's ears was roaring and she was aware of people looking at her. She wanted to leave the room or scream, or cry, she didn't know which. Instead, she sat as still as a statue, her eyes locked on the coroner as she listened to the police report. PC Lindon confirmed that she had broken the news to Mrs Paxton. She was of the belief that it was the first that Mrs Paxton knew of her husband's death. When she asked her how Mrs Paxton had reacted, Ari remembered her laugh with shame, and listened as the police officer described her as having an emotionally charged reaction.

The officers had then spoken to neighbours to find out the state of the marriage and whilst it wasn't happy there was nothing to suggest foul play on Mrs Paxton's behalf. Ari had been unaware that the police had spoken to her neighbours, but she supposed it made sense. As the reports concluded, the coroner addressed the room and ruled that the death of Gregory Paxton was due to misadventure and there was no suggestion of foul play.

This time Annette jumped to her feet and started screaming that Ari was a murderer. Spitting at her and raving that she was going to get the courts to take her children away from her. Nigel jumped up beside his wife and shoved a bench out of his way, shouting that he'd have justice one way or another as he barged his way towards Ari. Terrified she jumped away from him as court officials rushed forward to restrain him. PC Lindon came over to Ari and quickly moved her back towards one of the coroner's inner offices.

Out in the outer room Ari could hear shouting and banging until gradually the noise died down.

"Can she really take my children away?" Ari asked, her teeth chattering.

Meg Lindon took a deep breath and shook her head. "Not a hope in hell, dear. My advice? Issue a restraining order against them. After today's performance, a sympathetic judge will be on your side."

Ari told her about the hate-filled letter that they had sent her denying the children.

Meg whistled, "What a piece of work. I reckon that will make your case watertight. I'll have to write this up and will be happy to recommend a restraining order."

At that moment her partner, PC Moore stuck his head around the door. "All clear. The pair of them are being detained until they calm down. Mr Paxton punched a police officer in the face so he's going to be charged with assault. Mrs Paxton then called the coroner some pretty foul names, so she's also being charged, with racial abuse. I would suggest you file a restraining order."

The two women laughed weakly. "One step ahead of you, Steve. I was already telling Ari here that we'd be supporting any such motion. "Now, Ari, you know what to do next don't you?"

Ari nodded, "Go home, hug my boys, and put the kettle on?"

"Yes, indeed, and then call your fancy lawyer and get those wheels in motion. Where is he by the way? I'm surprised you're here on your own."

Ari shrugged, "I didn't want a fuss. Hey ho."

The two police officers walked with her to her car and once they were happy that she was fit to drive they waved her on her way.

"Do you reckon she'll be alright?" Meg asked concerned as she watched the car pull away into the traffic.

Steve snorted, "What with all that money and land and a big fancy title?"

"Oh, shut up you twonk. She just looked so alone. It took me right back to when we first met her, struggling to keep it all together. It's not like she's had an easy life so far."

"You're too soft you are. That girl has a backbone made of iron. She's going to be just fine. Especially now that scumbag family are out of her life. Now come on, we'd better go and write this up and then you owe me lunch for calling me a twonk."

Meg punched him on the arm. "Fair enough you twonk!"

As Ari drove home, she felt shivery and clammy, her head was throbbing, and her throat kept tickling. By the time she came up the drive she was beginning to feel lousy but decided it was the shock of the last few hours coming out. All she needed was a cup of tea and a good night's sleep. In the morning she would do what the officers had suggested and issue a restraining order. Calling out that she was home she made her way to the kitchen and put the kettle on and then went in search of the children. There was a note on the pinboard saying that Wendy had taken them for a quick bike ride around the estate and they would be home shortly. As the kettle started whistling, she picked it up off the Aga just as Dickie walked in. Taking one look at Ari she shooed her over to the chair and made the tea for her.

"Worse than you expected?"

Ari's head throbbed, she didn't feel like a chat, and the tea smelt wrong. Pushing it away from her she shrugged.

"I was accused of murder; Greg's parents started a fight with the coppers, and I have been advised to issue a restraining order on them. Other than that, tickety-boo. Do you mind, I feel crap. Can you ask Wendy to stay on and put the boys to bed?"

With that Ari pushed her chair back and slowly left the room, the cup of tea still steaming on the table.

The following morning Dickie arrived at work and walked into the kitchen to find a scene of absolute chaos. There were cornflakes everywhere and the cats were drinking the milk that was dripping down from the work surface. A chair had been pushed up by the counter and a bag of sugar was also spilt along the worktop. Every lower door in the kitchen was open and the fridge door was wide open. Walking into the playroom she found both boys eating cornflakes on the carpet in front of the television and taking turns to lick the spoon in the chocolate spread jar.

"Boys! What is this mess?"

The boys looked up at Dickie with her arms folded and realised that they might, somehow, be in trouble.

"We made breakfast!"

"All by our own," piped up Leo. "Mummy said we could," he added a bit defensively.

"Hmm," said Dickie, "and did Mummy say you could eat on the carpet in front of the television?"

Both boys looked at each other. She hadn't specifically said they couldn't, she'd just sort of mumbled a bit and carried on sleeping.

Heading upstairs Dickie knocked on Ari's door and when there was no reply she entered quietly. Ari was asleep in bed; her face was flushed and sweaty and when Dickie put her hand on her forehead, she felt the fever that was already obvious. Shaking Ari awake she was relieved that Ari grumbled and swore at her, got up to go to the loo, and then ignoring her went straight back to sleep.

Heading back downstairs she cleaned up after the boys and decided to call the doctors to see if they recommended doing anything or just wait for the fever to break.

That night both Dickie and Wendy slept over after Doctor Cooper had called in. He ran a few tests but felt certain that Ari was just run down. However, he also took some bloods because he wasn't prepared to rule out other conditions following her near drowning. Both women looked at each other in alarm.

32

The following morning Ari was drifting in and out of consciousness and the fever still hadn't broken. Dickie called up the surgery and asked Dr Cooper to come over and see what was going on. She then called Nicoletta; of all the sisters she felt that Nicoletta had the best skills to get things mobilised quickly. Paddy would panic, Aster wouldn't bother to call the others, and Clemmie would start shouting. Sure enough, by the time she put the phone down, she'd received instructions to make up some of the guest rooms and that hopefully, all the sisters would be there tonight or tomorrow morning.

Another day passed with Ari slipping in and out of feverish dreams. Sometimes Dickie heard her calling out for her mother, sometimes for Seb. Once she sat bolt upright screaming Leo's name and then fell straight back to sleep.

The following morning all the sisters gathered in the dining room to eat breakfast and discuss the situation.

Almost immediately Nick rounded on Aster, "What I want to know is why the hell you weren't at the inquest and why you didn't tell the rest of us about it!"

"Well, I didn't know," bristled Aster, "why should anyone have told me about it?"

"Because you were there that night," snapped Clemmie.

"Oh, right. Well, Ari never told the police that, she didn't want me to get dragged into it." Aster shrugged, glaring at the others. It was not her fault her sister was ill. She felt bad enough as it was, she wasn't going to have the others make her feel worse.

"It's not like she phoned any of you up to say what was going on either. What does that say?"

Paddy felt awful, she knew exactly what it said, it meant Ari was still trying to protect her little sisters, rather than leaning on them for support.

"And where the hell is Seb? I thought he'd be with her."

"Yeah, right," drawled Nick, "not really the done thing to bring your new fella to your old fella's inquest is it?"

"He's not here anyway," said Aster, glad that the blame had moved away from her. "He left her the same day that we all left, remember, but he hasn't returned."

"Jesus," snarled Nick. "What a creep. I thought he genuinely liked her but all he wanted was to get his land back."

Paddy protested that there must be another explanation. He was clearly head over heels in love with Ari, there was no way he would leave her. Aster agreed and Nick had to concede that she had thought the same. In fact, she wouldn't have been surprised if there had been wedding bells ahead, the two of them so clearly enjoyed each other's company.

Clemmie shuffled awkwardly. "Ari doesn't like Seb, they were just working together."

Instantly the other sisters rounded on her. "Rubbish. She was absolutely smitten with him. Every time we talked on the phone, she'd casually bring up his name once or twice in conversation."

"Once or twice?" laughed Nick, "more like all the bloody time. Did she not mention him to you, Clem?"

Clem shook her head.

"Probably because you were too busy whining on about your own problems," needled Aster.

"That's not fair," said Clem, "it's sodding tough up there." But yes, she had rather monopolised the conversations over summer, but it was only because she was desperate to make a success of the Scottish enterprise. Goddammit, why was she always screwing things up? She took a deep breath, "Right, this might be one of my messes." And Clem went on to tell the other three how she had rounded on Seb and told him to get out of Ari's life.

"MIGHT be one of your messes? Jesus, Clem!" shouted Nick, "How could you be so sodding stupid?" Angry that Nick was shouting at Clem who had always been there for her when Ari was out working, Aster started shouting at Nick. Soon the noise from the dining room was loud with angry recriminations until a voice roared for silence and all four girls spun round to see Dickie glaring furiously at them.

"Ariana is awake and asking if you lot would kindly put a sock in it. No, stop right there." She commanded as the girls rushed to see their sister. "None of you are going anywhere near her. The boys are in with her at the moment and I won't have them disturbed."

Nick was about to speak but Dickie cut her off again. "No, you don't. If your mother could see you now, she'd be appalled. I know you all have problems but life's like that and if you don't stick together, you'll all fall apart." Dickie stood and glared at four similar faces that all glared back at her. She wasn't wrong but they weren't used to being scolded. Reminding them of their mother only made the situation worse. Mostly because Dickie was in the right and they knew it.

"Now, sort yourselves out and then come upstairs and give your sister a hug. But not before you sort this catfight out." And with that she left, closing the door behind her.

None of the girls looked at each other and then Clem said, "Bloody hell, that's us told, then!" and catching Paddy's eye who looked ready to burst into tears she asked if she remembered when she had tried to flush Nick's doll down the loo and their mother had shouted at them. After a few shared tales of having been told off, the sisters calmed down. Each girl was quiet as she reflected on her own struggles and on the fact that she had been neglecting her sisters instead of them all pulling together.

"Right," said Clemmie, "here's my solution. We'll all go and say hi to Ari. Then we will spend the rest of the day talking about what is going on in our lives, yes even you, Aster, and we'll see if there is anything we can do to help each other. Maybe just talking about it will be enough. After that, I am going to find Seb, apologise and see if I can't make him come back. Finally, let's all come back here for

Christmas and make sure that we all have the best one ever. Is that a plan?"

#

"Seb? Sebastian! You naughty man. Where have you been hiding? We've missed you?!"

Startled, Seb looked up from his chair, a dark heavily silhouetted figure was standing in front of the tropical sun. Putting his pen down he stood up and found himself face to face with Clarice Kendrick.

"Clarice. What an unexpected pleasure. Here," he said pulling out a second chair, "please join me."

It was midday on the terrace of the Pink Sands Hotel and as such no one was around, the typical residents of Pink Sands tended to rouse late in the day and partied on into the evening. Seb had been staying at a friend's villa for the past few weeks but enjoyed the food at the resort, especially lunch when he would usually be left to his own devices.

The day after he had found Dragon he had packed up and told his parents that he was going to work from overseas for a few months. The planning case had been won and he fancied a change of scene and a rest. He knew his mother didn't believe a word of it and neither did his father but neither of them said a word as he got into his car. He'd noticed his mother's worried expression but he couldn't bring himself to tell her the truth. He had made a fool of himself mooning over a widow, playing at happy families.

He strode through the airport unaware of the appreciative glances as he made his way to the departure gate, a head taller than many of the men in the concourse, his mind lost thinking of a pair of blue eyes smiling up at him. What a fool he was. He needed some time away to try and distract himself. Now two months later he found himself looking at the perfect features of Clarice Kendrick. All at once his mood lightened, this was what he needed, some pleasant light-hearted company and a catch-up on all the silly gossip. Anything to distract his brooding mind. He hadn't been able to stop thinking of Ari, Leo or Will for a single day, and Clarice had just saved him from making a stupid mistake. He had been ready to admit failure. He'd been going to go back to England and tell Ari that he just couldn't manage without her. Thank God for Clarice and her perfect timing. Ordering two martinis, Clarice settled down and quickly began chatting to him about all the latest escapades and adventures of her crowd back in New York.

Just as he started on his second martini he wondered if he had had too many as he thought he might be hallucinating.

"Oh God, look," said Clarice gesturing to a girl struggling along the walkway. The boardwalk meandered along the front of the hotel, edging the beach and making it easy for those who didn't like to walk on sand. The girl was short, red-headed, and had a bright sweaty face. She was wearing a tight wool skirt and a fitted blouse, which was also soaked in sweat. In her hand was a pair of high heeled shoes. "She was on the aeroplane coming over from London. What a mess! Oh no, she's coming this way. She was up in first class with me, she must think we have something in common. How embarrassing."

The girl left the walkway and came to stand by their table as Seb stood up from his chair.

"There you are. Bloody hell, what a godawful place this is." Leaning forward Clem picked up Seb's martini and knocked it back then looked around for a waiter. Ordering a bucket of ice and a bath of cold water she sat down and looked at Seb.

"Is Ari alright? Clarice have you met Ariana's sister? May I introduce you to Lady Clementine? Clementine, this is an old friend of mine, Clarice Kendrick."

Clem looked Clarice up and down. If there was one type of person that Clemmie despised the most it was tall gorgeous willowy redheads that apparently never caught the sun.

"Do you think you could excuse us. This is a family matter."

Grinding her teeth and inwardly cursing Ari and her whole wretched family, Clarice made her excuses and hoped that she would be able to catch up with them both over dinner.

"Clemmie, is it the boys? Why are you here?"

The waiter arrived with a pitcher of water which, to Seb's astonishment, Clemmie promptly poured over the top of her head.

"God, that feels good. I am not kidding. I want to die. The heat is appalling and look what I'm wearing. I swear to God I'm going to melt."

Seb sat astounded. Clem was the most frustrating person he had ever met. He had decided it wasn't critical or else Clem would have said straight away. Deciding to take charge of the situation he called the waiter over again.

"Hello, Bobby, Lady Clementine is a guest of mine and her luggage has failed to materialise. Please, could you ask someone from the boutique to bring over a loose kaftan and some sandals, a sun hat, some sunglasses, sunscreen, and could we have another jug of iced water? And I'll have another martini, please."

Clemmie harrumphed but soon she returned from the changing room, suitably attired and she relaxed.

"Now, Lady Clementine. Please, why are you here?"

"Clemmie please, Clementine makes me feel like I'm being told off. Although I suspect in a minute I will be," and realising that she could put it off no longer, she began. "I was sitting with the girls back home and it became clear that I had jumped the gun in sending you off with a flea in your ear. I thought you were just chancing your luck with Ari and I wanted to protect her. The others put me right, so I got on a plane to come and find you."

"Just like that? Isn't that slightly impetuous?" said Seb incredulously.

"Well yes, that's sort of how I am. I tend to rush into things. Hence me arriving in the Bahamas dressed for an English winter."

"Good grief. You didn't even stop to pack a bag?"

"No, like I said," shrugged Clemmie, "I tend to think first and act later. And what with it being my fault that you weren't there when Ari collapsed, I felt I needed to fix things right away."

"Collapsed! I thought you said she was fine?"

"Well, she's getting better obviously, or else I wouldn't have left her. But once the girls showed me how much in love with you she was and how much I'd screwed that up by sending you away I figured it was up to me to fix it."

"In love with me?"

"Well, yes obviously. Haven't you been listening to me? So, the thing is, if my sisters are right and you did have a thing for her and still do then you need to get home and stop sulking out here, like some great Delilah."

Seb raised his eyebrow at being called a Delilah but decided to let it pass.

"When you say in love, what about her husband?"

"The dead one?"

God, she was exasperating.

"Yes, I know he's dead but surely she's still grieving. I want to respect her feelings."

Clem rolled her eyes. "Who told you she was grieving? She despised him. She was preparing to divorce him, but she won't speak ill of him in case it gets back to the boys. What are you doing?"

Seb had picked up the phone and was now speaking quickly in French. Pausing, he looked over to Clem, "Can you manage a flight home to the UK tonight or would you rather spend a day or two here to recover?"

Clem looked around at paradise and realised she preferred Scotland.

"Now's fine." And within the hour the two of them were heading to the airport ready to make the long journey home. Given that Clem's other clothes were still damp Seb also bought her a large shawl to try and keep her warm for when they arrived back in England. During the flight, he discovered that Clem was a dab hand at cards, and they spent much of the journey playing various card games. As they played, they chatted and Seb began to see a different side to her. When she wasn't trying to defend Ari, she was actually a funny girl. She was just fiercely protective of those that she loved. By the time they got to Heathrow, Seb realised that he quite liked her, despite also being a little terrified of her. Shouting that she had better see him at Christmas or she'd come and kick his butt, she headed off to catch a flight to

Edinburgh and left him to drive home to Norfolk, full of fragile hopes.

#

Ari was shuffling across the hall with a massive blanket wrapped over her grandfather's pyjamas and dressing gown. She'd rolled the legs up so she didn't trip over them, but they were the warmest bed clothes she could find so she had to make do. The antibiotics for the pneumonia had finally started to kick in but she still felt like death warmed over most days. However, today she had woken up restless and cross-tempered. She'd had a glorious bath and decided to come downstairs and make herself a mug of hot chocolate. She knew she was feeling better even if she did feel exhausted and she thought she would sit downstairs for a bit. Having watched the boys pull through from various childhood illnesses she knew this restlessness was a good sign. Hopefully, by Christmas, she would have knocked this bug into the long grass. Just as she was passing the front door the doorbell sounded. She didn't want to talk to anyone but as no one was around she opened it, only to find Seb standing in front of her.

As though she was on automatic pilot, she simply walked towards him. Opening his arms, he wrapped them around her small shoulders, kissing the top of her head and breathing in the smell of her hair. Then gently he stepped back from her. He looked down and took in how tired and pale she looked, standing in an open doorway, wrapped in a strange collection of clothes and blankets. Scooping her up in his arms he kicked the door closed behind him.

"Hello," he smiled gently, "I've missed you."

At that minute Dickie, thinking she didn't know how many times she had to tell the boys not to slam doors, strode into the hall and came to a sudden stop at the sight that greeted her. Ari, wrapped up in a bundle of blankets was cradled in the arms of Sebastian and both of them were grinning at her like a fool.

"Hello, Dickie, I think Ari was on her way to make a drink. Would you mind making it for her, I need to talk to her?"

Smiling he carried Ari over to the sitting room. It was already dressed for Christmas and there was a large log fire roaring in the hearth. Settling Ari onto the sofa closest to the fire he sat down beside her. He wrapped another rug over her legs and tucked a strand of her dark brown hair behind her ear. The warm orange glow of the fire brought a soft warmth to her cheeks. Seb looked around to make sure the boys weren't present, although the silence was enough of a clue.

"I was speaking to Clemmie yesterday." Ari groaned, now what? "Is it at all possible, and forgive me for being insensitive, that you haven't been grieving for your husband this past year?"

Ari's jaw fell. "Grieving? No, I couldn't stand him. I was so happy when he died that I have felt incredibly guilty ever since."

Looking back, Seb realised how easily he had mistaken Ari's expression of guilt for that of grief. She never spoke about him; she was quick to change the subject, and when he was mentioned her face and body would become closed and shut down. She was trying to master her emotions and he had misread which emotions those were.

"Is that why you left? Because you thought I was grieving? Oh God, I've missed you so much."

Seb hugged her towards him. "Not half as much as I've missed you. I love you, Ariana. Wait." He gave her another small kiss on the head. "I want you to know that I love you, but I am not going to rush you. You have had a roller-coaster of a year, so I am going to take things nice and slowly so that you can decide if I am who you really want. I am going to court you properly and in six months' time, I will ask you to be my wife and grant me the honour of adopting Leo and Will. What do you say?"

Ari stared at him in wonder. Was this another fever dream? "Can I say yes right now? I love you too!"

Seb laughed and squeezed her again. "No. You will have to learn patience. We're going to take this nice and slowly."

At that moment there was a huge shout from beyond the hall and two boys and two dogs came sprinting into the sitting room and threw themselves onto Seb, who wrestled them down onto the floor so they didn't accidentally hit Ari.

Seb, the boys and two excited dogs played Man Down whilst Dickie came in with two mugs of hot chocolate. Realising that Seb and Ari could do with a bit more time to themselves Dickie told the boys it was time to carry on with the baking; maybe they'd like to bring Seb and Mummy one of their mince pies?

As the children and Dickie left the room Seb noticed a sprig of mistletoe hanging from one of the chandeliers and, pulling Ari to her feet he pointed up to the green sprig and smiling at her he leant down and kissed her. Dickie and the boys spied on them across the corridor and as the kiss lingered, Dickie decided that it was time to leave them to it. As Seb swept Ari up into his arms still kissing her, her fingers wove through his hair. Dickie pulled the giggling children away. Now was a good a time as any to make gingerbread decorations for the tree and Dickie was certain that this Christmas was going to be the happiest that this house had seen in many a long year with many more wonderful years ahead.

Want to read more?

Read all about Ari's mother in *Dear Diary*

Sign up for your free novella at

www.lizhurleywrites.com/deardiary/

If you can't wait the first few pages are on the next
page.

Coming Soon

Book Two in The Wiverton Sisters Series

Heather and Silk

Hello and thank you

Getting to know my readers is really rewarding, I get to know more about you and enjoy your feedback; it only seems fair that you get something in return, so if you sign up for my newsletter you will get various free downloads, depending on what I am currently working on, plus advance notice of new releases. I don't send out many newsletters, and I will never share your details. If this sounds good, click on the following:
https://www.lizhurleywrites.com

I'm also on all the regular social media platforms so look me up.

Facebook /thewivertonsisters
Instagram @elizabethhurleywrites

Did you enjoy this book?

You can make a big difference.

Reviews are powerful and can help me build my audience. Independent authors have a much closer relationship with their readers, and we survive and thrive with your help.

If you've enjoyed this book, then please let others know.

If you read it online leave a review on the site where you purchased it.

Thank you for helping!

Dear Diary

The Diaries of Lily Fox
also known as
Lady Elizabeth Caroline de Foix
(Lilybet)

Elizabeth Hurley

Mudlark's Press

Autumn

New beginnings so a new diary. Picked this up in Jarrolds, typical isn't it? I trawled all over Norwich, had high hopes for the shops on Elm Hill but none were quite right, then I popped into Jarrolds and lo and behold this perfect diary. Sure it's not the prettiest but this reflects my new more serious outlook in taking control of my future. Me, new beginnings, new serious diary.

Anyway, what are these new beginnings? Well, I have only managed to finally convince Daddy to let me go to Art College! Lucinda's off to somewhere in Switzerland to learn to paint, whilst speaking French or something equally ridiculous. Honestly, when I think how stuffy my folks are, I thank my lucky stars that I don't have Lucy's parents, I mean seriously, finishing school? Who even does that anymore? Well, Lucy does, poor thing. She thinks it will finish her off permanently! I don't know if her parents have really thought about the consequences of letting her loose on Switzerland though. They were neutral in the last war, I can't imagine them remaining neutral if Lucy fills their fountains with washing-up liquid. God that was funny, how she didn't get sent down, none of us know. I reckon her father must have a filing cabinet full of incriminating photos of Headmasters. Always thought she was for the high jump when she drew a moustache on the Virgin Mary in chapel. She might have got away with it if she hadn't signed it!!!

Quite a lot of the girls are off to University in order to get a husband, which I have to confess I'm really jealous about. And I can say that here because no one will ever know, but I so want to go to university.

I tried to use that as an excuse to Daddy, as to why I needed to go to Uni, but he said I would get a husband the "normal" way and then harrumphed and refused to elucidate on what exactly the normal way was. I pointed out that arranged marriages were no longer a thing. Mummy mentioned a coming out party and I was so horrified by the notion that I skedaddled (is that how you spell it?) out of the room. I think that was pretty sneaky of Mummy, she knows I have no intention of getting married ever.

No, the reason why I am secretly jealous of the girls is that I would love to go to University. I know that makes me a bit of a swot but I really enjoyed school and learning stuff and the idea of going to a place where everyone wants to be there, and learning really great things, sounds so exciting. But not for me, oh no, I'm a girl, educating girls past 18 is a waste of time. Educating David is a waste of time, if you ask me. He's going to inherit the estate and become Lord Wiverton so why does he even need a degree? Even he agrees, school wasn't really his thing. The way he talks about Uni it just seems to be rowing, rugby, drinking and parties. And presumably girls. Girls looking for husbands. How funny if he fell for a bluestocking. Not that she'd have a bar of him. I don't think she'd be impressed by how many birds he can bag in a season and the arable yield of the lower fields.

He doesn't need Uni for any of that, he already knows so much about running this estate, he's going to be brilliant at it. Apparently though, according to Mummy, he's going to Uni to get a broader outlook on life and make new connections. David mentioned something about sowing oats so I don't know if we have changed our crop rotations. Must make a note to ask Daddy about it and show him that I am interested in the estate.

But anyway, what does Daddy think I'm going to do with myself? I'm not going to get married and have children, he doesn't want me to get a degree, so what am I to do? Work?! I told him I was going to apply for a position in the local shoe shop and I swear his eye actually twitched. Then I said I was going to work in Africa with the nuns, helping little orphaned babies, and both his eyes twitched. Cue Mummy, pointing out that Art School might be an acceptable solution for a year or two. Right, time for bed. My first diary entry has been a bit of a ramble but tomorrow, if nothing exciting happens, as if, I'll write more about my new college.

Dear Diary,

Nothing exciting happened today, well apparently, the village shop had run out of honey, so there's that piece of earth-shattering news from the epicentre of Norfolk, the buzzing metropolis that Wiverton is, but otherwise, nothing exciting.

So, ART COLLEGE!! It's this really beautiful building by the river and it is full of so many talented people. Honestly, they are incredible, I thought there's no way they'll want someone like me. I'm going to do a Performing Arts Btec, I'm telling Daddy it's an Arts degree, I think if I mentioned "Performance" it would be game over. Not that I will be acting, I saw one of their plays and they were incredible. There's no way I'd ever be able to be anything like them, plus I'm not sure I'd feel very comfortable with people looking at me. Anyway, I get to pick and choose the strands I'm interested in. I feel like I'm in a sweet shop. The admissions officer was so lovely, he said that with my three As I was a bit overqualified for the course so I had a bit of a panic, but a lack of a portfolio went against me a bit. Oh to have a portfolio! So I had a bit more of a panic.

Anyway, we went through the strands and together we picked Piano, Fashion, Architectural Studies, French and Photography. I can't wait to tell Lucy I'm basically going to Finishing School, but in Norwich, with boys and parties! Very excited. Mummy has been an absolute sport and given me money to buy all my course books so I've been reading through all of them ready for the start of term. Piano will obviously be a doddle but I'm really looking forward to photography. Daddy said he will consider lending me his Box Brownie. I tried to look grateful rather than appalled. I may have failed! I'm going to pinch David's.

Dear Diary,

Cycled over to Hever's to get some honey. They have also run out. This is getting serious. In other news… How can there be other news when honey levels are at an all-time low.

So basically no other news.

Dear Diary,

This is getting silly. Went for a swim over at Blakeney, fabulous cycle ride over there. Swallows are beginning to bunch up on the lines, summers almost over. Bought Mummy some honey from a local newsagent's and apparently, I bought the honey that foreigners use to preserve dead bodies in hot weather. That doesn't sound right to me but Mummy was deadly serious. I mean maybe they did in the past, and maybe they still do now, although it sounds a bit weird. Surely they don't then scrape the honey off the dead person and then put it into jam jars? Anyway, it's been added to the village raffle. God forbid we should eat mummified honey.

To read on, sign up at

www.lizhurleywrites.com/deardiary

45693783R00240

Printed in Poland
by Amazon Fulfillment
Poland Sp. z o.o., Wrocław